Praise for *The Mother Next Door*

"A witty, wicked thriller packed with hidden agendas, juicy secrets, and pitch-perfect satire of the suburban dream."
—ANDREA BARTZ

"This brilliantly paced tale of perfect-suburbia-until-you-scratch-the-surface is as compelling as it is twisted."
—HANNAH MARY MCKINNON

"A scintillating suburban thriller... *The Mother Next Door* promises to mix its feminist sensibilities with plenty of entertaining camp."
—*CRIMEREADS*

"Suspenseful, sinister, and just the right amount of spooky. A propulsive, expertly paced novel."
—KATHLEEN BARBER

"Packed with shocking twists and wonderfully complicated characters. I couldn't put it down."
—ALISON GAYLIN

"A wonderfully creepy and sinister read.... Tense, twisty, and intriguing."
—KAREN HAMILTON

Also by Tara Laskowski

Novels

One Night Gone
The Weekend Retreat

Short story collections

Modern Manners for Your Inner Demons
Bystanders

THE MOTHER NEXT DOOR

A Novel

TARA LASKOWSKI

GRAYDON
HOUSE

GRAYDON
HOUSE®

Recycling programs
for this product may
not exist in your area.

ISBN-13: 978-1-525-83668-8

The Mother Next Door

First published in 2021. This edition published in 2024.

Graydon House
22 Adelaide St. West, 41st Floor
Toronto, Ontario M5H 4E3, Canada
www.GraydonHouseBooks.com
www.BookClubbish.com

Printed in U.S.A.

For all the moms out there.

(You're doing a much better job than you think you are.)

HALLOWEEN

Ladies and gentlemen, skulls and boys: by the time our Halloween block party is over tonight, one of us will be dead.

And I don't mean dead as in dull, or dead as in zombified. I mean dead as in gone. Dead as in expired. Killed.

Murdered.

You may be feeling distressed about this, knowing what you know about Ivy Woods—the great neighborhood it is, the sweet, loving families that live there. How could such a tragedy happen in such a wonderful place? You may have traveled here yourself, as a child or as a parent, lured in by the local fame of the street and its ghoulish decorations each year. The lights, the smoke, the gravestones, and the moaning. The witches, cackling and handing out candy. The swarms of little Frankensteins and cowboys and robots and ballet dancers lugging their pillowcases and plastic pumpkin buckets filled with sugar and junk.

But Ivy Woods isn't perfect.

Far from it.

Look closer. Look under the makeup and the masks, look into the windows of the perfect houses. Dig under the surface of those freshly mowed lawns and you'll find the worms. I've looked—believe me, I've looked. There's something about this street. There are secrets. I know from watching through the windows, from hearing the hushed conversations, from lingering on their faces when they think everyone else has looked away.

Oh they think they are perfect. They pat themselves on the back for throwing such good parties, for raising such fine children, for living in such big houses.

But they are pretending.

They don masks on this one single night to dress up as someone or something else, but in reality they live their lives this way.

We all do.

We hate ourselves. We are too fat, or too thin. We should work hard, be smarter. We are lonely and depressed. We are worried about money. We are ashamed of the way that our friends and family treat us. But we lie about it all. We hide behind a protective façade, fragile glass figurines inside elaborate dollhouses designed to look like perfect, safe, happy places.

Tonight it will all shatter.

Watch closely and you'll begin to see what I see. There's trouble in the air, a cold wind blowing in from far away, and it's settled on Ivy Woods Drive. The secrets and the lies we tell ourselves and others will emerge tonight like spirits of the dead. Lines will be drawn. Sides will be taken. Someone won't make it out alive.

I can't save that person, but I'll tell the story. Turn over the rocks, expose the worms. Pull back the masks.

Because I know their secrets, secrets that will destroy them all.

If they don't destroy themselves first.

SEVEN WEEKS
BEFORE
HALLOWEEN

ONE

Theresa

The moms were having a party. I watched from across the street, through my living room window, as I ate my dinner of chicken piccata on the couch, sipping a hefty glass of merlot.

At dusk, they arrived one by one from the houses around the cul-de-sac, the glow of their phones like fireflies in the dying light. Dressed stylish but casual, ponytails and makeup, jeans and heels.

Viciously, effortlessly powerful.

The blonde mom was hosting. The one I'd noticed walking an oversize dog around the cul-de-sac, cell phone to her ear. She seemed to know everyone, always paused by one porch or another while her dog sniffed in the grass. Yes, my new neighbors were social butterflies. I observed their fluttering hugs as they converged in front of the house. My view inside was limited—a hallway beyond the screen door, painted red, like the inside of a mouth, and at the end, the corner of a giant island in the center of the kitchen where I imagined they set their Tupperware trays and booze.

I turned back to the TV. A wispy woman in a white nightgown was making her way down a dark hallway with one flickering candle. Lily must have been watching it before she'd gone out; my daughter binged on these kinds of movies, Halloween season or not. She loved all things creepy, Frankenstein and ghosts, serial killers and porcelain dolls. If it was undead or moaned in the attic, Lily was all about it.

Just before the woman reached the door where the knob was rattling violently, there was a loud bang outside, and I jumped. Another woman, getting out of a car this time. I shut off the TV, the fate of the wispy woman forever unknown, and went into the kitchen to wash my plate.

It was 7:30. Lily was at a friend's house, and Adam had dived headfirst into his new job as principal of the local high school. He wouldn't be home from Parent Night for another couple of hours at least. I was on my own and knew I should get out, go for a walk. I enjoyed wandering the streets of our new neighborhood, getting the lay of the land, especially at night.

I put on my sneakers and slipped a light cardigan over my T-shirt as I stepped outside. The sky was clear, the moon a ripe banana. I'd always been in love with this neighborhood—Ivy Woods—and my love had continued to grow since our family had moved here from Philadelphia three weeks ago. Our cul-de-sac ran up against a small lake that separated our homes from a town house community across the way. And even though we were only a dozen miles from DC, the woods around the neighborhood made us feel like we were in a secluded forest retreat, private and protected.

It felt so easy, so normal. The kind of place you saw on a dated sitcom, with large and wholesome families and golden retrievers and everyone learning important lessons. The kind of street that made you wonder how different your life would be if only you lived somewhere like that.

And now I did.

I walked down our driveway, turning left to leave the cul-de-sac. I passed these houses often, but I'd been so busy unpacking and getting us settled that I hadn't actually met any of the neighbors yet. I'd seen them pulling out of their IKEA-organized garages in the mornings, jogging on the weekends, gathering at the mailboxes at the ends of their driveways. Never a hair out of place. Pencil skirt suits or designer yoga pants, whether on their way to work or instructing their gardeners where to trim the boxwoods. I'd been studying—their habits, their style. Figuring out how they operated, so that when the time was right, *I* would fit in.

Just as I reached the giant old oak tree at the opening of the cul-de-sac, I realized I'd forgotten my cell phone. I headed back, but crossed to the other side—where the party house beckoned to me like a big bright lamp.

As I approached, I slowed. The moms were chatting animatedly around a table, one woman's words tripping over the last's. Beautiful creatures, at ease in their lives and their homes. Several bottles of wine out, like they were planning on staying for a while.

I inched onto the dark lawn to the dogwood tree and pressed myself against the brittle trunk for a better view. One of the women was standing now, stretching her arm from beneath a purple-and-green pashmina to show off a delicate bracelet on her wrist.

I willed one of them to look up.

To notice me.

The blonde mom, perfect highlights framing her face, nodded her approval of the jewelry. I was betting she was the leader, the take-charge one who never flinched during an emergency, who would wrangle all of us behind her and face the tigers first.

I watched.

I waited.

A dog started barking in the distance, then another nearby, in the house. It rushed to the front door and pawed, heavy breath creating condensation on the glass.

The blonde mom frowned. "Cut it out, Barney," she yelled. She took a sip of her wine.

I watched.

I waited.

Then she looked up. She seemed to gaze right at me through the window. Flecks of bark snapped off the tree trunk as I squeezed, and they fell at my feet. Even though I knew the woman couldn't see me out here in the darkness, I held my breath until she turned away.

TWO

Theresa

Adam had warned me the Welcome to Woodard event wasn't going to be fancy, and unfortunately, he was right. They hadn't done much to transform the gymnasium of the high school—public school budgets, I supposed. The bleachers were pushed to the wall like unclimbable ladders, and they'd arranged a mix of low- and high-top tables throughout the gym. Near the doors, a microphone and two bulky speakers had been set up for remarks. No mood music, unless you counted the squeak of the men's shoes on the waxy floor. The local community newspaper I'd worked for back in Philly had Christmas parties swankier than this, and those had been in the basement of a chicken wings place.

It was as one might expect—lots of *hellos* and *nice-to-meet-yous* and handshakes and forgetting people's names as soon as they said them. Five hundred and fifty *and this is my wife, Theresa*s. There were jokes about sports teams—"Coming from Philly, you know you can't be an Eagles fan anymore, right?" After a while I felt like my smile needed to be propped up by toothpicks. Much of the conversations were shoptalk about the school, the classes, the kids, and I drowned it out until I could finally excuse myself, feigning thirst.

The woman at the drink table appeared to be a parent volunteer, dressed as she was in a Woodard High T-shirt and khaki pants. Her shoulder-length hair curled with humidity, and her facial features naturally arced downward so that even when she threw a smile my way, it came off as defeated.

"You're Adam Wallace's wife, right?" she asked as I took a flat-looking Coke. There was no alcohol. "We're so excited to have him here."

I got a little thrill noting the clout Adam's name brought here.

"That's me," I said brightly. "Theresa Pressley." I held out a hand.

"Oh wow, it's so nice to meet you. I'm Georgeann. Georgeann Wilkins." She handed me a thin white cocktail napkin. "Do you need anything else?" We both glanced at the table—there wasn't anything else—and the woman let out an embarrassed chuckle. "Well, I guess if you need any help with anything, I've been here forever."

After all the polite small talk at Adam's side, Georgeann's awkwardness made it easier to relax. "Oh you just must know everyone then," I teased.

"I don't know about that," she said, but my flattery had pleased her. Her cheeks blotched red. "I mean, not everyone."

Above us a section of basketball hoop netting had wrapped around itself, and I kept glancing up at it, wishing I was tall enough to fix it.

Georgeann busied herself rearranging soda cups. "Some of the folks here are more up on that stuff. I just volunteer where I can, help out. My son's on the swim team, so I go to the meets…" She trailed off, her eyes focused behind me.

I turned. She was staring at my neighbor, the blonde woman who lived across the street. The woman stuck out from the crowd in a chic plaid dress with a pretty fall-colored, striped scarf. Like she was going to a wedding shower instead of a meet and greet in a dumpy gymnasium.

"Who's that?" I asked.

Georgeann started waving in her direction. "Hi, Kendra!" she called, but the woman didn't notice her. Georgeann dropped her arm. "Well, that's your neighbor, Kendra McCaul. You're on Ivy Woods, right?"

I nodded.

"Their Halloween block party is famous, you know," Georgeann added.

"Is it?" I asked absentmindedly, as Kendra crossed the room in heels in a way that would've made my aunt Ruth—who could cover forty New York City blocks in stilettos—proud.

"Oh yeah. Hundreds of kids come by every year."

Kendra was greeting another woman, pressing her hands in hers, air-kiss at the cheek.

"Hundreds?" I asked, facing Georgeann again. "Our daughter loves Halloween. That might make the move less painful for her." Adam would like it, too—he'd grown up in a big family and loved reunions and parties and socializing. Halloween was one of those holidays I could take or leave, but this year it sounded like I would learn to love it. Which was fine. If it was tradition, we'd be going all in as good new neighbors.

"She'll love it," Georgeann said. "You guys are living right in the middle of the in-crowd. They know everyone." Georgeann fanned her face with a clump of napkins. "I'm sorry. I shouldn't gossip."

"Oh no," I reassured her. "You know what they say, 'What happens behind the drink table stays behind the drink table.'"

She laughed, grabbed one of the watered-down Sprites, and took a swig like she was shooting vodka. "Kendra is the one who heads it all up. Rumor says she's pretty militant about it, too. You know, that everything has to be *perfect*." She smirked and did a scan of the crowd. "There's another one of your neighbors. With your husband, actually."

She pointed to a petite woman with a tiny knob of a nose, black hair cut into a severe bob that grazed the tops of her shoulders. I recognized her from the other night, too—despite her size, something about the way she squared her body suggested command. She was leaning in close to Adam, talking with her hands, and he threw her the warm smile that made you feel like you were the most important person in the room. I knew that smile well.

"That's Bettina Price."

Georgeann identified another neighbor, Alice Swanson, who was wrangling three young kids around a table. Alice was a good name for her, too—she seemed like the type that might slip curiously down a rabbit hole. She was as bouncy as her ponytail, moving swiftly to open plastic snack containers and set out toys. And at the same table sat the woman with the bracelet I'd seen through the window, head bent, oblivious, scrolling through her phone. Pia Burman, Georgeann informed me.

"They're the Ivy Five," Georgeann said. I made a mental count. Just four. I wondered who the final member of the band was. "But my friend Maggie calls them the Ivy Hive. You know, busy bees and all. But don't worry. They'll love *you*." Georgeann's tone was edgier now, like she'd drawn some sort of line between us. "I mean, you're perfect. The principal's wife, living on their street."

The principal's wife. I wasn't sure if I should be offended. My sister-in-law, Trixie, had warned me that suburban moms sometimes trended back to that old-fashioned mentality—*just wait, they all sit home and bitch about their yoga instructors*—but Trixie always had a sore spot for anyone who she thought had life easy.

I heard my name and saw Adam signaling from a corner of the room. He finally had a moment alone.

I said goodbye to Georgeann and hustled over. "I'm meeting the whole state of Virginia, feels like," he said quietly, though I could tell he was pleased about it. He fixed my necklace clasp, which had fallen forward.

"I saw you talking to one of our new neighbors," I said, curious.

"Ah, yes." Adam's eyes twinkled. "She told me they'd love for you to join in on their Halloween party planning meeting this week. I said I'd allow it, but that would count as the one time per month I let you out of the house without my supervision."

That made me laugh. I bet it had made them laugh, too. He was going to be very good at his job. I could tell from the way everyone melted around his messy mop of hair, round wire glasses, his earnest talk about education and making a difference.

"Come on, I'll introduce you," he said, tugging me along before I could protest. I caught Georgeann's eye as we passed, and she winked.

Kendra McCaul was in the middle of a story as we approached. "—and I was like, I completely had told you not to go with him, so what did you think was going to happen?"

"Excuse me, ladies," Adam interrupted. "I just wanted to introduce you to my better half. This is my wife, Theresa Pressley."

The women stood between two cafeteria tables, four of them with slight smiles, heads cocked at the same angle, a united front. An army with moisturizing sunscreen and Kate Spade purses, doused in Yves Saint Laurent perfume.

"Well, I'll leave you all to it," Adam said, patting me on the back and disappearing into the crowd. He forgot sometimes that not everyone was comfortable meeting new people.

Bettina broke the silence and introduced herself. "So, you've been married for a year?" she asked after we shook hands.

"Well, it'll be a year in March," I said. "Still newlyweds."

"How did you meet?" Alice bent down to fish one of her children out from under a table. "I'm Alice, by the way," she called from the floor, snatching a dirty penny from a toddler's clutches.

"Uh, on a plane actually," I said. They didn't seem like the type, but I always braced myself for a "Mile-High Club" joke whenever I shared that fact.

"A plane! That's so funny." Pia, the oldest of the group, held out her hand and introduced herself.

"If the only way to get married was to meet on a plane, I'd be single forever," Bettina said. "The second I sit down and buckle my seat belt, the headphones come on. Small talk with someone you're trapped with for hours like that is my nightmare."

I laughed, feeling myself calm. "Normally, me, too," I said. "But I spilled my ginger ale all over him."

I'd been mortified. I wasn't usually that clumsy. I was the girl who always checked all angles in the mirror, who showed up ten minutes early, who beat herself up over every small mistake. But Adam had been laid-back about it. So charming. By the end of the flight, I'd completely forgotten my embarrassment and was plotting instead how to make sure he didn't vanish from my world when the plane touched down.

Pia's turn to laugh. "Now that's a good move, honey. I may have to try that myself." She had an air like she couldn't be bothered, though her eyeliner was applied perfectly and she kept twisting her bracelets to make sure the jewels were on top of her wrist for all to see.

"Please do not go dumping your wine in poor men's laps all over town," Bettina said.

Kendra McCaul was the only one who hadn't spoken. I couldn't read the look on her face, but when she shifted, the gym lights glinted off a pin affixed to her scarf. It was the shape of a leaf, shiny green enamel with tiny jewels embedded along one side.

Ivy.

"So, is Adam your second marriage, then?" Bettina again.

"Bettina!" Alice swiped at her arm, then rolled her eyes at me. "Ignore her. She's nosy."

This assessment didn't seem to bother Bettina. "It's not like I'm Maggie Lewis and it's going to end up on the six o'clock news," she murmured.

The four of them cracked up—clearly an inside joke. I glanced over my shoulder at Georgeann behind the drink table. She'd knocked over a cup of Coke and was trying to mop up the mess.

I'd been a Georgeann all my life. The self-conscious introvert whose mother was always pushing her to fit in despite not having the right clothes or the right hair or the right name. Who had to work twice as hard only to settle for good enough.

Starting now, starting here, those days would be over.

"This is my first marriage, actually," I said, making sure to stand up as straight as the others. *Don't hunch, Theresa Ann*, my mother would say. *Makes you look weak.* "I raised Lily on my own."

Alice gave a sympathetic smile. "I can imagine that was hard."

I shrugged. My response in this scenario was always to downplay. "It is what it is." I spread my arms out wide. "But we're here now, so…happily-ever-after?"

The conversation dead-ended there.

I checked the time. Adam would be making quick remarks in a few minutes anyway. "If you'll excuse me, I've got to—"

"Well, you are the star of the show." Kendra finally spoke, and her voice was catlike, a smooth and low purr. She pursed her lips, which were stained a shiny plum color so dark it was almost black. There was a look in her eyes that I recognized, had seen before in colleagues, classmates, friends, reminding me I needed to prove my worth. A reminder it wouldn't be so easy to press myself into this life like dough into a cookie cutter.

I slipped away to the bathroom. The harsh lighting made me seem tired. I took a few deep breaths, powdered my face. In a stall, I pulled out my phone and scrolled through Facebook. Someone from Woodard had already posted a photo of Adam and me in the gymnasium. "Please extend a warm welcome to Woodard's new principal, Adam Wallace, and his wife, Teresa." They'd spelled my name wrong and caught me in a grimace, gripping someone's hand, my necklace askew.

But we'd done it. We'd shaken the snow globe, and once the flurry of flakes descended, what would be left was our grand four-bedroom, four-bathroom, two-car garage, screened-in porch dream at the top of a cul-de-sac, snug as a bug in a rug. And the three of us, together and happy.

I'd make sure of it.

So it hadn't come without a cost, without risk.

So I'd had to call in a favor.

We deserved it.

THREE

Kendra

They could say what they wanted about us, but we knew how to throw a killer party on Ivy Woods Drive.

It was the highlight of the year—never got old, no matter how many times we'd done it. Think hordes of shrieking kids. Drunk parents, good food. Think the most amazing, epic, terrifying Halloween decorations in the county. And this year? A band. Live music, trivia contests. I. Was. Ready.

Halloween had been my favorite time of the year since I was a teenager—armrests pushed up in theaters, the killer with a chainsaw, your eyes buried in a guy's sweatshirt, his hand on your skin. Drinking on haunted hayrides and in corn mazes. Driving too fast on dark roads. Ghost stories in backyards. The chance to let your hair down, be reckless. What was not to like?

Of course, we all grow up. Get married. Have kids.

Move to the suburbs. But who says us moms can't still have some fun? We *deserve* fun after all we put up with. That's one reason I started the Ivy Woods block party, grew it from an annual neighborhood tradition to a community *phenomenon*. I was its mastermind. Maybe that made me sound vain. But everyone knew it.

Grandma Betty insisted, *If you want something done right, you have to do it yourself.* So I did. I made the plan, stuck to it. As I always did. Let's just say I held shit together in this place.

From Paul's perspective, I was a control freak (my husband wouldn't know what to do with himself if I suddenly dropped off the face of the earth, but he liked to pretend my constant planning was a flaw because it made him feel better about himself). But for everyone else, I was a miracle worker. It was why I was told, constantly, *"I don't know how you do all you do, Kendra."*

And, yes, I'll admit it. I took satisfaction in hearing that.

This year was going to be our greatest show yet. The best decorations, the biggest crowd. I said that every year, but this year I meant it. I was really going to outdo myself. My youngest son, Cole, was graduating. Next year he'd be in college with his older brother, Sam, and Paul and I would officially be empty nesters. Maybe then it would be time to pass the legacy on to someone else. Or end the party altogether.

But I'll tell you this: if it was going to be the last Ivy Woods Halloween block party, we were going out with a bang.

———

The first nuts-and-bolts planning meeting was on Friday, always six weeks out from Halloween. Which is why I was surprised when Alice texted us on Wednesday night with an urgent message:

Bonfire meeting tonight. 8 p.m.

I stopped chopping the green pepper for the dinner salad. We'd just seen each other a couple days ago at the new Woodard principal's welcome event and before that, over the weekend for girls' night. Did something happen?

Whenever there was a crisis—like the time Pia found a lump (it turned out to be benign), or when Alice lost her full-time nanny, or when Bettina caught her first husband tapping into their retirement account to pay gambling debts—we'd meet in Alice's backyard, around her firepit, and strategize how to fix it. It was all in the details, and you couldn't get those kinds of details over the phone. We'd coined them *bonfire meetings*.

But we hadn't needed a bonfire meeting in several years.

I kept my reply breezy: I love you guys and all, but three get-togethers in one week?

Will explain later. See you then.

Alice had three kids, and her husband was away on military duty. She rarely had the time to just hang out for fun. And it wasn't like Little Miss Sunshine, who oozed happiness out of every orifice, to be so terse. Her texts were usually filled with *pleases* and *love y'alls* and emoji hearts. She was our Southern belle: sweet, soft, and smiley. We joked that someone could burn her house to the ground and she'd find a reason to bake them strawberry fig bars. Still, that was our Alice.

I washed the lettuce and set it aside in the salad spinner, then called Bettina. "What's up with Alice?" I asked.

I could hear pots and pans clanging in the background. Probably her husband making dinner. Bettina rarely lifted a finger when it came to cooking, the lucky bitch.

"No idea. I wondered the same thing." The noises stopped, which meant Bettina had moved into another room. I imagined her in the spare bedroom off the back, finding her way through the darkness to sit on the edge of the bed. We knew each other's houses like they were our own.

"Maybe she's stressed about planning the block party," I offered. "Or Full Moon? Two major events in one month can be a lot for some people."

When I got to Alice's backyard after dinner and lifted the rustic gate latch, the old firepit was roaring. Pia and Bettina were already sitting in lawn chairs close to the flames. They were drinking wine—well, for Pia, water—from Alice's plastic goblets.

"Where's our host?" I asked as I walked up and poured myself a goblet.

Bettina jabbed her thumb toward the house. "Hildie started fidgeting on the monitor, so she went in to check on her." Sure enough, in the grainy black-and-white feed of the baby monitor on the table, Alice was bent over the toddler bed, fussing with the blankets.

"Any hint as to what's going on?" I checked a seat for spiders with my phone's flashlight before settling in.

Pia shook her head. "No clue." She was closest to the fire, so close I thought her sweater, a geometric pattern that had to have cost a fortune, might start to smolder. It was pretty, but too snug on her. "I just hope this doesn't take too long. Michael's supposed to call me tonight."

Bettina's eyeballs seemed like they were going to roll out of her head. "The twenty-six-year-old?"

Pia sniffed. "He's twenty-nine. And very mature for his age."

"Cradle robber," I said. Ever since Pia shipped her kids off to college, she'd been playing the role of affectively bored divorcée, including her obsession with online dating sites and men way younger than her. "Speaking of men, what did you think of the new principal?" I asked them.

The fire danced in the lenses of Bettina's glasses, glasses she didn't need but just liked the style of. Bettina was always about the accessories. "I hope he'll be good for Woodard."

I pinched my lip. Adam Wallace was a decent-looking guy. Goofy, maybe, but in an attractive way, if you squinted. He was about Paul's age but still had all his hair. And a nice jaw. Earnest smile.

"I bet they have good sex," Pia said.

"Do you think they role-play teacher and student?" I pressed. *"Spank me, Mr. Wallace,"* I said in a low, husky voice. *"I've been a bad girl."*

"You guys are disgusting," Bettina said. "I don't want to imagine this." But she was laughing.

"I've got his wife volunteering at the game next weekend," I said.

"Yeah. You sure strong-armed her into it." Pia pulled out her phone and checked a notification on the screen, then slid it back into her pocket.

"No, not really. Just a polite *nudge*. She's the wife

of a key figure here, and the mother of a student at Woodard, so she's got to hold her own." I flipped my hair over my shoulder and smiled. "Plus, she'll be good. She seems eager."

"Whatever," Bettina said. "Fresh blood in the water. You're like a shark."

I hummed the *Jaws* theme as Alice came out, the screen door slamming behind her. "So sorry, guys. Hildie's been peeing the bed lately, and I wanted to make sure she didn't need to go." She scooted her own chair next to mine, twisted her hair into a messy bun, and secured it with a hair tie. "I just didn't want to put it in writing over text. But someone's messing with us."

"What do you mean?" Pia asked.

"Did y'all get any weird messages?" Alice looked at each of us.

We all shook our heads. In the firelight, we might've been witches around a cauldron. My mind flitted to the scene in my high school's production of *Macbeth*, the old crones dancing around the flames. Trouble. Toil. Tumult. *Something wicked this way comes.*

"Nothing? On Facebook? Did you see Neighbor-Who?"

"NeighborWho?" I laughed. NeighborWho was a hyper-local neighborhood group that people used to swap recipes, find lost pets, make business recommendations, trash local politicians, spread rumors, and sell shit they no longer wanted. Paul loved it because he traded old yard equipment and rated restaurants. I deleted my account after the year I'd run for school board and anonymous bitches had used it to campaign against me in ugly ways. "I can't believe you even still read that trash."

"Hush yourself and look," Alice said.

I held the phone away from me (unlike Bettina, I did need reading glasses) and read it aloud for the others' benefit:

Subject: Halloween Party in Ivy Woods
It's been 13 years. This is the Halloween I take revenge.
~Ghost Girl

I handed her phone back. "Ooh so spooky," I said sarcastically. She'd called us all out here for this?

"That's targeting *us*. *All* of us."

"Oh come on. That's some kind of bad spam." I gaped at Alice, searching for a sign she was joking. "You can't be serious."

"It's not spam," Alice snapped. "They mentioned me, too. Look." Alice thrust her cell phone back in my face:

Does what you did keep you up at night, Alice?

Uh-oh! I hear a buzzing sound around your hive...

Better watch out!

"See? They mention my hives. They *know where we live*."

"So someone doesn't like your backyard bees," I said calmly. "You always said you were going to get complaints about it so close to the walking paths."

"Let me see it." Pia wiggled her fingers, and I handed the phone over. "Well, that's better than some of the messages I get from guys on OkCupid anyway. Lame." She passed the phone to Bettina, who read it without comment.

"Don't y'all see who it's from?" Alice asked.

I took the phone back and clicked through to the person's profile, but Alice narrated it for everyone. "Ivy Woods. And look at the profile picture."

I squinted. "Seriously, Alice. It's so small. Can't you blow it up?"

She snatched it back from me, annoyed. "It's the Browns' house."

A piece of wood popped and crackled, shooting sparks. In the trees that framed the back of the yard, we could hear an animal furiously burrowing. We could hear the leaves rustle.

Pia sighed. "So, what you're saying is the Browns—who don't even live here anymore—are sending you cryptic notes about bees?"

"The principal lives there now," I added incredulously. "I highly doubt *he's* into anonymous threats."

"I don't know," Alice said, tossing up her hands. "But I don't like it, y'all. Thirteen years. That's an unlucky number."

I turned to Bettina, who was hunched low in her chair, unusually quiet. "Surely you don't believe in this shit." The last thing we needed right now, as party planning geared up, was for Alice, or any of us, to lose it over an urban legend.

It took Bettina a second to come around, and I almost thought she was going to jump on Alice's little bandwagon. Finally, she said, "It's just a snotty message, Alice. Don't flip out."

I grinned, stood up. "Now, since we've got such a nice fire here, I'm getting more wine. Anyone else?"

HALLOWEEN

The mothers are so selfless. So giving. They do the party because they love it. They work so hard, little bees buzzing and buzzing, for the good of the neighborhood. For the reputation of Ivy Woods. They say they can't remember year from year from year—a blur of sugar and strobe lights.

They will remember this year. I'm certain of it.

It's their houses that are always the centerpieces of the party. Look there, the house with the giant spider, eight feet tall at least, even taller if you're just a kiddo. It moves, too, which will scare you shitless the first time you visit, but the next year you'll remember it and after a long time it becomes just another part of the story, the nostalgia, the memories.

And there's the zombie house, with the frosted screens in the upstairs windows and those shadowy hands pressing, over and over, trying to get out. The graveyard with the moaning werewolf. And the house at the top of the slope, Casper's mansion, graveyard in front, a glittery, dancing projector-image ghost darting from window to window like magic.

They invite us to come inside their homes this night, but they don't really think anyone's paying attention to them. And yet, if we peek, we see so many things. There's a mom in an upstairs window, adjusting her cape. Adding darker eyeliner than she would for any other day. Is she crying? Hiding the puffy circles under her lashes? In another window, a dad steals a miniature candy bar from the bowl, swipes it while his wife's in the kitchen, putting the finishing touches on the casserole she prepped for the pre-party potluck, the smaller get-together before the get-together, the one exclusively for the Ivy Woods gang. A few stray kiddos are already outside in their costumes, running across lawns, chasing each other with plastic swords and light sabers.

Someone wheels out a cooler. Card tables get unfolded. Cheap plastic orange tablecloths fight the breeze. The grandparents show up with cameras that don't take good pictures in the dark. There's a howl deep in the woods, but no one hears it because of the one house that always blasts "Monster Mash" on repeat.

The party starts out the same, but it isn't going to end the same. Not this year.

In the corner of one of the houses, on a porch, two masked shadowy figures huddle. One's shaking, with fear, or rage? We can't really tell.

"I won't let them do this to me anymore."

"Yes. They need to pay."

They slip off the porch and join the others.

They'd hate to ruin the festivities.

SIX WEEKS
BEFORE
HALLOWEEN

FOUR

Theresa

Lily and her new friend, Ellen, were in the living room watching a movie, each sprawled across an end of the sectional with a bowl of cheddar popcorn propped on her belly. Lily's long hair was splayed out on the pillow, and she was twirling it around her finger.

"You guys look comfy," I said as I came down the stairs.

Ellen sat up and snatched the remote to pause the movie. *Candyman*—one of Lily's favorites.

"You didn't have to stop it," I said. "I'm heading out."

"I didn't want to miss it. This is a really good part," Ellen said. Her hair was about as long as Lily's, but with blue streaks running through it, and she was wearing a long cardigan sweater and a T-shirt that said in black block letters, I CHALLENGE AUTHORITY. She was a senior, on her way to valedictorian, Adam had mentioned when I'd wondered why a senior was hanging out with a freshman. *Good role model*, he'd pointed out. Clearly they had horror and ghosts in common.

"Mom hates this movie," Lily said, sitting up and grinning. I'd noticed she'd painted her fingernails black.

"Why on earth?" Ellen asked. She pushed her large, round glasses back up on the bridge of her nose and stared at me, evoking a kind of confidence I wasn't used to in teenage girls.

"I can't stand the bee part, where they swarm all in his mouth," I said.

"She's allergic," Lily added.

"But mostly that part where they find out the guy was coming in through the bathroom medicine cabinets," I said, fake shivering. "Just creeps me out."

"She makes us check them whenever we go to a hotel or anything," Lily said, a little too gleefully. "Like someone's going to be waiting there in the walls."

"Lily!" I tossed a pillow at her to get her to stop. She shrieked and ducked. These days she wavered between kid and adult, one minute giggling over Adam's impressions of *Sesame Street* characters and the next lecturing me about the importance of composting. I held my breath for the day she'd wake up and realize that I was not just her mother but a flawed human who, even at thirty-eight, had no idea what she was doing.

"Well, I think the movie has a lot of really interesting things to say about race and class and the way that myth and superstition can encourage prejudice and stereotyping," Ellen said, punching at the remote so the movie resumed. "Plus it's got an über-creepy urban legend."

"And so do we," Lily said to me. "Right here in the neighborhood. It's so exciting."

"All the best things," I said, trying to avoid being pulled into a long conversation, but they were already absorbed again, forgetting me.

As I walked the few houses to Bettina's for the block party planning session, a barred owl in the distance gave its throaty hoot that sounded like—*Who cooks for you? Who cooks for you-all?* It was a phrase Adam, intrigued by all the wildlife, had discovered on a nature website when we'd first moved here. We'd certainly seen our fair share already, fat slugs on the sidewalk in early morning, deer feeding off grass in the woods by the lake, and an alarmingly large snakeskin Adam found when organizing the garage that I hadn't told Lily about. I liked the red foxes the best. They ran free, unafraid. I'd often wake in the morning and see one curled up sleeping on the tree stump in our backyard like a big house cat, not a care in the world.

I followed the stone path up to the porch, running my fingers over my navy-blue wrap dress. I was going for simple and classy, hopefully effortless, like earlier that day I hadn't yanked out nearly every piece of clothing I owned. I felt like my twelve-year-old self, all braces and no breasts, wanting desperately to be invited to Carley Aronowitz's bat mitzvah, but then later worrying I was only included because my mother called her mother and insisted on it.

You want to be the popular girl, just once, the voice inside me nagged.

And why shouldn't I be, this time?

I rang the doorbell, and Bettina answered, drink in hand, lips painted a deep red. She flashed me a tight smile but didn't say a word, just unlocked her screen door and pushed it open.

I could hear the others talking inside. "Hi there," I said. "Hope I'm not late."

"Not at all." She gestured for me to enter.

The house felt cold, and not just the temperature. One of those modern homes that looks sophisticated but not inviting. Weird marble pots and angular stone doll statues. Metal wall sculptures that could've doubled for torture devices. Tiny, lumpy, twisted gourds lined the fireplace mantel. Everywhere I glanced, there was something decorative that could hurt you.

"What a beautiful home," I said anyway.

The women were sitting in the sunken living room. Three of them, plus Bettina. I wondered about Georgeann's nickname, the Ivy Five, if that had been a mistake. Or if they were still waiting for someone else to show up.

"Theresa!" Kendra McCaul said. "Come, sit." She attempted to rearrange a stack of small hard decorative pillows on the couch to make space for me.

In the corner on the other side of the room, Pia flipped through a catalog, but Alice jumped up right away, sticking out a cool, slim hand. Her perky demeanor made her seem younger than I suspected she really was, around my age. "I know we met before, briefly, but I'm Alice. It's so great you're here. You just have the greatest hair," she gushed. "Is that weird to say? It's probably weird to say, but you do."

"Thank you," I said. To tell the truth, I didn't know if it was weird. "I just dyed it a few weeks ago, actually. It turned out redder than I'd thought."

"What? Don't ever admit that, honey. It's all natural, remember." Pia looked up from her catalog, tossed it on the side table. She pointed at my dress. "That's a Boden, right? I think I have it in green."

Bettina interrupted, "We're drinking gin and tonics tonight. Are you in?"

"Definitely," I said. I could use it to settle my nerves.

She handed me a short, heavy glass with one giant skull-shaped cube in the middle. I sipped it gratefully and sat next to Kendra on the couch, which was by far the most comfortable-looking seat in the room. The others were on modern leather chairs with hard wood arms, in a semicircle, Bettina closest to the sidebar. I'd watched them just last week through Kendra's window, and now here I was.

"So, Theresa," Kendra said. She straightened a giant beaded necklace. "Dish it. Tell us everything about you."

I laughed, even as I was taken aback. *Don't hunch.* "Well, I don't know where to even begin with that."

"What do you do? For work."

"I was a reporter—in Philly. But now I'm freelancing, until I can figure out my next steps."

"What kind of reporter?" Bettina asked. "Investigative?"

I took another sip of my drink. "Education, mostly. I covered some K-12 stuff for the *Inquirer.* But honestly, I'm open to anything."

"Easy. We'll find you something." Kendra waved her hand as though it was a done deal. I was beginning to see how she could go from businesslike grilling to warm and friendly in a matter of seconds.

"Speaking of jobs," Alice said. "I reckon a toast is in order." She held up her glass, and everyone followed suit. "Congrats to your husband, for getting the job as principal and bringing y'all here to Ivy Woods."

We clinked glasses, except for Pia, who was drinking a bottle of water.

"Thank you," I said. The gin had started to take effect, warming me. The women seemed much more welcoming than last week at the high school. It was a relief. "We're glad to be here."

Kendra took a sip and turned to me again. "I can imagine it's a big change, moving somewhere totally new."

"For Lily, yes. For a while there, we were sure she was going to run away and join the circus to enact revenge. I mean, to be fair, I've thrown a lot of changes her way over the last few years." I paused, cleared my throat, tugged on my hair, a nervous tic. *You're blabbering on.* "But it's not totally new for me, actually. I went to grad school at Gunston University. Lived near campus, like two miles from here?"

"Really?" Kendra's expression shifted, as if she was processing this new information.

I nodded. "Actually, this whole neighborhood is familiar." I made a sweeping gesture with my hand, the alcohol carrying me on a light wave. I'd remembered the houses right away. Tucked up around the lake. The mothers, the strollers, the creaky swing sets. The sun glittering on the surface of the lake. "My professor lived around here. He used to have our class over every month or so. Down by the water?"

"Who's that?" Bettina asked.

"Greg Hendricks?" I wasn't sure why my voice was suddenly making everything into a question. *They don't need to hear your life story, Theresa.*

"The superintendent's son?" Kendra's eyebrows had disappeared under her bangs.

Pia chuckled. "Someone has friends in high places."

I pressed my finger into the ice skull and it cracked, breaking in half.

"Yes, well. Speaking of," Kendra said. She pulled a folder from her purse. "I wanted to talk about the guest list."

A guest list? For a block party?

Pia rolled her eyes at me, as if to say, *I told you so.*

"Doesn't that take care of itself?" I smiled. "I mean, don't the neighbors just invite their friends?"

"Oh, Theresa. Don't you know if you want something done right, you have to do it yourself?" Kendra sighed, looked down again at her papers and clicked her pen. "We like to increase the prestige of the party each year. Up the game, I guess you'd say. One of the reasons we're excited you're here is because we wanted to see who you might be able to bring in."

"You mean, like, friends?" I asked.

"Well, yes and no." Kendra made notes on her papers, but held them at an angle where I couldn't see. "Sure, if you have friends in the area with kids. But we are thinking more like…celebrities."

"Celebrities?"

"Well, local celebrities."

Alice piped up. "It's so nice. We have the mayor every year. He brings his grandkids trick-or-treating. We almost got the governor one year, too, but then at the last minute he changed his mind. They are just the sweetest family, too. We're— Kendra's thinking of getting a band this year."

"Which is why"—Kendra waved her papers—"we

need to get the word out ASAP. I'll take care of pitching the local media, of course. I mean, the calendar listings and whatnot. That's easy. But what I'm hoping for from you, Theresa, is more like personal invites."

She handed me a printout, an Excel spreadsheet titled "The Ivy Five—Halloween Block Party Guest List," followed by names and addresses. "These are the kinds of people we're talking about." She moved her pencil down her spreadsheet efficiently. "Maybe Adam knows someone?"

The list was alphabetical and organized by category, with different shades of color for each mother's guests:

Red for Kendra.

Orange for Bettina.

Green for Pia.

Pink for Alice.

Four mothers. Four colors.

"The Ivy Five," I said without thinking, my reporter's instinct kicking into gear. "But there are only four of you?"

I expected them to tell a cute story. Maybe someone liked the sound of the rhyme, so they just went with it. But I was met only with an awkward silence and blank stares. You could cut the tension with Kendra's chunky gold hoops.

Oh god. What if the fifth member had died or something? I tried to recover. "I'm sorry, was that a bad question? Georgeann had just said—"

"Georgeann Wilkins?" Kendra asked. She adjusted her necklace again.

I wished I'd kept my mouth shut. "Yeah. She..."

Kendra broke into a wide smile. "Oh it's fine. Sorry. Honestly, it's just one of those names that stuck all these years. We forget it doesn't make sense anymore. Our fifth friend moved away ages ago."

"Career opportunity," Bettina added.

"We haven't seen her in forever," Alice said. "You know how it is when someone moves away. I mean, it's awful to say, but if I don't see someone…they might as well have just…"

Pia looked up from her phone. "What they are trying to say is we buried her in the basement."

"Har, har, Pia," Kendra said.

"Do you need another drink?" Bettina asked. When I shook my head, she got up and poured herself another. "We need another toast," she said. "To the shrewdest moms in town."

"To the best-dressed moms in town," Pia added with her water bottle.

Kendra slid her spreadsheet back in her bag, and picked up her drink, too. "To the most reliable moms in town."

"And the prettiest, of course." Alice giggled.

They all looked at me expectantly.

I held up my glass. "To the most popular moms in town?"

"Hear, hear." We clinked. Some gin sloshed. I tilted my head back and let it roll down my throat. I wasn't used to drinking this much liquor this fast, but I liked how light I felt.

Alice set her glass down on the table. "I almost forgot! Bettina, you've got to show Theresa the— They're almost ready, right?"

"It's probably too dark…"

"Not with the porch light. Come on." Alice grabbed my hand. "You'll love this."

Alice, Bettina, and I tromped out onto the back porch. Alice flicked on the light and started down the steps to the yard. "Come on." She wavered in her clunky heels through the lawn. I followed, glad I'd chosen ballet flats instead of the pumps I'd been eyeing in my closet, though I hoped it wouldn't be mucky out there anyway. It was dark, but I could make out that Bettina's back-yard was shaped like a slice of pizza, rounded on the left side and tapering into a long triangle down to the right, where her neighbor's yard cut it off with a tall fence. Alice headed toward the wider end, where the grass stopped at a darker weedy section that bumped up against a small shed.

"Hold on, Alice," Bettina called, striding past us. "I don't want you messing anything up."

Bettina stepped into the growth, which swallowed her legs to the knee. As I got closer, I saw it was a mass of vines twisting around one another. Bettina gently pushed some aside, and the light from the porch illuminated a giant, plump pumpkin, nestled on a bed of soil. It had shifted slightly when Bettina moved the leaves, as if it we'd interrupted its slumber.

"She grows them every year," Alice gushed. "Just for the party."

"They're autumn golds," Bettina said, brushing aside another set of vines so I could see another hint of orange below. "For jack-o'-lanterns." Bettina's head was in shadow, and I imagined her as a fairy-tale sorceress, vines tightening around her toothpick legs and dragging her into the ground.

"Very cool," I said. "I'm impressed. Even my fake cacti die on me."

"You have to be pretty persistent about it," Bettina

said. "I have to grow them inside for a few months. If you plant them outside too early, the cold will kill them. And then, once they start to grow, you have to come out here and turn them, so they don't grow lopsided. Every year I lose a few, even so."

"But there's usually one for each of us girls." Alice beamed, clapping her hands. "And this year there's five. It's like it's meant to be."

Meant to be. I felt myself getting that warm feeling again. The universe was shifting, all the pieces fitting together. It was meant to be—the house, the street, the party.

The Ivy Five.

"Wow, five good ones," I said, trying not to sound too excited.

And five good moms. Shrewd. Well-dressed. Reliable. Pretty. Popular.

"Well, I won't know that until I cut them off the vine in another week or so." Bettina's chilly voice returned. "Sometimes one rots."

FIVE

Kendra

It's a fact: swim moms look younger. We get free facials sitting by the humid indoor pool for hours. We aren't exposed to UVA rays like the soccer or baseball moms. We may spend hours inhaling chlorine fumes, but at least we don't have to deal with lightning or snow. And unlike the wrestling moms, our meets aren't in gymnasiums stinking of sweat.

I climbed to the top of the bleachers and watched the boys warm up for the meet. Cole was a great swimmer, broad shoulders, long arms that sliced through the water like daggers. He was best at short runs and currently held the school record in the fifty-meter freestyle, beating out Bo Lewis by less than one second. It was electrifying to watch him race.

Some parents seemed to think their children's sports or other activities were a burden, complaining at every turn about where they had to be and when, like it was a chore. My mom had been that way. She'd hardly ever gone to my softball games or theater productions, bitching about how *hard* the bleachers were to sit on or how *crowded* the high school auditorium was. My mother had made sure my sister and I knew we were her "burdens to bear," and I'd sooner eat glass than ever make my kids feel that way. I tried my best to get to every one of their events—whether Sam's concerts and marching band halftime shows, or Cole's swim meets.

I opened my email. As communications director for the local hospital, I had to constantly check in. You never knew when a malpractice suit would hit, or a research breakthrough would go big. During Cole's events, I'd often bring my laptop to knock off a few press releases or media pitches or proofread an invitation to a research symposium. To survive as a working mom, you needed to multitask.

Nothing urgent in my email, so I scrolled through Facebook. A college friend just returned from a Hawaii vacation. Another friend had posted dozens of photos of her annoyingly adorable Portuguese water dog. The usual hateful political posts from Paul's niece.

Alice had also forwarded us the message from "Ivy Woods."

Does what you did keep you up at night, Alice?

Uh-oh! I hear a buzzing sound around your hive…

Better watch out!

It was ridiculous, even more so when not read outside in the dark next to a fire. Beyond the childish taunt, the excessive use of exclamation points annoyed me.

It was clear that someone wanted to spook Alice. Or at the very least, rile her up. You think kids are bullies? Parents are even worse. A few years back, when Alice had gotten approval for her hive, everyone suddenly had an aggressive honeybee story. One guy, who, thankfully, has since moved away, left notes on her porch in black marker that he was going to sue her for bee stings. This had to be something similar—some neighbor being an asshole.

Not everyone in Ivy Woods fell under our spell.

Still. Someone had gone through the trouble of creating a dummy account. And the profile picture of the Browns' house...the new principal's house...

That house.

"Well, hello there."

I looked up from my phone. Maggie Lewis was sashaying up the bleachers with Georgeann Wilkins in tow. Maggie Lewis, who thought she was a big shot because she reported on fire alarms and burglaries for Channel 7. She was wearing boot-cut jeans and a tan cardigan, the same exact one I'd bought last season from J. Crew, except hers was covered in cat hair. Georgeann was wearing her usual L.L.Bean boxy khaki pants and a long-sleeved polo shirt. While Maggie was at least stylish, Bettina and I had often joked that we wanted to throw Georgeann in one of our trunks and drive her to Neiman Marcus.

"Hi, ladies," I said, humoring them.

"So your boy stole our record," Maggie said, getting right to it. She plopped herself down on the bleachers below me.

Our record? Like she'd done anything. Her son was the one who worked his ass off to make the swim team. "Yeah, I guess he did." I smiled sweetly. "Sorry about that."

I, of course, wasn't the least bit sorry. Maggie couldn't stand that Cole was better than Bo. She couldn't stand being second fiddle anything.

"No worries. He'll get it back." Maggie smirked. Then she changed subjects. "Bo turned in his scholarship application, by the way."

"I'm assuming you'll be at Full Moon, then?"

Everyone was always *very* interested in the merit scholarship, but less so in donating to it. Full Moon was our fundraiser, an annual event at the lake behind our houses right before Halloween. I liked to think of it as rehearsal for the block party.

"I'll be covering it for the news. I'm doing a whole feature on Halloween, the party, all that stuff." She crossed one leg over the other and leaned in. "It'll be all the *buzz* of the town, I'm sure."

Buzz.

I studied her face for any hidden expression, but she was about as clever as a pipe cleaner. Still, if some of the mothers in this town wanted to screw with us, Maggie Lewis would be the one leading the charge. And it would be her MO to go for the weakest of us, too.

"Uh-oh." Georgeann laughed. "Looks like Kendra doesn't like that." She gulped, putting her hand to her mouth. Georgeann was *so bad* at being snarky—it was uncomfortable to watch.

"Of course I do," I said. "A story would be great. We love spreading the word about the party."

The JV heat began with a short blast of whistles. Which meant Cole's race was next.

"So you've got the principal living across the street, eh?" Maggie asked.

"Guess so."

"I'm totally going to ask his wife up to come to my poker game."

I couldn't decide if she was trying to goad me or if she was serious. Either way, the thought was incredibly ridiculous. Theresa Pressley at Maggie's monthly poker games? Where the women swore and smoked and pretended they were still freshmen in college? Yeah, no. Theresa seemed more like a nature hike or afternoon tea kind of woman.

"I don't really think Theresa's the gambling type," I said.

"We'll see." Maggie picked a particularly long cat hair off her arm and let it disappear between the cracks in the bleacher seats. "It's important to get on her good side, after all. Never know when it might come in handy."

"Oh god," I said. "You. Are. Insufferable."

"Like you weren't thinking the same thing." She eyed me up, and I had to will myself not to look away. "I just wish her husband was as good at his job as he is at schmoozing."

"Someone needs to tell him to ask you for advice," I said, laying on the sarcasm. "Maybe next time I see him outside raking leaves, I'll let him know you have some tips for him."

I would have been satisfied just to get a scowl out of Maggie, but that one shut her up.

"He seems like a really nice guy," Georgeann, ever

the optimist, added. "But I'm still shocked they gave the job to him over Diane Bloomington. I thought she was a shoo-in."

So had Diane. When she'd found out she'd lost it, she'd called me, crying like a baby who dropped its pacifier, raging mad, too, saying it was a con job, calling Miles Hendricks names that would make even Pia blush.

They announced Cole's race, and as the swimmers prepped, I stood to get a better view. He was on the starting board, white cap, goggles, red shorts, bouncing like he always did. Then whistle, and Cole and the others plunged into the water. The shouts echoed through the gym.

"Go, Bo! Go." Maggie was all fist in the air, obnoxious voice bouncing off the hard walls as she cheered on her son. "Come on. Push it. Push it!"

Not me. I was not one of *those* moms who screamed and made a mess of herself trying to prove to everyone how much she loved her kid. I was the silent missile. Exploding only when he touched the pool side.

Cole and Bo separated from the pack, well ahead of the swimmers from the other school. *Come on come on come on*, I thought hard.

Slipping into the home stretch, Cole was leading by just a hair. But then Bo made a final push and gained on him.

It was close, so close it seemed like the boys touched the side at the very same time.

As we waited for the final times, Cole heaved himself out of the water, shaking the droplets off his shoulders. My son was competitive, just like his mother. I was sure he had it.

The announcer came over the speaker, his voice

breaking up, at the same time the results appeared on the scoreboard. "…a new record at Woodard…"

Cole had broken the record he'd set.

Yes.

But Bo had broken *that* record by a fraction of a second.

Shit.

Maggie screamed, her face red. She hugged Georgeann, who, to her credit, looked mortified. "Yes!" She fist-pumped, nearly losing her balance on the bleachers, and I wanted to smack her, watch her tumble down each tier like a sack of potatoes.

She turned to me. "I'm sorry," she said, with the smile of a devil on her face. "Can't be winners all the time."

SIX

Theresa

There was something exciting about a football game on a crisp, clear fall evening. The crowds, the lights, the cold bleachers against your thighs, the smell of hot oil and sugar, and the poor PA system.

Lily had accepted a ride to the high school with us, but as soon as we pulled into Adam's parking spot, she hopped out, smashing a knit cap onto her head. "See you guys later," she said, then scampered off before anyone could say more.

It made me nostalgic for the times she and I used to go to the local high school's games and huddle under a bright quilt my mom had made, cheering on the team and buying too much cotton candy and caramel popcorn. She'd always wanted to be right by my side.

"Hey," Adam said quietly, as if reading my mind. "It's okay. She's just testing her independence. She still loves you. Don't worry."

He rubbed my chin, forcing a smile out of me, but if anything, his words made me feel worse.

I was used to arriving early and snagging a good seat at these kinds of events, but I quickly learned that when you're arm in arm with the principal, people stopped you every minute to say hello. By the time we got to the fifty-yard-line, the stands were a dense sea of blue and purple school spirit—Woodard was apparently a good team. As we looked for an opening, a waving arm caught my eye. It was Kendra, calling my name.

There they were, a few rows into the stands, front and center. Kendra, Bettina, Pia, Alice, and their families. As we headed up, Bettina and her husband stood and moved behind Kendra, making room for Adam and me on the end of the row.

"You don't have to move," I said once we reached them, concerned she'd be irritated.

"No worries," Bettina said. I didn't detect an edge to her voice.

Adam and I took our seats on the cold metal benches.

"So good to see you guys," Kendra gushed. She was wearing a gray Woodard hoodie and blue gloves. She introduced us around again, mostly for Adam's benefit, though I did get to meet Bettina's husband, Joe, who kept passing Kendra's husband, Paul, a small football-shaped container that I suspected was a flask. Pia was in front of us with her sister. Alice was on the other side of Kendra with her kids, who were waving mini Woodard flags while Alice attempted to keep them from smacking people.

"I love your earrings," Kendra said to me.

I touched the silver hoops I'd found at the bottom of my jewelry box. They'd been my mother's. Way bigger than I normally wore—even Adam had said something as we left the house. Just like the gold ones Kendra always had on.

"It's like you're twins," Bettina said from below a dark blue knit cap, her hair carefully combed across her forehead, and I blushed at her words.

It was a chilly evening. The others had come prepared with foam stadium seats and blankets, and Kendra insisted we take one of her blankets. I slid my hand into Adam's and squeezed, snuggling against him.

After the first quarter, Adam spotted someone he needed to talk to a bunch of rows over. Once he was gone, Kendra poked Pia. "Come up here for a minute," she said. Pia shifted up beside me, creating a kind of triangle of the five of us. "I wanted to talk costumes. Any ideas for this year?"

"Yes!" Alice said, her kids now busying themselves with her phone. "Y'all, I was thinking famous moms? Wouldn't that be so cute? I could be one of those 1950s mamas with the big skirts and apron."

"It's a tradition," Kendra said, filling me in. "A new theme every year."

"That sounds great," I said. "Famous moms? I've always thought it would be fun to dress up like Marge Simpson, with all that blue hair?"

"Well, that's not decided yet," Kendra said, smoothing a lock of her hair, then tossing it over her shoulder. "I had a *really* great idea, in fact. I thought we could be forest animals."

Pia burst into laughter. "Animals?"

Irritation cut across Kendra's face, but it was gone before she noticed me staring. "We live on Ivy Woods. The woods, get it? Woodland creatures," she said. "We could be sexy woodland creatures. Like a squirrel, a fox, a fawn…"

"A skunk," Pia said, nudging me with her elbow. "Bettina, you could be a skunk and just wear that awful patchouli perfume you use."

Kendra glared at Pia. "Grow up."

I imagined myself in a puffy bear costume, staring through a jaw. Or worse, stuffing myself into a cheap furry sweater dress with a tail and trying to maintain my dignity. The last time I'd dressed in a group costume was in graduate school, at a house party just a few miles from Ivy Woods, somewhere on the other side of campus. I'd been engaged to my then-boyfriend, Brad Fontaine, and we'd all gone as characters from *The Wizard of Oz*. Brad had been the Cowardly Lion. I'd crafted a Good Witch/Bad Witch costume, sewing half of a black dress to half of a cheap gold princess dress, decorating half of a black witch's hat with sequins, and crafting half my face in green and half with sparkly eyeshadow. I'd always been just a little too clever back then, hadn't I?

"Anyway, we can chat about it more," Kendra added.

Just then, one of the Woodard receivers caught a long pass, and the whole section erupted in cheers. When we sat back down, Pia whispered to me, "There won't be any chatting about other ideas, trust me."

I laughed, and Kendra turned to me. "Shouldn't you be on lollipop duty by now?"

"Not 'til fourth quarter," Bettina broke in, leaning forward.

I was surprised she knew, but I nodded to confirm.

"Okay, just making sure you haven't shirked your

duties." Kendra winked. "Oh! By the way, Bettina has something for you."

"Right," Bettina said. She set down her cup of steaming hot chocolate and pulled out her purse, handing me a business card. She spoke so softly that I had to tip back to hear her. "This is a friend of mine at *The Washington Post*. I told her you were looking for a job, and she said to call her."

I clasped the card in my palms, reading the black letters in the famous font. This was a far cry from the community newspaper, even the *Inquirer.* "Wow, thank you."

Bettina shrugged. "No guarantees. I don't know anything about their education editor or if they're even hiring."

"Point is, this is how we roll." A gnat hovered between us, and Kendra swatted it away. "If there's a need, we usually know someone who can help. I'm sure you're the same way?"

I recognized it for what it was—an offering and a challenge.

"I'm always willing to help," I said.

"Then you'll fit right in here. It's that kind of place," Kendra said. "It's why we've all been here forever, right, Bettina?"

"Sure." Bettina sat back, loosening the purple scarf around her neck, and that's when I saw it affixed to her jacket. The green ivy leaf pin, same as Kendra's the night of the school welcome party.

When I peered over, I saw the same pin peeking out from under Alice's jacket. I was willing to bet Pia had one, too.

They sparkled in the stadium lights like a dangerous promise.

"I'm so lucky to have landed here," I said.

———

When there were five minutes left in the third quarter, I said my goodbyes and made my way to the concessions stand under the bleachers for lollipop duty. The lollipops were homemade by members of the Parent Team and the Booster Club, and apparently they were famous. "People go nuts for them," Kendra had said proudly. "You'll see. It's always packed."

Indeed, there were two lines, several people deep, when I arrived to relieve the third-quarter volunteer. She gave me a brief tutorial on how to use the cash register, then grabbed her purse and ran. Not a good sign.

The booth was small, four folding tables in a square that we volunteers stood inside. On the back table were several trays filled with lollipops of various shapes—a *W* for Woodard, a lion for the mascot, and a football— and in different flavors—cinnamon, fruit punch, strawberry, root beer, cherry, watermelon, and grape.

"Hey there." I turned and saw Georgeann joining me behind the tables. I was glad to see someone I knew. "Looks like we're it now, eh?" she said.

"I guess. You can teach me the ropes?" I'd already forgotten most of the details the prior volunteer had thrown at me before rushing off.

"Sure. It's easy. Just watch and learn." She fanned herself with a Booster Club brochure and then started waiting on customers.

Georgeann and I were a team. She gathered the lollipops; I handled the money. It was a bit of a cluster at first, but after a while I got the hang of it.

Near the end of my shift, I was rearranging the root beer, which seemed to be the most popular flavor, when a voice to my side startled me. "Well, hello stranger."

I spun around, and there was Greg Hendricks, hands thrust into his jacket. I was suddenly twenty-five again, heart slamming, palms sweating, unsure of myself. When was the last time I'd seen my former professor? Over a decade. He'd aged, of course. The skin around his eyes had a few more wrinkles, his hair had a few more silver streaks. But he was still as handsome as he'd ever been, that same glimmer in his blue eyes that everyone fell for.

He surveyed me with a smile. "Look at you, stepping up already. They saw you coming a mile away, didn't they?"

"That's me. The good little soldier." I saluted, then felt stupid about it.

"I feel incredibly neglected," he said, shifting closer. I could smell his aftershave. "You've been here, what? A month now? And not a peep from you."

"I know. I got your email. It's just been so busy…" I felt light-headed, like I was in a dream, warp-speeding back to the past, when everything had simultaneously come together and fallen completely apart.

"I'm joking, Theresa." He took a strand of my hair and rubbed it. "I like this look. Red hair flatters you. I almost didn't recognize you."

I stepped back, smoothed my hair back in place. Georgeann didn't have any customers now, and I could feel her hovering behind me, drinking in every word. When I glanced back at her, she tapped her watch. "Only a few minutes left in the game. I can close up here if you want."

"Thanks, Georgeann. I owe you one." I gathered my things and waved goodbye, and Greg and I walked away from the concessions.

We'd kept in touch over the years via email, and he'd sent flowers after my mother died, but I knew so little about him these days. All our recent correspondence had been businesslike. I felt selfish—asking and taking and not bothering to check in with him personally. How long had he been divorced now? I knew I should ask about his daughter, Nora—god, she'd be a few years older than Lily by now, maybe even in college—but I didn't want to bring up family. Not now.

"I heard you were coaching a team here at Woodard," I said instead.

"Yep. Debate. Going on six years now." He stopped near a pillar just off the trafficked path. Above, the stands vibrated with cheers and foot-stomping. "And still teaching at Gunston. And still working with the study abroad program."

Greg's ticking off of accomplishments—that do-it-all mentality that everyone around here had—was something I'd forgotten about this area. In grad school, it had seemed natural, and I'd been prepared for it since my mother was always pushing for perfection. Even now I could feel the tug of it—that desire to always be the best, to prove you belonged. Prove your worth.

"And you're liking the new house?" Greg asked.

"I love it. It's keeping me busy, too." I changed my voice to sound proper. "I'm learning all about paint shades and wallpaper and brushed nickel cartridge faucets."

"Wow. You're becoming an interior designer."

"Hardly." I laughed. "I'm just starting with our powder room. But Lily has taken to calling me 'HGTV' to be mean."

Greg threw back his head and laughed. "I take it she likes the new house, too?"

"Are you kidding?" I said. "It was really the one thing that sold her on moving. She barely ever comes down from her bedroom in the attic."

"Oh. The attic," he said.

"Yes, weird, I know. Adam says that he's never seen her so happy."

I caught a flash of something in Greg's eyes—anger? sadness?—and realized it must've been my mention of Adam. Greg had always seemed slightly unhappy, lonely—even when I'd known him all those years ago—and I wondered if seeing me now, finally happy with someone else, was triggering him.

I put my hand on his arm. "Listen, Greg," I said softly. "I just wanted to tell you how much I appreciated—" I stopped. The crowd was spilling down from the bleachers, and I could see Adam, tall above the crowd, coming toward us. I dropped my hand, something like a cherry pit rising in my chest. "Look, Adam doesn't know. Any of it. Okay?"

Greg's brow rose. "Really?" He noted my expression, then whispered, "Our little secret, then. I like that. I can hold it over you."

Adam reached us, eyed Greg, then me. Were we standing too close?

"Hi, honey," I said cheerfully and clutched his arm. "Adam, this is Greg Hendricks. My former professor."

"Ah, Miles's son." Adam held out a hand. Miles, his boss, the superintendent. *Friends in high places*, like Pia had said.

"Yes. No matter how old I get, I'll always be Miles's son." He laughed, ran his fingers through his hair. "I suppose it could be worse. But anyway, I've got to get back to my dad. I shall see you both again, I'm sure. 'The pain of parting is nothing to the joy of meeting again.'"

"Charles Dickens," I told Adam as Greg waved and disappeared into the crowd. "He likes to quote literature." Above us, the sound of the fans stomping down the metal bleachers made it seem like the world was exploding.

Adam shrugged. "I'm starving," he yelled over the din. "Let's go get a pile of greasy food."

HALLOWEEN

She's new to town. This is her first Halloween party, and she doesn't see the flaws. She only sees perfection. She loves these people, this community. She loves wandering around the eerie lake in fall. She loves the house, so big and beautiful, especially the giant round attic window that looks out onto all of Ivy Woods. She's happy that her daughter seems to love it, too.

And now, this party. This night. Where everyone can pretend they are someone else and bask in the orange glow of pumpkin light and kiddie laughter.

I can understand that feeling. It's getting dark, after all. It starts getting dark so early now. And look, even the weird neighbor, Mrs. Tressle, is here, and she hates Halloween. Her house is usually as dark as tar. I've never seen a bowl of candy on the porch, not even one sign of a skeleton.

But here she is, walking around, eating food, a glob of icing stuck to her cheek. The neighbors soon realize she's watching. They make witch jokes behind her back but mostly ignore her. Mrs. Tressle's presence doesn't stop anyone from behaving badly.

If anything, she enhances the mood. The music seems louder. The drinks stronger. Conversation takes on a pattern, and if you close your eyes, you can hear it.

Murmur, stop. Murmur murmur—laughter.

Like an irregular heartbeat. An underlying condition you can't see.

Potentially fatal.

An impromptu dance party starts up in the middle of the cul-de-sac, and a bat and her mummy husband start waltzing, trying not to trip on his unraveling bandages. Someone hands out glow sticks, and in the dimming light of the evening, the children streak like lightning bugs, green and yellow circles moving around and around.

And perhaps here is where she begins to relax. Here is where she decides that everything's going to be okay. That all her past mistakes don't matter. She can transform here, become someone new. The moms like her. They trust her.

But do they really accept her?

Can she ever really escape her past?

Or will they begin to wonder just what her intentions are?

Is here where the spark catches, a slow burn that will suddenly turn to fire?

FIVE WEEKS
BEFORE
HALLOWEEN

SEVEN

Kendra

Paul and I were watching television in the den when Bettina called. More like *he* was watching, and I was focused on checking things off my to-do list. I stepped to the front of the house to take the call.

"You busy?" She was in the car. I could hear the whoosh of her driving, her voice cracking in and out.

"I just emailed you the website for the Halloween costumes. Send me your size and preference soon so I can get the order in and out of the way." I checked the time. 8:30 p.m. "What are you doing out so late?"

"Massage. Last appointment of the night."

"Must be nice." It was never good when Bettina had nothing else to do but lie around thinking for an hour. After last month's massage, she'd roped Pia into a makeup consultation, and now they couldn't get the woman to leave them alone. I needed to find a task for her.

"Do you have a sec?" Hesitation.

I pressed my phone closer to my ear. "Spill it. But no way I'm starting a nonprofit with you."

When she didn't laugh, I sank into a chair near the front window, where I had a view of the street. I'd see Bettina when she drove up and into her driveway.

"Alice and I...we were talking about those messages," Bettina said. "It just doesn't feel right."

The cul-de-sac was empty this late at night. One of the streetlights was blinking on and off in rapid succession, then pausing, only to start again. The wind had kicked up. A branch on my dogwood tree was swaying like it was about to fall off.

"It's one of the bitchy moms," I said. "Got to be. Remember how horrid they were when I ran for school board?"

A pause. Bettina must have stopped at a light, because all was silent on her end. Then she said, "We think it could be Jackie."

Her name was like a shot. I almost dropped the phone.

Bettina continued quickly, like she was afraid I might hang up. "When was the last time any of us heard from her?"

I ran my fingers through my hair, frustrated. Were they all losing it? I didn't have time for this bullshit. I had a party to pull off. We couldn't afford to unravel like this, not now.

"That's ridiculous," I said. "Utterly ridiculous. Why in the world would you think it was her?"

If not for the whoosh of the car, I'd have thought we got disconnected.

I hadn't thought about Jackie in a long time. Tried not

to think about her. We'd been such good friends back then. One for all, all for one. I'd have done anything for her. And then she'd gone and ruined everything, and I'd wanted nothing but for her to disappear.

"I tried to google her, and I couldn't find her," Bettina said.

"Good," I said.

Karma was a bitch.

I stood, paced the room. Outside, a car pulled into the cul-de-sac, but it drove by Bettina's house and then ours, headed toward the pipe stem. When it passed, its headlights illuminated the dogwood.

That swaying branch wasn't a branch. There was something in the tree.

I put on my flats and stepped outside, into the front yard.

"Don't you think it's weird?" Bettina asked. "She's not on Facebook or anything either. I can't find any trace of her."

"Did you really think she'd become a big star?" I asked, half-distracted. Whatever was in the tree was thin and white, whipping around, bashing into the trunk. I walked over, reached up to grab it, but it flew just out of reach.

"Jackie's been gone all these years," I said, balancing the phone between my ear and shoulder as I stretched up again. "There's been no trouble. Why now? It doesn't make any—"

My phone fell into the grass. I'd finally gotten a grip on the thing in the tree.

The white was lace. A dress. A doll.

"Kendra?" Bettina's voice, tinny and high, sputtered from the phone on the lawn. "What's wrong?"

I turned it around. And that's when I saw the face. I bit my cheek and felt a salty warmth in my mouth. Blood.

————

Cole was in his bed, covers askew, headphones on, playing that goddamn Xbox again. Multiplayer games, open worlds. He and his friends would rather meet in some virtual pirate land and pillage a ship or set up an apocalypse and fight zombies than see each other in person. I regretted buying him a TV for his bedroom.

I threw the doll on his lap. "Too early, Cole," I yelled, hands on hips, pissed I'd fallen for that crap.

After I'd hung up with Bettina, I'd unhooked the doll from the tree branch and brought it inside. It was a foot long, white fabric stuffed with grass and twigs and dressed in lace. Someone had painted two slits for eyes and a round O of a mouth that made it look like it was screaming.

He sat up, took off the headphones. "I'm in the middle of battle here." He picked up the doll with two fingers, cringing. "What is that?"

"You tell me. Your friends left it in our tree. A little early in the season, don't you think?" Every year around Halloween, the Woodard teenagers committed pranks against one another. Sometimes they were nonsensical—one year a giant, busted air-conditioning unit was hauled in the dead of night to a new kid's front yard, decorated with Christmas lights—and other times the "gifts" were darker. But Prank It Forward, as it was dubbed, didn't start until a week before Halloween.

"Chill. It just looks like that stupid Ghost Girl." Cole held the doll out in my direction. His eyes went back to the TV, where a swarm of monsters with horns was attacking his avatar.

Ghost Girl. The urban legend all the teenagers talked about. I thought back to the message Alice freaked out about. *This is the Halloween I take revenge.*

Childish.

Ridiculous.

Of all the stories that had to stick around here, why the hell did it have to be that one?

I took the remote control and cut the screen to black. "Get rid of it."

"Mom, Jesus Christ. They're going to take back the river."

"Hello? Real life here?"

"Real life? As in all this stupid haunted girl stuff?" He shook his head dismissively. "I hate this holiday. It's the worst."

His comment stung. This type of behavior always seemed to rear its ugly little head right around this time of year, just when things were busiest, when I had so much else on my mind. As a kid, it had been night-mares—no, night terrors—a semi-conscious state where I couldn't get him to wake up and he'd sit howling in my arms for what felt like hours. These last few years, he had been acting sullen, disinterested. He'd decided he hated Halloween, as if just to hurt me. As if to shun all the work I put into it.

He shook the doll at me, pieces of grass dropping to the floor. "Ooh spooky voodoo magic." Then he shot it, free throw style, into his trash can, where its twig feet stuck up over the lip. "Two points for the win."

EIGHT

Theresa

I was now a person who attended bake sales in high school cafeterias. A joiner, a helper. Eager and willing. If Lily's old school had ever had anything remotely like a bake sale, I'd never known about it. The closest I'd come to attending a parent event in Philadelphia was when I'd gone to get the laptop Lily had left in her locker and accidentally walked in on a school board meeting.

Yet here I was on a Saturday morning with a bright smile and a tray of mini blueberry tarts that I'd bought at a local bakery. They were fancy enough to impress, but not so fancy that I couldn't have whipped them up myself. Considering my baking skills ended at brownies from a box, there was no way I was going to show up with anything homemade.

The room was bustling with women. All women, in fact, which was not surprising. The mothers in this town, I'd learned over the past couple weeks, were the ones that made things happen. And once I'd started showing my face at events—Adam's welcome night, the football games—they wanted me to participate in everything. I was a new recruit. I'd been invited to chair the library's book donation project, judge a student journalism contest, and join Alice's weird pyramid scheme lotion-selling business. I'd even attended an awkward Pilates class with Pia. It was nice to feel in demand. The only person I hadn't really seen was Kendra, who was always busy with work and various projects. Each time I tried to return the blanket she'd let us borrow at the game, no one was home.

I carried my tarts into the cafeteria. I didn't recognize anyone, but that was fine. I was here to mingle, to prove I was part of Woodard, one of them. *What would Adam do?* I asked myself, trying to envision it. He was so good at forced social events. At our wedding, he had been as comfortable doing the chicken dance with our nieces and nephews as he was listening to my uncle Stan go on about where to find the best cheesesteaks in downtown Philly and how someone was going to die someday running over a pothole in his neighborhood because the director of the Highway Division was corrupt and only cared about his box seats at the Wells Fargo Center.

But I wasn't a natural, not like Adam.

I was improving. Baby steps. The Theresa Pressley from several years ago—heck, even six months ago— would've gotten hives just thinking about walking into a den of overachieving mothers, but things were different now. If the Ivy Five liked me, everyone else would, too.

Two women were chatting with each other next to

the water fountain, and I decided to introduce myself. "Hi, I'm Theresa Pressley. Principal Wallace's wife." I said it with authority, confidence, then had no idea what to say next.

"Oh we know who you are," one of them said, almost bitter-sounding.

What would Adam do? I thought again. Say something witty? Kill them with kindness?

"It must be my legendary tarts that gave me away," I said, gesturing toward the tray. "My mother always said I'd be famous someday for my baking."

That was a bald-faced lie. I added a dazzling smile.

"Those *do* look good," the friendly one said. They introduced themselves—Kathryn and Diane (the snarky one). "Are they a family recipe?"

"No. They're actually super easy to make. Just short-bread and some apricot jam and the blueberries." I recited what April, the helpful woman behind the counter, had told me. "You can even cut the dough into rectangles, so you don't waste any."

"Interesting," Diane murmured. "You can just set them over there on the table and someone will price them for you."

"Thanks," I said. "And while we're at it, I'd love to pitch in and help. It will keep me from wandering the tables and gaining fifteen pounds with all these temptations. Anyone in need?"

Kathryn glanced around, then gestured toward someone across the room. "Yes. Yes. I'm sure Maggie could use some help with the register, if you don't mind?"

"Not at all. Lead the way."

I followed her to a table where a very busy woman

was standing with a cash box. "Maggie. I've got a ready volunteer."

Maggie looked up at us as she counted a stack of ones under her breath. Her straight brown hair brushed her shoulders and framed a roundish but shrewd face. Something about her seemed familiar, but I couldn't place where I'd seen or met her before.

"Awesome," Maggie said when she finished. "I've had to pee for like an hour."

I took my place behind the table. I'd not worked a cash register since my part-time grocery store job in high school, but already I'd used that valuable skill set twice since volunteering at Woodard. By the time Maggie came back, things had died down.

She whipped out a lint roller from her purse. "Cats," she said, pushing it across her sweater. "They lie all over me before I leave the house, and it's not until I'm staring at myself in the mirror that I notice the fur. I'm Maggie Lewis. My son's a senior at Woodard."

"I'm Theresa."

We shook hands.

Suddenly Maggie's eyes lit up. "Oh you're Adam Wallace's wife," she said. "It's so nice to finally meet you. You have a daughter here, right?"

"Lily. She's a freshman."

"How lovely. She'll find her place. That's the nice thing about Woodard—there's a club for just about anything. My oldest is a swimmer, and my youngest is like a chess genius, and I can't do either. Isn't it weird how we give birth to these beings and then they grow up entirely different than us?"

"Totally weird." I thought about Lily's temper. So sudden and fiery. Like the time I'd forbid her twelve-year-old self from going to a rock concert in Camden without me and she'd exploded, face beet red, eyes wild. *You and I are nothing alike*, she'd screamed, and I'd had to agree.

Maggie continued talking, almost as though she'd heard my thoughts. "Ugh, you've got a girl, though. Girls are hard. Oh the hormones. My boys are smelly and loud, but at least we've dodged some of that girl drama."

"It hasn't been that bad so far," I said. "Lily had good friends in Philly, and she seems to be fitting in here, too. It's the boyfriend thing that I'm worried about. I'm sure that will be starting soon." I wasn't sure why I was confiding in Maggie about Lily's future love life, but it felt right. This was what women did, wasn't it? Plus, I wanted her to like me. I wanted them all to like me.

Maggie tsked. "Overprotective mama, eh?"

"Well, not really. I just—"

She pointed at me with the lint roller. "You're the stereotypical parent of an only child. I've got three boys. I don't have the luxury of lording over them. I just want them to get the hell out of my house and give me some peace."

I laughed. That blunt kind of talk didn't seem too popular among most of the moms around here. It was refreshing.

"Ah, I'm just joking." She exchanged the lint roller for ChapStick and rubbed a liberal amount on her lips. "Where were you before here?"

"Born and raised in Philly."

Maggie nodded. "What did you do?"

"I was a reporter."

Her face softened. She pressed her hand to her chest. "I'm a reporter, too. Channel 7 news."

"Ah, that's where I've seen you," I said. "I knew you looked familiar." And now I saw it—the husky voice, heavy makeup. Like she was always on camera. Always *on*. "I was in newspapers, not TV."

"Still, though, it's in your blood."

Maggie chatted my ear off while we worked. I heard about the four cats she'd adopted, her sons' bathroom habits, all the recent stories she reported for the news. When Diane, the unfriendly woman from before, wandered by, shooting me another look, I asked Maggie about her.

"Diane Bloomington. She's an assistant principal at Jackson Middle School, but her son's here at Woodard. Why?"

"Just wondering. I met her earlier and I worried I upset her in some way," I said.

Maggie laughed. "That's because she was a finalist for your husband's job. She's probably pissed she didn't get it."

Ah. That explained the attitude. She'd played the same game, but we'd won.

Just before lunch, as my stomach started to growl, a short elfish woman strolled up to the table, gazing at all the trays. Maggie introduced us. "Beth, this is Theresa Pressley. The new principal's wife."

"Right! How nice to meet you. I'm Beth Posniak." Beth's nails were long, probably fakes, manicured with a bright pink-and-black swirl design and a tiny sparkling gem in the middle of each. She held out a hand, and I shook it gently, worried one of her nails might snap off and fall into the Rice Krispies treats. "I'm on

Parent Team. Part of the Daphne Brown Merit Scholarship committee this year."

"How nice." I had no idea what the Daphne Brown scholarship was. Was this something Lily should be applying for?

"My god, look at these. Oh my. They must be Liz's turtle bars, right? I can tell her work anywhere." She peeled away the cellophane with Maggie's help. "Oh god, I need like three of those. And these over here, too. Do you guys have boxes?"

I stepped aside while Maggie packed Beth's sweets.

"So, tell Theresa here that she needs to come to my poker game," Maggie said to Beth.

"That sounds fun," I said. "When is it?"

"I usually do them monthly. I'm right down the street from you. A few blocks down, so not too far. You can easily stumble back to your bed if you drink too much."

"You're in Ivy Woods?" Beth turned to me. Seeing the envy in other people's eyes when they talked about Ivy Woods hadn't gotten old yet.

"She's right there on the cul-de-sac," Maggie said.

"You're so lucky! I just love it there. Beautiful houses, beautiful people. My friend Alice lives there, and she just adores it."

"I know Alice," I said.

"She's a doll." Beth directed one of those claws at me. "But don't get on her bad side. She might seem like a pushover, but nope. She can be fierce when needed, especially if someone messes with her kids."

"Really?" I tried to envision Alice telling someone off, but the image was comical. She seemed more like the type who avoided conflict at all costs—to a fault.

"Oh yeah," Beth said. "Maggie, don't you remember when that Connor kid was bullying Greta a few years ago? She marched right over to that kid's house and chewed out the mom. And the mom got all defensive. It was a big thing. And then Kendra McCaul and all them got involved."

Maggie smirked. "You don't want the *Ivy Hive* on your bad side." I remembered Georgeann mentioning that name at Adam's welcome event.

Beth laughed. "Do they still call themselves that?"

"I think it's *five*," I said. "The Ivy *Five*."

"Right, but there's a reason there aren't five of them anymore," Maggie said mischievously.

A customer arrived before I could ask what that reason was.

"Oh my god. That. I'd forgotten," I heard Beth say as she shifted behind the table now, dipping into her bag to sample the sweets. "I was in that mommy group with Bettina Price, remember? At the hospital. Sloane was born like two weeks before my Jenny."

I tried to eavesdrop on their conversation, but my customer had a lot of annoying questions.

"How much are those?" She gestured at the pumpkin streusels.

Maggie said something I couldn't hear, and Beth answered, "No! She wouldn't even speak of her."

"Fifty cents?" I guessed.

"Hmm. Did you make them?"

I shook my head as Maggie said, "She was too good-looking for them. It was a threat."

"I honestly don't know that I'd recognize her if she walked in here right now," said Beth, walking over to a tray farther down that had caught her attention. My tarts. "But I remember when she had too many wine coolers during Casino Night and they had to call a taxi to send her home."

"Oh my god. She was like movie-star pretty. And no one ever really knew what happened." Maggie tapped her finger to her cheek. "There's a story there."

Thankfully, Beth moved away from the tarts. "Look at you, putting on your investigative reporter hat."

My customer whipped out her cash, started to count it, muttering to herself. "Here you go." She jammed several bills at me.

I handed her a bag, finally free, and turned to them. "Who are you two gossiping about?"

"One of the old Ivy Hive," Maggie said, twisting a lock of hair around her finger. Her eyes were glittering. "Sorry, *Five*. Before they ran her out of town."

I raised an eyebrow. "Ran her out of town? Wow, that's dramatic. You make them sound like the mafia."

"There was definitely some sort of scandal," Maggie insisted. "She did something they wouldn't forgive."

"Maybe she slept with one of their husbands." Beth wiped powdered sugar off her blouse. "Every time I tried to ask Alice about it, she sort of blew me off."

"Or she just got a job elsewhere and the family moved away." I shrugged.

Beth stared at me funny. "That woman? She never worked a real job a day in her life. She was some sort of *ar-teest*, or fancied herself as such."

"Yep," Maggie agreed. "I'm not trying to be a bitch or anything, but those women are cold. One day they were all tight, like sorority sisters, and then the next… boom! She was completely cut out."

HALLOWEEN

Darkness comes fast.

And with it, the mothers light their jack-o'-lanterns, the candles baking the insides of the gourds.

The party is a raging success, like always.

Here come the kiddos—see them? Hear them? The small ones first, toddlers begging for sweets they'll never eat. The mothers perch on their porch steps with bags of candy or stand at the end of their sidewalks. The children come in droves, eager little beasts with pillowcases and recyclable grocery bags. More more more, they chant. Trick-or-treat trick-or-treat trick-or-treat.

The fathers, who are largely invisible in this story, mutter at the edges, already three or four beers in, trading stories about how when they were kids they used to have to sing songs or tell jokes or dance for their candy. They exaggerate and they burp and the mothers overhear and are secretly disgusted by them.

The kids come and come, a seemingly never-ending

trail. But our five mothers—the ones who deserve focus tonight, the ones who are to blame for what is to transpire—will not run out of candy. They have unopened bags behind them on their porches—Mounds and Kit-Kats and Hershey bars and mini bags of Skittles and plastic eyeball rings and glow-in-the-dark necklaces—and they will continue to refill.

They smile and ooh and aah at the little bats and rain clouds and mummies and princesses—so many goddamn princesses—as they bend down and present their bowls.

"Just take one," they say.

Notice how similar our five mothers look—it is hard to tell them apart sometimes, especially tonight. So much shared between them. Recipes. Gossip. They have keys to each other's houses. They know each other's dress sizes (mostly). They've found each other jobs. They offer to drive each other to scary doctor appointments. There was that one time one of them threw up in another's car after a strange night at the bar.

A friendship hard to break, solid, smooth. Only by the light of those jack-o'-lanterns might you be able to see the beginnings of a fissure. For they also share something darker. Secrets. Shame. Jealousy. A desire for control.

A desire for power.

A desire to be loved.

A desire to kill.

Yes, it's nearly pitch-black now.

NINE

Theresa

You could only see part of Alice's backyard from the lake path that ran by her house—the small deck and the concrete pad with the firepit. The rest of the yard was shrouded in trees and was much bigger than I'd expected. Big enough, in fact, to host a swing set with a slide and monkey bars, a trampoline, and a giant storage shed she called the Barn.

Alice had texted us late last week about going through the Halloween decorations she stored there. I wasn't sure we needed any extra decorations, but I couldn't imagine saying no to the Ivies.

Turned out that only Kendra and I could make it. And she seemed distracted—something with work, I supposed, since she kept checking her phone. I was also in my head. I'd been trying to draft an article about instructional coaching budgets for my former editor at the *Inquirer* all day and was still mulling it over.

Alice tried to fill in the silent spaces with chatter. "Is anyone thirsty? I made lemonade. Literally squeezed it myself." She held up her hands. "My fingers are crazy sore right now, but Jonah's been asking about it, he loves it—Greta, just give the doll to your sister, darlin'. Honestly it's not that hard to be nice."

When we declined the lemonade, she pulled a large key from her pocket and ushered us to the Barn. Her kids tumbled over one another, rushing to be the first ones on the trampoline.

Alice was still talking. "Theresa, brace yourself. We have a lot of stuff. It's such a blast. But it terrifies my kids, of course. They won't set foot in here."

The Barn was dark and smelled of rubber and wood. Alice ventured inside and yanked a chain hanging from the ceiling, an exposed bulb that threw light into the center of the room. Although the corners were still in shadow, I could discern enough. The Halloween props were on the right, black and white, cobwebs and drifty gray hair, knives and swords and fake blood.

Alice clicked on another light. "Welcome to your nightmare."

I could see why Alice's kids steered clear. There were several life-size figures in front: a Frankenstein and a hooded, cloaked Death complete with scythe. Plastic gravestones were stacked against the wall, and on top of them were body parts, arms and legs, skulls and hands and feet. The cobwebs looked fake, but I couldn't honestly tell. When I leaned in to get a closer look, there was a loud cackle.

"Death is calling. Are you home?" droned a maniacal voice, followed by a shriek.

I jumped, squeaked, as the women burst into laughter.

"It's a door knocker. We haven't replaced the battery in over ten years," Alice said. "It's definitely possessed." She moved past me and hugged Frankenstein to lift him out into the yard. "This guy's mine. He's my darlin'."

"You have to save the spider for Bettina," Kendra said.

Alice put her hands on her hips, scowling. "Uh-uh. He's mine this year. I already said that."

Kendra shrugged. "She said you had it last year."

"I did not," Alice said. "Y'all skipped me because Pia's cousin was visiting and she wanted him. Remember?"

They went back and forth like this for a while before Alice gave in. I understood the battle even less when I saw what they were fighting over—a giant, hairy spider that came in pieces you had to assemble. We had to help Alice drag it out.

"What's your theme for the house this year, Kendra?" Alice asked, blowing her hair out of her face as she worked up a sweat lugging more figures around. Her theme was classic monsters. Besides Frankenstein and his bride, she had Dracula, a werewolf, and two creepy green children. Her house was deemed the Monster Mash-ion.

"Scenes from famous urban legends. Think—guy with a hook for a hand and a radioactive alligator in the sewer." Kendra opened a box with what appeared to be a projector inside. "We'll see what kind of time I have. Just save my zombies as a backup."

We sorted through the rest, setting aside decorations for each of us. Above me, a buzzing started.

A large bee twittered near the ceiling. I eyed it warily.

"Oh don't worry about it," Alice said breezily. "It won't sting you."

"I'm allergic," I said.

She gently swatted in its direction, and it flew away. "My bees are generally harmless unless you get close to the hive. They're just foraging for food at this point, getting ready for winter. Looks like one got trapped in here, bless his heart."

"Your bees?" I asked.

"I have a hive out back, in the woods there." Alice pointed out past her yard, toward the lake. "You can't see it. It's tucked right behind my fence. It's a hobby. You know they're in trouble? Going extinct. But seriously, don't be scared. There's a fence around the hive. They're really quite peaceful creatures."

"Plus they make delicious honey," Kendra said. "Alice gives it as Christmas presents."

I made a mental note to bring my EpiPen whenever I walked the lake path in the future.

Kendra dug farther into the shed, clearing out decorations from a wall shelf. "Theresa, didn't you say you were doing a graveyard?" she said. "We've got these gravestones. Lily would love more, wouldn't she?"

"I'm sure she would," I said. "But I don't want to take anyone's decorations."

"It's no bother," Alice said. "That stuff on the back shelf there doesn't belong to anyone anymore."

There were five of them, until they ran her out of town. I watched as Kendra and Alice stacked and restacked the decorations, wondering if what Maggie Lewis had said was true. My neighbors seemed so nice, so polished. They'd been generous. Welcoming.

Friendly. Fun. I couldn't really imagine it, or didn't want to.

So why was that gossip bothering me?

"Is this left over from the friend of yours?" I asked, then inwardly winced. *Way to be subtle, Theresa Ann.*

"Probably," Alice said. She held up a zombie mask and grimaced at it, tossing it in the pile. "I honestly can't keep track anymore."

"Oh I forgot about these," Kendra said, pulling out what appeared to be a pair of skeleton gloves.

"What did she do again?" I asked as I hauled a dusty box from the corner. Several crickets skittered away into the shadows. "I mean, for a job?" The Ivies had implied that's why their friend had left, but at the bake sale, Beth and Maggie had insisted she didn't work.

Silence. I looked up. Alice was staring at me. "Why?" she asked, and it wasn't in her usual tone.

I felt my face flush. I sounded like a weird jealous girlfriend, paranoid about an ex.

Kendra spoke up. "She was in theater. Went to New York City." She glanced at Alice. "To be honest, she wasn't very good. We didn't want to say anything mean about her, but...well, let's just say you're a way better addition to the neighborhood."

"If that ain't the truth," Alice said. They both flashed warm smiles my way.

I stood up, brushing off my jeans, embarrassed that I'd fallen for the petty gossip. "Aw, thanks, guys." *We* weren't in high school—our kids were. "And you're right. There's amazing stuff here. I'm sure Lily will want some of it. Is it okay if I ask her what she needs before I lug it all over? It's kind of supposed to be her thing."

"No problem," Alice said. "I can give you one of the extra keys, and you just come by whenever and grab it."

"Here, take mine," Kendra said, just as her phone started ringing. She frowned at the screen. "Hang on, I've got to get this."

"Please make sure my littles haven't broken any limbs," Alice called as Kendra left the barn.

"Does Kendra ever stop?" I asked. "The poor woman is eternally busy, it seems."

Alice waved a hand in dismissal. "Oh she's always worn slap out around the party. It's extra bad this year because it's the last one before her youngest goes away to college. You know, like the end of an era."

I hadn't thought of it that way, Kendra as an empty-nester. "She's so involved at Woodard, too. That will be weird for her."

"I know, right? It's like a million years away for me, so I can't even." Alice yanked another heavy box from a corner and started rifling through it.

"So, will you be taking over next year on the party? You know, like pass the baton?"

Alice paused. There was a smudge of dirt across her cheek that she tried to wipe away. "Are you messin'? No way. I've been here long enough to know that as long as Kendra lives in Ivy Woods, she'll always be in charge."

TEN

Kendra

Finally, a family dinner. Cole didn't have swim practice. Paul had actually been home from work on time
for a change. I had no fires to put out for my boss or
urgent tasks for the party. And I hadn't heard anything
in days from Bettina or Alice about threatening messages. They had to have come to their senses and realized that Jackie's lack of a social media presence didn't
mean she was on the lam and coming our way. I wasn't
even annoyed when Cole walked in with Ellen, who
was dressed in camouflage boots, black leggings, and
an oversize crocheted sweater.

"Your house is going to look great, Mrs. McCaul,"
she said as we all sat down at the table. "Appropriately
macabre."

"I haven't even scratched the surface, but thank you."
All my decorations from Alice's shed were currently in

a heap in our sitting room. It looked like a crime scene in there. But my plan was starting to shape up. I'd found a giant plastic alligator online and plastic jail bars that I fashioned into a sewer grate. I'd repurposed one zombie with a hook hand and was finishing up on a girl with baby spiders bursting from her face.

It was going to be epic, indeed.

I had a right to be proud. I was a good party planner—not to mention a damn good mother, too. I worked hard, made dinner, raised my kids to be good people. I was there for them when they needed me. For everyone. And here we were, in a beautiful home, in a great neighborhood, our contented dog under the table waiting for scraps. Cole's friend was comfortable enough to eat with us—comfortable enough, even, to just assume she was welcome.

I'm a better mother than Jackie ever was.

It was satisfying to know that. To know that I would never end up like her.

When Theresa had asked about Jackie in the storage barn, I'd wanted to tell her all about our old friend. About her "career," about her failures. She deserved everything that had happened to her. She was weak. She was not cut out to be a wife. To be a mother. She'd fucked all that up. All she ever wanted was to be a "star."

And now she was. A fading, dying star, somewhere out there. A nothing.

She couldn't touch us. She wouldn't dare.

"Cole, please say grace," I said, and while he mumbled it, I bowed my head. *Yes, thank you, god, thank you, fate, for all you've done to keep us safe.*

I'd made an easy favorite—a ravioli bake that looked

fancy but took five minutes to prep. Cole and Paul ate quickly, like wolves, but Ellen took her time, cutting each ravioli with a knife and chewing thoughtfully.

"I'm putting up our decorations this weekend," Ellen said. "Lily's coming over to help me."

"Lily Pressley?"

Ellen nodded. "We're dressing up like the Ghost Girl this year. It's going to be amazing."

Here we go. That absurd urban legend again. I thought about that damn doll in the tree. Had Cole told Ellen about it? Was she the one who'd left it for him in the first place? Seemed right in her wheelhouse.

"If by *amazing* you mean *stupid*, then yeah," Cole said.

Ellen smacked him. "You're so boring," she said. "I've been sensing a lot of energy out there. It's like the woods are getting ready for all the souls to return."

I ignored her, handing everyone napkins. Ellen liked to act all sweet, but the girl wasn't as innocent as she made out to be. I needed to warn Theresa about her, if she was hanging out with Lily. Cole had never admitted it to me, but I strongly suspected that Ellen had been the one to lure him to the football field last year to drink when he was caught and suspended. She'd gotten away with it, like she always did. Too bad we hadn't had the principal and his wife living across the street at that point.

"There's still a ton to do for the party, of course," I said. "Mr. McCaul needs to hang the orange lights on the garage roof."

"Well, if you need any help with the party, I can do it," Ellen said, ever the wannabe adult.

"That's generous of you, but we're good. Plus, I know you have a lot going on with your senior year."

"Not really," she said. "I mean, I got my early decision applications in. My counselor says I'm pretty much guaranteed to get into NYU and Oberlin, but I'd much rather Princeton." Ellen shrugged. "I've worked hard enough that I deserve Ivy League. Just depends on how much financial aid they can give me."

"We need to get Cole motivated like you are," said Paul, pointing his fork in their direction. He'd already finished his plate. Was he going to get seconds himself or wait until I offered to get them for him? My money was on the second.

But Paul was right. Cole could use motivation. A kick-in-the-ass reminder to keep him going. We all needed that sometimes. I tried my best to be there for him, but I'd been distracted with work and party planning. When was the last time I'd told Cole how proud of him I was?

"Cole is motivated," I said to Paul. "You should've seen him tear through the water the other day. He's going to get his school record back. Right?" I winked at Cole.

Cole grinned. "I'll let him have it for another week or so," he said.

"Bo won't let it go that easily," Ellen said, taking another small bite of ravioli. "He's so freaking competitive. It's like Suzanne Jennings thinking she's going to snatch valedictorian out from under me. Please."

"Could she?" Paul asked, curious.

Ellen's eyes narrowed as she shook her head. "No way. I could probably coast the rest of the year and still make valedictorian."

"Oh lord." Cole poked her with his finger. "Turn down the humbleness."

"What? It's true. Once I hear back from Princeton, it's pretty much a done deal." Ellen looked over at me as she sipped her water, then smiled. "Unless I, like, murder someone before graduation or something."

––––––––––

The sink was filled with crusty dishes and silverware when I got back from walking Barney. Cole had, as usual, poured a giant glass of Coke (no ice—seriously, how did I manage to pop a child out of my uterus who doesn't like ice in his drinks?), took about three sips, and left the rest to flatten and die on the counter. I considered yelling and rounding him or Paul up to clean everything up, but the energy wasn't there.

Paul was in bed watching TV in his boxers, sipping dark liquor on the rocks. He'd been drinking more than usual lately, I'd noticed. Work must have been rough these days. Tell me about it.

I curled up and put my head on his shoulder. When we'd first started dating, Paul was nervous around me, like he couldn't believe his luck. After my asshole boyfriend Mark, I liked that. Paul was eager to please. He bought me flowers, then concert tickets, then diamonds. He let me pick where we went to dinner, where we took vacations—happy if I was happy. I'd thought it was nice. That he was trying not to be some controlling alpha male. But after all these years of marriage, I realized it was more that Paul just didn't really care what we ate, saw, did. He left it for *me* to do everything. Like everyone else in my life.

He kissed me vaguely on the top of my head. "Georgeann

called while you were out on your walk. Something about the swim team fundraising event."

"Again? She keeps wanting to host it. It's my last year. She's not taking it away from me."

I pushed closer to him.

"Maybe you should let someone else do it," he said. "Give yourself a break."

"What if I don't want a break?" I whispered into his ear. "What if I want to play? Do you want to play?"

"Kendra," he said, craning to see the TV. "Stop. I'm watching this."

He was lucky to have me as a wife. Didn't he know that? I sighed, slid out of bed, and rubbed my arms. "Do you have the window open again?"

"I like it," he murmured. "Cold air is good for sleeping."

"Well, I'm closing it if those goddamn foxes start screaming again," I said.

I changed into my pajamas and brought my laptop into bed. There were fifty new emails since last I'd checked. Helen Boorman from work wanted a report on the marketing plan. Finance needed me to complete my time sheet. Laura Scott from high school was asking for Girl Scout cookie orders for her daughter. The dentist had sent a friendly reminder to schedule a six-month checkup.

And I had a new message request on Facebook.

Reluctantly, I logged into my account. I rarely received messages and usually just spent my time scrolling through friends' photos.

The message was from Ivy Woods—that same thumbnail photo of Theresa's house as the profile picture.

My heart started thudding as I accepted the request.

Oh, dearest Queen Bee. Just 28 days until Halloween! Enjoy the spotlight while you still can—soon you will be nothing. Are you going to tell everyone what you did? Or should I do it for you?

I'm watching you! Don't screw this up.

Attached to the message was a photo. I blew it up. It was pixelated, but large and looming on my screen, and I could still make out the image.

Alice's firepit.

And the four of us sitting around it, our faces illuminated by the flames licking the black sky.

HALLOWEEN

Let's take a break from the party for a moment and go down to the lake. It's dark down here—shh—and the moon isn't quite full, but it's still big and bright. It feels like the kind of place where terrible things can happen. So dark. No one's around. You can still hear the murmur of the party, still feel the faint bass of the music, but you're on the edges. You're invisible.

If you stand right by the water and look up, you can see all the houses. Their wooden decks, their fancy grills. The lights inside are blazing. No one ever thinks to close their blinds. No one ever thinks anyone's watching back here.

I once read a book about a serial killer who chose his victims based on who he could watch. He spent his time, months and months, just standing outside in the dark, observing. Finding routines—because we're all creatures of habit, we all fall into patterns, we're all easy to track down—and then plotting his kill. He knew when they ate dinner, when they left for work, and when they returned.

He knew when they went to sleep.

The point is, we're all predictable. And that makes us vulnerable.

A place like Ivy Woods makes the mothers feel protected, and with that sense of security, they feel invincible.

They begin to think they can do anything they want.

They believe they deserve this perfect life on this perfect street. Their rosebushes grow no thorns. Their roofs spring no leaks. Their husbands always love them. They are heroes to their children. They've been planning this life since they were children themselves, working hard to make sure it all unfolds just the way they want it to.

And nothing—or no one—is going to stand in their way.

ELEVEN

Kendra

The photo was taken the night of our bonfire meeting. I could see the geometric pattern of Pia's sweater and my UGG boots. Someone had been lurking in the woods, watching us, capturing an image with their camera to prove they'd been there, too.

These messages weren't just Halloween pranks. Someone *was* targeting us. Knew what we'd done.

And was nearby.

Had Alice and Bettina been right after all?

I called Pia on my way to work the next morning. She answered groggily—I'd woken the princess up.

"Does Jimmy-O still owe you a favor?" I asked as soon as she registered who was calling. Jimmy-O was an old friend of Pia's, a retired detective from the police force and a part-time PI.

"Kind of. I'd probably have to go on a date with his cousin, though. He's been talking about it forever."

"You may have to take one for the team, then." I told her about the photo.

"Um, I don't like that." Pia was awake now, her voice clear. She often went through life underwater, but when you needed her, she surfaced, armed and ready for battle. "So this creep is getting creepier. And has a lot of fucking time on his hands."

Or her hands.

"Send it to me," Pia said.

I copied the photo and texted it to her. A ding on her end, and then she sucked in her breath. "No message with this?"

Just 28 days...soon you will be nothing.

"More of that vague threatening crap about bees again," I said, hoping she wouldn't ask for another screenshot.

"So what...you want Jimmy-O to patrol our street more often? Look out?"

We look out for each other. That's what friends do. Isn't that what I'd told Jackie all those years ago? *We can't ever tell anyone what happened. If we did, we'd all be ruined.*

"No. I want him to find Jackie."

"Jackie?" Pia asked. "What would she have to do with..."

Everything. Jackie's joke... *Dearest Queen Bee.* Her nickname for me all those years ago. It was too much of a coincidence. And she still had ties here to the area. Family.

"I don't know," I said to Pia. "Probably nothing, but we've lost track of her. If someone's threatening us like this, I want to know where Jackie is. I want to know if she's involved."

I wanted to remind her that we had things we could hold over her if it came down to it. And who did she think everyone would believe?

"Last I heard she was in New York," Pia offered. "So unless she decided to hop an Amtrak just to come down here and take our picture, I doubt she's got anything to do with it."

"Can you just ask him anyway?" I said impatiently. "Get him to do a search? Current address, job, that sort of thing? Maybe find a phone number for her or some way to get in touch? We may need to have a chat with her. Remind her what she agreed to."

"I'm sure that would go well." I heard a noise. The phone dropped, then Pia cursed.

"What happened?" I asked.

"Tried to light my cigarette and dropped the phone," she said. I heard the strike of a match and her intake of breath.

"You're smoking again?"

Pia had always been on and off, but she hadn't smoked in years.

"Don't judge me. Stress."

I couldn't blame her. The stress was getting to me, too. I closed my eyes. We'd been okay for so long. Had put stuff behind us as much as possible. I couldn't let us collapse now. Couldn't let Pia's bad habits, my nightmares, Alice's omens, and Bettina's anxiety come back. *Goddamn Jackie.* I wasn't looking forward to having it out with her, but at this point it was necessary. "So, can you ask Jimmy-O or not?"

"Sure, yeah," Pia said, exhaling smoke from her lungs. "Though that would mean me in a Red Lobster watching his cousin slurp lobster meat out of a shell."

"I'll love you always and forever."

"Okay…but I'm still not convinced it's Jackie," Pia said.

"First steps first," I said. "Let's find our dear friend and see what she's been up to. I have a feeling she'll be able to give us some answers. Oh and, Pia? Don't say anything to the others."

There was a pause. "Are you sure? If someone's taking photos of us, they should know."

It would be hard for Pia to keep her mouth shut, but I'd have to trust her. "I will tell them. In a few days. Promise. Let's just get more info first."

So if I need to, I can strike fast.

———

I got through the workday on autopilot. I left right at 5 p.m., chatting with two other coworkers on the way to my car so I wouldn't be alone. The days were getting shorter. It was getting darker.

I kept thinking about the photo. That took some nerve. It was brazen. Cocky. Not really Jackie's MO, but then again, I hadn't seen her in so many years. People change. That was the worst part of it: I didn't know what was next. Or when.

And I *hated* feeling out of control.

The house was empty when I got home. Cole was at swim practice, and Paul was at work. I entered the mudroom, my brain still running through the message, then stopped. The door that led to the kitchen was closed. We never closed it because Barney's water bowl was in there.

I snatched Cole's old baseball bat and threw open the door. "Hello?"

Barney came tearing up, jumping on me, tail wagging. I lowered the bat. "Hey, boy, okay, boy, calm down." He bounded off, probably to go fetch me a toy.

Still, the air in the house felt strange—I smelled a faint burning smell, like charred food or a recently extinguished candle. On the kitchen linoleum, I spotted a small, hard semicircle of dried mud that had fallen off a shoe sole. Like someone was there, or had just been there.

The hair on my arms bristled. "Hello?" I called again, moving into the living room. "Paul? Cole?" I opened the front door, checked the porch. Nothing was hanging in the tree in the front yard.

In the hallway outside the powder room was a sock of Cole's that Barney had fished from the laundry and chewed to death, but nothing else seemed out of place. I walked through the rest of the house, making noise just in case some creep really was inside. Barney wasn't much of a watchdog.

Nothing.

I went back downstairs and let Barney out, then stepped into the living room.

Someone grabbed my arm.

I screamed. Leaped back.

"Kendra!" a voice cried. "I'm so sorry. I didn't mean to scare you." It was Theresa. She pointed behind her. "Your front door was wide open, so I wanted to make sure everything was okay."

I put my hand to my chest. "Fuck, Theresa. Call out or something." I must've forgotten to close the front door when I looked outside.

"I'm so sorry." She held out a bundle. "I kept forgetting to return your blanket. Thanks for letting us borrow it at the game."

I took the blanket and tossed it on the couch. "You could've kept it. We have a million."

She slunk back, as if I might bite. I was being unfair.

"Sorry, it's been a long day at work," I said. "I'm just extra on edge."

Theresa did the polite thing and shrugged it off. "That kind of thing happens to me sometimes, too. Especially in the new house. It's so much bigger than anywhere else I've lived. I hear noises all the time. Something about the space. I don't know."

The attic especially, I thought. But I couldn't talk about that house, not now.

Barney barked in the yard, scratching at the door.

"I need to let Barney in. Come back with me."

"Oh you sure?" Theresa tugged the end of her ponytail. Something about the gesture—I felt a strong sense of déjà vu. Some memory, some vague sense of alarm descended over me, but before I could name it, it was gone.

Lord, what the hell was wrong with me?

"You were talking about your house being big?" I asked in the kitchen as Barney bounded in, nearly knocking Theresa over. I gave him a bone to settle him down.

Theresa leaned against the kitchen counter. "Yeah, when I was growing up, we were always in apartments. My dad died when I was eight, so it was my mom and brother and me. We did have a duplex once, and that was nice…" She trailed off. "You can imagine this neighborhood is like my dream come true. I love everything about it." She crossed her ankles, kicking dried mud onto the linoleum, which reminded me of the scuffs I'd seen when I'd first entered the house. How bad had it gotten that I let myself get scared over dirt?

"Shoot. Let me clean that up," Theresa said. "The paths by the lake are so stinking muddy right now." She wet a paper towel and picked at the mud flecks, her ponytail whipping around.

"Don't worry about it. It gets everywhere," I said.

Theresa tossed the dirty towel in the trash and stood up. "Ugh, I feel like such a mess sometimes. I just hope Adam didn't expect a homemaker when he married me. Because that I am not."

This was the first time I'd seen her with her hair in a ponytail rather than curled down around her shoulders, and she looked much younger this way. She was in workout clothes—navy blue yoga pants and a white fleece jacket, dewy, flawless skin. I had to admit, Theresa Pressley was a classic beauty. I was betting she was the type of woman who could eat whatever she wanted (and did) and stay slim. Meanwhile, I'd been gaining a steady five pounds every couple of years even though I hadn't changed one thing about my diet.

Theresa didn't seem to realize how good she had it. If anything, she seemed desperate to please. She hadn't pushed back once about planning the party or volunteering at the school. It was like she was trying as hard as she could to be our friend. And right then, with the way everything was going, I was enormously glad to have her, a loyal soldier, at my side.

"I would imagine he married you because you're smart and ambitious, not for how well you can cook a casserole," I said.

She laughed. "You're always so put together, so confident. I wish I could be more like you, Kendra."

Ah, flattery will get you everywhere, my dear. I would be lying if I said I didn't enjoy it. And I needed it right now.

I ran my fingers through my hair. "Usually, yes. Not today, though."

"I did scare you, didn't I?" Concern washed over her face. "Do you want me to stay and hang here for a little bit?"

"Oh stop it," I said. "The guys should be home any minute now."

Theresa shook her head. "No, no. I've been spooked before, and it's not fun. Besides, no one's at my house either." She smiled. "We can keep each other company. Won't that be fun?"

TWELVE

Theresa

Kendra's house felt two-sided. The front half was fancy, a formal sitting room in all white, oil paintings of her boys on the wall, an upright piano with expensive-looking ceramic haunted houses on top. But the back of the house was like the nerve center—kitchen counters cluttered with bills, newspapers, vitamins, coats piled on breakfast table chairs. I liked it best, the reality of it, the sense of family and a life packed full of energy. The small den, where we settled, had two well-worn love seats, fluffy and cozy to sink into, and a massive TV mounted on the wall.

Kendra opened a bottle of wine and poured it into two glasses with skeleton hands as their bases. She was still wearing work clothes—sleek black slacks, a floral shirt, and a blazer—and I wished I'd had on something other than yoga pants. I hadn't worn any of my business clothes since we'd moved, and I missed that powerful feeling that came from a well-tailored pair of pants and the right heels.

Thanks to the Ivies, though, it looked like I might get to wear them again soon.

"Oh hey. I meant to tell you. I got a call from the *Post* yesterday." I grinned. "This girl may or may not have a job interview next week."

Kendra handed me my wineglass. It was surprisingly light, the skeleton bones made of a flimsy plastic. "That's great. Was it Sharita?"

I nodded. "It's exciting. But I'm also nervous. I haven't done one of these things in ages, it feels like."

I wanted that job, a big step up in my career. Adam and I could be that power couple people envied. But I also wanted to show my new friends that their string-pulling was worth it. That *I* was worth it. I was already imagining the happy hour celebration we could have with the crystal champagne flutes Adam and I had gotten as wedding gifts last year but had yet to use.

"You'll kill it." Kendra held up her wine. "Cheers to new adventures."

We toasted, and I eased back into the cushions.

Kendra drank her glass fast and poured another. "I don't usually drink during the week. But after the day I've had—the week—I really needed this."

I chuckled at this confession. "Your secret's safe with me."

"I'll be hungover tomorrow and regret it." She sighed. "God, in college we would start drinking right after class and then go to a party at ten and be out all night. I'm old."

"Yeah, but would you really want to still do that now? I for one am glad that life is behind me."

"I keep forgetting you went to school here," Kendra said.

"Yeah, it's actually nice to return to the area," I said. "I mean, things were so different then. It feels like a million years ago."

Kendra tipped the bottle my way. "But you had a good time?"

I let her top up my glass. It felt nice to talk to someone—a friend—one-on-one. I hadn't really spoken about that time with anyone except Trixie and Adam.

"Actually, no," I admitted. "It was one of the hardest times of my life. I was working like three part-time jobs when not in class. And I was engaged—did I tell you that? Oh god, we kept hoping to make it work and it just didn't."

Brad. I had filed him away in a locked box in my mind, but since we'd moved back here, he'd returned to haunt me. "We were very different people. But when Lily came into the picture, I thought we'd do better. Have a purpose. A family. He didn't see it that way."

Her mouth fell open. "He ditched you? With a baby?"

"Oh yeah. And he's like this California playboy now. Inherited a lot of money. Has nothing to do with us." I'd dodged a bullet there. Brad was never going to be the family guy that Adam was.

"Men. They can be such selfish bastards." As if to prove her point, Barney padded in and plopped himself down right on top of her feet. She reached down and absentmindedly petted his head.

But could I really blame Brad for what happened? I'd certainly done my best to sabotage our happily-ever-after with all my bad decisions. "I can't put all the blame on him," I said. "I made mistakes, too. But I vowed I wouldn't let Lily suffer for them. I've always tried to give her the best life I could."

"Ah, mothers," Kendra said. "We really are the heroes. And we don't get any credit for it, do we?"

"Hear, hear." We toasted again, my wine almost tipping over the side of the glass.

"I'm going to need some food to soak this up." Kendra picked up her phone. "I'll just order pizza. Screw it."

I checked the time. Five thirty.

"You should stay." Kendra looked up from the screen. "The boys will take their food and hole up in front of their devices and I'll be on my own anyway."

It was tempting. The wine, the couch, the conversation. I didn't want it to end yet.

"Let me just check in on Adam and Lily." I texted. Can you guys fend for yourselves tonight for dinner?

They responded almost immediately. Lily sent an emoji of a plate of pasta. Adam said, Don't worry about me. Work to do.

"I'd love to stay," I told her. "If you don't mind?"

———

The sky outside darkened fast, and Kendra finally switched on a light and drew all her drapes closed. Around 6 p.m., Paul and Cole stomped in, said hello, and, as she'd predicted, retreated to their separate spaces. When the pizza arrived, we kept one pie in the den for ourselves.

We were nearly through the wine bottle by then, and I could feel my head loosening and floating, my limbs heavy. Kendra had kicked off her shoes and burrowed her feet between the cushions.

"So, tell me what you think of everybody," she said, sitting back.

"Who?"

She waved her hand. "The girls." She took a sip. "What's your impression of them?"

"They're great," I said. I knew I had to tread lightly. This was the first time I'd hung out with Kendra alone, and I didn't want her to think I was a gossip.

"Nah. What do you really think?" She grabbed another slice of pizza and sunk her teeth in.

I didn't know what type of answer Kendra was looking for. Did she want me to point out weaknesses, flaws, to prove I was perceptive? Or gush about how great everyone was, to demonstrate I was loyal? I decided to hover in the middle. "I'm not sure I know them well enough to form an opinion yet. I think Alice is very sweet"—Kendra smirked—"and Bettina is...really stylish."

"Stylish?" Kendra laughed. "Yeah, she is. She can also be totally hard to read, right? Like, you have no idea if she loves you or hates you? It's okay to say it."

I shook my head but started laughing. I was drunk, but also high on the moment. There I was, in Kendra's house, like we'd been friends since second grade.

"And Pia is way better at Pilates than I'll ever be. And she gets through life without alcohol, which is a heroic thing in my book."

"Oh god, she fooled you?" Kendra threw her head back and laughed. "Pia is a total lush. Well, that's not fair. She *was*. After her divorce she tried to quit, thank god. She gets all high and mighty about it sometimes, shaking that water bottle in our faces, going on about how many days sober she's been. But her willpower can be pretty shitty. We all know where she hides it in her house."

"Wow," I said. I imagined Pia stashing airplane bottles of whiskey behind boxes of rice in the pantry, the way my aunt Carol used to between stints in rehab. "I guess we all have our secrets."

Kendra aimed her crust at me. "So, what's yours?"

"Mine?" I took another bite of my slice to buy myself time. *How many hours do you have?* "I'm afraid I'm just boring old me."

"Bullshit. That innocent ponytail and those killer reporter instincts are a dangerous combination." She dusted off her palms and set her plate on the coffee table. "Come on. I know you've got something sneaky behind that 'who, me?' expression." Kendra stretched her foot across and nudged my knee. "Spill it, you witch."

It was a challenge, same as that night at the football game when she asked whether I was willing to help out. *Are you one of us?* she seemed to be saying.

"Okay, well, since we were talking about moms having to do everything and wanting what's best for our kids..." I drew a deep breath. There were multiple things I could tell her that might be shocking. I decided I could let one slip for a good cause. "I'm the reason we landed here."

Kendra had that tiger look on her face now. I thought back to the night I'd seen them all through the window, talking, laughing. Back to driving through these neighborhoods as a grad student, visiting my professors' beautiful houses, meeting their beautiful families. And even before that, tagging along with my mother to the expensive houses she cleaned, seeing how the other half lived. Like that first time Adam and Lily and I toured Woodard High School, how big it was, all the offerings. Smart kids, good grades, an excellent rating. So much opportunity—for Lily, for Adam, for me.

My mother had been harsh at times, hovering over me. Making sure my hair was combed, my homework was done, my friends were respectable. She'd taught me to strive for something more, always dream big. To believe I deserved it.

All those years, I'd wanted in.

When you think about something so much, you need it even more.

And you'll do even more to get it.

"I really wanted Adam to get this job. Like, really." Another sip. Liquid courage. "So I called in a favor. I asked Greg Hendricks to put in a good word for him."

"Whoa." Kendra whistled low. She was leaning forward, her elbows on her knees.

This was the exact type of secret she'd craved.

"That's quite the favor," she added. "Miles Hendricks is no pushover. Greg must be a *very* good friend."

My cheeks grew hot with embarrassment. I knew what she was hinting at, but there was no way I was going there. "It's not like that," I said.

But it was. It was exactly like that.

The images came before I could stop them. Professor Greg Hendricks with the sparkling eyes, stacking his papers, shoving them in his briefcase. *Theresa, can you stay after class for a minute?*

Then, outside, slipping between two buildings. His face, so close. My back pressed against concrete and bricks. His kiss, soft, then firm, my heartbeat responding before my brain could even register what had happened. Dinners three towns away. Secret meeting spots after dark. Sheets tangled between legs.

Yes, it had been exactly like that. But I wasn't spilling *that* secret.

"Greg and I just go way back," I told Kendra. "And I did him a favor once, so he owes me."

"Damn, girl," Kendra said, winking. "I underestimated you. Nice job." She set down her wineglass. "I've got something for you. I'll be right back."

She left the room, and I checked my messages again. Adam had texted.

Enjoy! Love you, my love. See you tonight.

All the air went out of my sails seeing those words. I'd said too much.

I'd called Greg when the Woodard position opened up because I wanted what was best for our family. Adam hadn't been happy in his old job, had ambitions to move up to principal. But I didn't want us to land in a school district in the middle of nowhere, with no opportunities for Lily. Woodard was the perfect chance for Adam— and for us. So what if I had to nudge it along? Competition was intense, and if you're going to win, you've got to play the game. My mother's words had echoed in my head. *You think I'm scrubbing these toilets for fun, missy?*

"This is for you."

Kendra had come back in black lounge pants and a soft-looking sweater, hair pulled up into a clip. She handed me a small, deep blue velvet jewelry box.

I held it in my palms. It had a tiny gold clasp on the side. "Kendra," I said. "You can't tell anyone. About Adam and the job. He doesn't know. He'd kill me if he found out."

"Oh, Theresa. Please don't worry," she said, sitting back down on the couch. "I'm not going to tell a soul."

"I just wanted what's best for Lily. And for us."

No matter how many favors I had to call in. No matter how many lies I had to tell.

"Stop worrying! You can trust me." She gestured toward the box. "Now open it."

I removed the top. Inside, a satin cushion, and then: a green leaf pin.

Ivy.

"We all have them," Kendra said, picking up her wineglass again. "I got them for everyone for Christmas years ago. I thought you might like it."

My mind flashed to Georgeann Wilkins. Maggie Lewis. Beth Posniak. The way their eyes glittered when they talked about my neighbors. *The Ivy Five.*

"I love it so much. Thank you." I held the pin up to my fleece jacket, but it looked too fancy in contrast, so I set it back in the box.

"Of course." She smiled. "Like I said, we mothers need to stick together. I'm a Scorpio. Fiercely loyal to my friends. To a fault."

I rubbed the velvet of the box in my hand.

I'm doing this so one day you'll have a place like this of your own, Theresa Ann, my mother had said when she took me with her to clean houses. *For now, though, you just look.*

I'd been looking all my life. Now it was time to be on the other side. On the inside.

I was still nervous. I'd exposed myself when I couldn't afford to.

But power came with a price. I knew that.

TWENTY-FIVE DAYS UNTIL HALLOWEEN

THIRTEEN

Theresa

Lily was getting anxious to put up the Halloween decorations. It was the first week of October, after all, and she and Adam wouldn't be around over the weekend. They were driving to Philly—the real estate agent had finally sold our condo and Adam was going to handle the paperwork. Normally, I'd have jumped at the chance to get back and see my brother and sister-in-law, but I'd already volunteered to help out at a Parent Team event. Plus, as Adam pointed out, the time alone would give me a chance to prep for my interview.

We'd already gone to several stores for graveyard supplies. Adam had splurged and bought a smoke machine, rigging up a timer so it would start spewing fog just as dusk hit. I wanted to make sure everyone knew we were taking our first Halloween here in Ivy Woods very seriously. Though I'd drawn the line at digging holes in the yard to make the graves look "realistic." We'd bought a few extra-large bags of potting soil at the garden store for dirt piles instead.

My mom had always loved Halloween, but we'd never been able to afford much in the way of decorations. I remembered stringing up orange and black streamers from corner to corner of our living room and clustering unscented white pillar candles on the fireplace. We always had a pumpkin—Mom would spend a long time walking around the patch, rolling over gourd after gourd to find the right one, the perfect one, and then she'd carve it into something amazing, a gruesome face or a black cat that sat on our front stoop until it grew white fuzzy mold.

I didn't have that kind of talent, which I'm sure would've disappointed my mother. But when Bettina had brought one of her treasured Autumn Golds over yesterday, Adam had promised he would turn it into a work of art. Until then, it sat on our porch step like a contented little orange pet.

I moved the wireless speaker to the porch, and we listened to a Halloween playlist while we worked in the yard, warm breeze, no clouds in the sky. As soon as Adam got home from the school, he cranked open the garage door and set up a table saw in the driveway to take advantage of what daylight was left.

I walked over, absorbing it all. "What in the world are you doing?"

He grinned, flipping down a pair of safety goggles, but not before I saw him wink. "I've been put to work by Lily."

"I had no idea you were a handyman," I said, astonished at how much I still had to learn about Adam, the new things I kept discovering, like turning a corner in a city I thought I knew only to find a delicious-smelling bakery or a cozy bookstore.

"Ah, I come from a long line of woodworkers. Almost all of the furniture in my parents' house was made by my dad."

"Wonderful," I said. "You can make our new coffee table then." I still hadn't found the right one. We'd been using an old brass monstrosity that my mother had picked up at a discount furniture store decades ago, and I wanted it gone.

I watched Adam line up a board and press through it with the high-pitched saw. His movements were precise and confident. Which was the way he did everything, including his job. The job he deserved.

"Let him work," Lily called. She was trying to untangle a long string of orange lights I'd never seen before. Perhaps they'd been Adam's at some point. "He's making me a stage for the grave robber."

I shook my head as I sauntered back over. "I don't even want to know."

"You know what else you don't want to know?" Lily asked. "We have a ghost."

"What?" I took one end of the lights and tried to make sense of them.

Lily snatched them from me and began stretching the strand along the sidewalk. "In the woods. By that lake down there. Ellen's going to show me."

Ellen again. I was grateful Lily had made a friend so fast, but was she the right friend? At her old school, Lily hadn't exactly been popular, but she'd had a core group. Here, though, the last thing I wanted was for Lily to be branded as strange before she even had a chance to blossom at her new school. Once you were labeled one way or the other in high school, it was impossible to shake it. I knew that from experience.

"I don't know that I like the sound of that," I said.

"A girl ghost." I could hear the smile in my daughter's voice. "She haunts this creepy railroad bridge down there."

"Great," I said. "Is this that urban legend you've been going on about?"

"Yeah. She's a bride, too. Plunged to her death in her wedding gown."

"Probably because the appetizers weren't hot enough," Adam called from the driveway, an old joke from our wedding where his mom wouldn't stop complaining that the mushroom puffs were cold as ice.

"Sounds morbid," I said. "Just don't hang around railroad tracks. I don't like that idea."

Lily groaned. "I'm not going to fall off or get run over. Don't worry. Ellen wants us to dress up like her for Halloween, and we just need some inspiration."

Somehow a dead bride was more appealing than woodland creature costumes.

Lily got the lights untangled—turned out she'd borrowed them from Ellen—and we strung them up along the porch rails. As we incorporated body parts in our dirt piles, I grabbed a severed arm, chasing her around. "Give me your blood," I called. She picked up a giant leg and we started dueling, until my arm (the fake one) flew out of my hand and sailed across the yard. As I turned, I saw it nearly hit Bettina, who was standing on the sidewalk, watching us.

"My god, I'm sorry," I said. "I didn't hear you coming."

She tilted her head in the direction of Adam, whose saw was making a high-pitched whine.

"Right," I said.

"I'm sorry to interrupt," she said formally, dressed, as always, like she'd stepped out of a fashion magazine with her black pencil skirt, pale pink silk shirt and cardigan, and pearls around her neck. "But I wanted to ask before I forgot. Sloane usually babysits the smaller kids the night of the block party, but she got invited to a friend's house. I wanted to see if Lily might be interested." Lily heard her name and walked toward us, still wielding the giant leg. "It's pretty decent money, for not that hard work. We usually just corral them in someone's living room after trick-or-treating and put on a movie. Half of them fall asleep by nine."

Lily was alarmed. "Oh I don't know—"

"That sounds great," I interrupted, throwing a side eye at her. "Funny you ask, since Lily's been talking lately about how she wants to be more independent. This is a great opportunity, don't you think, hon?"

"I've never babysat before," she blurted out.

"What are you talking about? You watched your cousins all the time."

"Well, that's different. But, Mom, Ellen and I were going to..." She trailed off, frowning, then murmured, "I just don't want to babysit on Halloween."

"Maybe you could talk to Sloane and she could give you all the insider scoop," I said, wanting to help Bettina out. Broadening Lily's friend horizon couldn't hurt either, and the girls were close in age. But Lily gave me a face like I'd just suggested we all hold hands and skip down the street singing "We Are Family."

"I'm sure she'd be happy to," Bettina said. "We are

having a little family and neighborhood gathering for her birthday this weekend if you guys want to come?"

"Oh," I said, surprised. "Well, Lily and Adam will be coming back from Philly, but I can probably stop by."

Bettina pursed her lips. "Great. Well, just let me know about the babysitting thing."

"Will do. Oh and, Bettina,"—I stepped onto the sidewalk and lowered my voice as Lily went back to decorating—"thanks again for the hookup with Sharita. It's a big deal to get a call from the *Post*."

"I know." Bettina didn't warm to gratitude, though I did note a small smile. "I hope it goes well. Sharita and I have been friends for a—" Bettina stopped, her eyes focused on my sweater.

I looked down. She was staring at my leaf pin. I'd affixed it to my wool sweater because it went well with the yellow color.

"Nice pin," she said, in a tone that did not suggest nice.

I touched it self-consciously. "Kendra gave it to me the other night," I said.

"I didn't realize she'd gotten that back." She tucked her hair behind her ear, staring at the pin as though it might jump off my chest and bite her.

"Gotten it back?" I asked, flustered. "From who?" But I already knew. Of course. Kendra had said, *I got them for everyone for Christmas years ago.*

"It's funny," Bettina went on as if reading my thoughts. "You kind of remind me of her. You are both very…ambitious."

FOURTEEN

Kendra

The bathwater was scorching. Just like I wanted it. Hot enough to turn my skin bright red. I snuck away after dinner to take a midweek evening soak and think through everything swirling in my head.

I want whatever is best for my family.

Wasn't that basically what Theresa had said? I respected that. I *lived* that. Everything I'd done, I'd done for my family.

No matter the sacrifice.

Theresa Pressley wasn't a softy after all. She had those mellow eyes and dewy skin, but the other night I saw a fire inside her. She'd raised a kid on her own after her lousy ex-fiancé dumped her, after all. And got her new hubby a fancy job in an elite school district. She wasn't afraid to take risks to get what she wanted.

Now I knew why she had seemed so familiar to me,

why I'd felt like I knew her from somewhere. Because she reminded me of myself.

Yes, Theresa Pressley was a fighter. Like me. We both had secrets to keep, things we'd done to make sure our kids, our families, would succeed. The problem with a secret was that you had to be constantly vigilant about keeping it. Not tell it to the wrong people. Time made us soft. It blurred things. If you weren't careful, you could forget what you most needed to remember.

Everything had been fine for so long now, for so many years, that we'd all become complacent. I blamed myself.

I'd let Jackie off my radar. Figured she'd moved on. Figured everything was long buried and forgotten.

I'd been wrong.

Dearest Queen Bee... Those words. Jackie's words. I knew it. It had to be her.

When had she first started calling me that as a joke? *Our Queen*, she'd said. *What would we do without you?* She'd meant it in an affectionate way—I'd been the one to organize the book club, the holiday party, and later, the playdates. One year for my birthday, she'd even bought me a gilt crown that I still had somewhere in the back on my closet, half its plastic "jewels" fallen off.

That nickname didn't seem affectionate now, though. Jackie was trying to open a crack in what we'd sealed. I wasn't sure why, or what she hoped to gain. But I did know I wasn't going to let it happen.

I hoped Jimmy-O would be able to track her down and give us more information. Because Bettina had been right—Jackie was hard to find online. Oh there were headshots of her, cast photos from some of the plays she'd been in years ago. An outdated actor résumé on a theater association website. But unless she was using a different name, she had no accounts on any of the major social media apps, no email address or phone number.

I didn't know how long it would take Jimmy-O to get back to us, but until then, I'd stay calm. Be vigilant. Continue planning and decorating and moving forward. If Jackie was nearby, I wasn't going to give her the satisfaction of showing her threats unsettled me.

I could handle myself. And I knew Bettina could hold her own. Even Pia was pretty steady. It was Alice I worried about, Alice who wore her emotions on her sleeve. The woman sobbed at dog food commercials and couldn't lie to save her kids' lives. She'd always been the weakest link, and I couldn't let her collapse now. Not after all this time.

Pia had gifted me expensive lavender sea salts last year for my birthday, and I relished the feeling of the slick oil coating my skin and soaking into my pores. I was a deep sea creature, powerful and steady, suspended in a safe pool. But ready to attack, to strike, to sting, whenever necessary.

We had twenty-five days left until Halloween. Twenty-five days to find out what Jackie was up to. She'd better be ready for a fight.

HALLOWEEN

It's been a very strange month for the Ivy Five. So many things to be stressed about. So many worries and suspicions. Even now, when the party seems to have gone off without a hitch, they wonder. They worry.
Can they trust one of their own?

She has shared a secret with them, and they are a group that prides themselves on righting wrongs. They will do their best, for now, to help her. As long as she doesn't fuck it up. As long as she holds her own and stays loyal. Fidelity is very important to the mothers of Ivy Woods. They are nothing if not faithful.

She is a little too pretty, of course. She looks a little too good in her Halloween costume. She laughs a little too loud. She is one of them, but she is also a threat. Even if they don't admit it to themselves.

There she is, sitting with the other four. Telling a story about something from long ago, something grand that uses lots of hand gestures. The mothers are notic-

ing how the fathers watch, too, for their friend has that charm about her, and it's not just about the extra eye liner and mascara and blush, not just about the short dress and long legs. It's some inner shine, some burst of energy and passion. It is a sense of instability and mystery that surrounds her—do any of them really know her? Do they understand why she's chosen to live here, of all places, when she could be anywhere else at all?

And with that uncertainty comes a colder judgment. They have chosen to let her in, but they also want her to know that she can, at any time, be removed. Maybe she knows that, too. They've done it before, haven't they? Maybe this is why she seems to try extra hard to win their approval.

Watch now as she swings her arms out, leans forward to finish the punch line. Her hand hits the table next to her, where one of them has set down her cell phone. Because the pavement of Ivy Woods Drive isn't as perfect as the people, there are small divots, uneven planes, and the table's legs aren't entirely stable. Her wild, nervous motion sends the cell phone arcing into the air. It falls with a skitter and a clatter, directly into the center of the small firepit set up in the middle of the cul-de-sac.

There is a flurry of activity. Someone finds a metal stick used for s'mores and tries to fish it out, but by then it's clear it's ruined. Toast.

"I'm so sorry, I'm so sorry," she says. She is burning with embarrassment. She cannot be consoled.

It's Queen Bee's phone. The woman who's always been in charge. The fixer. Watch her blow it off. She's a martyr. She's a saint. She says she's just glad no one got hurt. "Cell phones can be replaced," she intones with gravity. And everyone appreciates her kindness.

"This is turning out to be a very weird block party," someone whispers with a tragic look.

Little does she know.

FIFTEEN

Theresa

In the circular window of our attic, Lily had fixed a translucent image of a witch riding a broom. When it was dark, the lamp from her desk made it seem like the witch was riding all the way to a full moon.

I saw it as I slipped down to the lake late Saturday afternoon, soon after Lily and Adam had left for Philadelphia. I was alone, for once. Just like that witch.

And up to trouble, too.

It was growing dark as I wove down the path past Kendra's house to the lake, but I knew the way by now. I'd been walking it nearly every day since we'd moved in.

The air was cool, and I drew up the collar of my flannel shirt, wishing I'd worn a coat. I tucked my hands in my jeans pockets. It was quiet and foggy on the path, but there was always some sense around here of activity, of families living their lives. At dusk, you couldn't open a window without smelling charred meat from someone's grill or hearing the solitary *thunk, thunk* of a teenager shooting hoops in their driveway.

"The whole weekend to yourself," Adam had said as he kissed me goodbye earlier. "Just don't throw a wild party and burn the house down."

I'd laughed, kissed him back. "I'm just a boring old person," I'd said, feeling guilty as the words, the lies, tumbled out of my mouth. "Catching up on Netflix."

Or meeting up with ex-lovers in the dark.

I sat on the bench at the edge of the lake and glanced at my phone, hoping Greg wouldn't be late. After my conversation with Kendra earlier in the week, I'd been worried about what I'd told her, whether she'd keep my secret. Whether I'd thanked Greg enough for the favor. Since I'd run into him at the football game a few weeks ago, he'd emailed several times asking to meet for coffee—*Wherefore art thou, Theresa?*—but I hadn't responded, justifying it to myself as having been too busy. Now I wondered if that was a mistake. After all, I needed him on my side.

This had been our old off-campus meeting spot, right near his house, easy for him to sneak away to. Almost thirteen years ago, and it felt the same. It was surrounded by a copse of pines, so we'd be sheltered if anyone did pass by. Close enough to the black water to see the bubbles and ripples from fish feeding. I was a woman disappearing into the shadows. Invisible. Something about that both terrified and thrilled me.

What would Kendra think?

I waited, a lone witch. For weren't witches almost always depicted alone? One solitary caped figure, pointy hat askew, flying high above the treetops. She might

have a cat if she was lucky, or friends—other witches—
but they met rarely, and only to exchange recipes or con-
duct a complex spell that required numbers. Witches
did not have husbands. They didn't get married off or
sent on a happily-ever-after.

I heard gravel crunching, and a dark silhouette filled
the space.

Someone in a black hooded sweater drew closer to
me.

I stood, confused. The figure was too small to be Greg.

Then the figure lowered the hood, and in the fading daylight, I saw it was Ellen, Lily's friend. Chunky
eyeliner and metallic lipstick. Her wavy hair streaked
with pink this time and piled atop her head.

"Ellen. You scared me."

She surveyed me carefully. Tucked a small notebook
in the front pocket of her sweater. "Meeting someone?"
she asked bluntly.

"What? No. I was just—sitting here. Thinking." I
was stammering. "This time of year, you know. It just
puts me in that kind of mood."

Ellen's eyes narrowed, as if she knew I'd lied. And
Greg would probably be here at any moment to confirm it.

"I figured since Lily and Mr. Wallace were out of
town that you might have plans or something."

This girl didn't miss a trick.

"Getting excited for Halloween?" I asked, changing
the subject. "It's all Lily can talk about."

"It's why I like to walk here at dusk," Ellen said.
"This is the time when the barrier to the spirit world is
thinnest, and it's always easier to cross closer to Hallow-

een." She shut her eyes, breathed deep. Then her eyes flew open. "We're going to be Ghost Girls."

I nodded encouragingly. "Lily told me."

"Have you seen her bridge?"

I shook my head, but Ellen tugged my arm. "Come. I'll show you."

"I don't really—"

"It's not that far. It's the perfect time to see it. If we're lucky, we might even see her."

I followed. I didn't want Greg to show up and prove me a liar in front of her. He was late anyway. It would be his turn to wait.

And it wouldn't hurt to know more about this friend of Lily's and their obsession with this story. I didn't believe in ghosts or spirit boundaries, but Ellen's cold grip on my skin made me wonder.

Ellen moved fast, and I had to rush to keep up with her. The leaves were crisp and fragile, and they crushed in a satisfying way as we stepped, sending acorn shells scurrying around us.

The path wound around and down, deeper into the woods, ending at a fork. In front of us was a small wire fence and, beyond it, railroad tracks.

We turned left, walking parallel with the tracks until the path began to incline. Then suddenly ahead of us loomed a large bridge that the tracks went under. Graffiti was painted on the side: *Ghost Girl Lives* in bright pink, and below that, *Where Are the Children?*

I stopped to take it all in. The bridge was an eyesore, an imposing concrete monster in an autumn woodland. It snuck up on you, with its rusted grating, concrete pilings, and overgrown weeds. It wasn't hard to grasp how such a structure could inspire an urban legend in a sleepy privileged neighborhood.

"Come on," Ellen said enthusiastically, heading toward the incline. "How often do you get to see a haunted bridge?"

I was wary of going up there. A crude wooden barricade had been placed at the top, and signs screaming NO TRESPASSERS and DANGER STAY AWAY warned against lingering, but the wooden planks had been pushed aside, probably by teenagers like Ellen, who gathered here after dark to smoke and drink and lord knows what else.

I could see the appeal for Lily. That tragic, dramatic tale. A young, depressed bride, scorned and outcast, feeling like there was no other choice. Leaping to her death in a wedding dress.

"The story goes that if you're out here late at night, very quiet, you can see her appear at the top of the bridge." Ellen pulled my hand, trying to drag me up. "I've seen her," she said. "Many times."

I trailed her to the top but stopped at the wooden barricade. I wasn't going to walk out on that bridge. It looked, despite the hulking pile of concrete, precarious, as if, in the dying light, it could all crumble to dust.

"Are you scared, Theresa?" The way she said my first name was off-putting. Lily's friends in Philly had called me Ms. P.

An animal howled in the distance, and a tree poking out over the top of the bridge swayed.

"No," I said. "I just—I don't think I have the right shoes…"

Ellen left me there, walked onto the bridge with confidence until I lost sight of her. But I could still hear her voice traveling clearly through the air.

"There's one thing I don't agree with. Everyone says she's sad. That she comes here to reenact her death. That they can hear her crying."

Something creaked—how sturdy was this structure? "Ellen, I think maybe you should come back…"

"That's bullshit, in my opinion. I think she returns seeking revenge."

Behind me, the sound of crunching gravel on the path. I shifted, saw someone coming fast, and stepped back. A loose rock in the incline tripped me and I fell, let out a scream as I slid down toward them.

"Theresa?"

I looked up. Greg was looking down at me, holding out a hand. He lifted me to my feet.

"You okay?"

"Yeah, I—I just—" I brushed the dirt and leaves from my clothing. "How did you find…?"

"Sound travels around here. I heard voices." He checked over my shoulder, and I followed his gaze. Ellen, coming down from the bridge. In her all-black garb, she almost blended into the landscape. A spirit-shadow.

I dropped Greg's hand, not sure if she'd been able to see.

She stopped in front of us and sized us up like we were strange wildlife she'd stumbled upon. I was about to introduce them when Greg spoke. "Out here in the dark again?"

She curtsied, then grinned sarcastically at him. "Yes, Father."

SIXTEEN

Theresa

Father?

I was still trying to regain my footing, literally and figuratively, as Ellen's word hovered in the air between us. I turned to Greg. "She's your daughter?"

Greg looked confused. "Last I checked."

"I thought…" I trailed off. "I thought your name was Nora."

A memory, unearthed from long ago, of a giggling little girl. Chasing her into a dark bedroom, a flash of silk hanging out of a drawer. *Come out of there, Nora, we aren't supposed to be in here—*

Ellen rolled her eyes. "Nora was such a childish name."

Hadn't Nora, the little girl I'd known, been precocious? I remembered when I'd played board games with her a few times, she asked me to rewrite the rules in *Chutes and Ladders*—not to make the rewards more lavish, but to make the punishments harsher.

"Eleanora is her full name," Greg said. "But she decided on Ellen a few years ago. I guess it sticks now."

"I had no idea," I said, feeling foolish.

"Why would you?" Ellen asked in a snappy tone. Her eyes fixed on me, brimming with hostility.

And then, as quickly as it had come, her expression changed. A fast smile, shoulders relaxed—so warm I must've imagined the other. "It's been so delightfully fun, kids, but I must be off," she announced. To me, she added, "I trust my father can lead you out."

She disappeared down the path.

"I can't believe I didn't make the connection," I murmured once her footsteps faded.

"Well, she was like three feet tall the last time you saw her," Greg said. "And a lot less sarcastic. Come on, let's get out of here."

We reached a narrow part of the path, and Greg grabbed my arm to steady me. The familiarity of that gesture, how effortlessly we attuned to each other even after so long, was a little unsettling. The path widened and led us back out to the lake, where the houses along the water were all lit up. Shadows moved across the frames, families watching television or making food, doing homework.

"So tell me," he said as we walked around the lake. "Why are we meeting in the woods, like old times?"

I laughed. "Habits die hard, I guess."

He cocked an eyebrow. "Is that it? Or do you not want your fancy neighbors to see us together?"

"Well, it is a gossipy place," I said.

Greg ducked to avoid a low-hanging branch. "Just don't give them anything they can hold over you." I was glad it was dark so he couldn't see my embarrassment.

Did Greg somehow know I'd told Kendra about the job? He'd always had an uncanny way of figuring out my innermost thoughts, plucking them out and highlighting my worst fears. "Joking, kind of." He ran his fingers through his hair. "This does bring back memories, though."

"Agreed. I was just talking about those dinners you used to have at your house every month."

"Until Grady nearly choked on a peanut."

My hand flew to my mouth. "Oh my god. I'd forgotten about that." I couldn't help but laugh at the memory. "Everyone was trying to do CPR on the poor guy, and then it popped out—"

"Right into MaryBeth's wineglass," Greg finished.

"Poor Grady."

Greg jabbed me playfully with his elbow. "The only thing that freaked me out more was when *you* called me that time from the emergency room to come pick you up."

I groaned. "It was urgent care, but yeah. Bees and me don't agree." How stupid I'd been to go down to the lake, in a field of clover, without my EpiPen.

"Anyway, enough about the past," Greg said. "The present is so much more interesting. Like our kids. Lily and Ellen have really hit it off, it seems," he said. "You've done well."

"Thank you."

"Adam seems to be doing well."

"Yeah, you think so, too?" I asked. "He really does love the job."

"My dad hasn't said one grumpy thing about him, which is a high compliment, you know."

I stopped on the path. Above us, somewhere in one of the rows of town houses, a man shouted, and a dog barked. I lowered my voice. "Greg, I feel kind of bad for asking you to help out with that."

He threw me a lazy smile. "Oh please. That type of thing happens all the time with these high-profile jobs." His broad shoulders seemed to block out the moon.

"Maybe." I bit my lip. "But it's Adam more than anything else. He'd be furious with me if he knew. He's so ethical about stuff. Never cuts any corners."

"A Boy Scout, eh?"

I nodded. "An Eagle Scout, actually."

He laughed. "You sure know how to pick 'em, Theresa."

We started walking again. It was colder now, and my hands and cheeks were numb. Above us, a passenger jet's lights blipped as it soared past. When Lily was a toddler, she'd thought they were aliens keeping watch over us.

"Look," Greg continued. "You've got nothing to worry about. We go way back, right? You did me a favor once, and now I've done you one. This is what old friends do."

The way he said it—*a favor*. As though I'd let him borrow a book or picked up his dry cleaning. As though our past hadn't stamped its mark on us, changing us forever.

"It's not just the job, Greg." I felt the frustration boiling inside me. "Adam doesn't know about any of *that* either. Neither does Lily." I stared hard at him, hoping it would sink in without me having to say the words out loud. "And they never can."

SEVENTEEN

Kendra

I loved Bettina. I did. But she spoiled the shit out of her daughter.

Sloane's birthday parties were always grand affairs. The child had an airbrushed Peter Rabbit smash cake when she turned one. When Sloane was in fifth grade, Bettina rented a pony to prance around the yard giving rides to the kids. Next year, when Sloane was old enough to drive, I was sure we'd all be gasping with faux surprise at a zippy Volkswagen Jetta with a big red bow affixed to the hood.

Alice and I strolled into their backyard for this year's festivities. As Alice's kids ran out, on the hunt for things to destroy, we spotted Bettina attempting to tape down an unruly tablecloth. Sloane's friends offered dismissive looks and checked their phones. I had a massive headache that I was hoping wouldn't tip into a migraine. I should've skipped this whole affair, but here we were.

We said happy birthday to Sloane, gave her our gift cards. She was wearing fur-lined knee-high boots and a cowboy hat with a dress that was so short I wouldn't have let her out of the house.

"I'm so glad I had boys," I muttered as we approached the food table, where Bettina had set out a buffet of sugar. Pumpkin-shaped cupcakes, candy corn cookies, and a giant sheet cake with a picture of Sloane twirling a baton in the middle.

"Tell me about it," Alice said. "Poor Greta's going to have a rough time. You remember that ruthless Connor girl, what a little *bitch* she was." Alice bit off the word *bitch* with distaste—she hated cursing, but any threat to her kids riled her up. "And now there's a girl in her day camp passing her notes saying her teeth look like horse teeth. I swear to sweet Jesus I'm going to tear her dirty hair out of her head before it's all over."

Alice snagged a handful of caramel popcorn. "But while we're on the subject of notes," she said, "I'm glad you were right, Kendra. I haven't gotten any other messages."

"I'm always right," I said. Which technically wasn't a lie. Alice hadn't gotten any other messages. Did I feel guilty not telling her or Bettina about the bonfire photo? Sure. But it had only been four days. Soon Pia would have answers, so why worry them when we didn't have all the facts straight yet?

Speak of the devil, Pia sauntered over, draped in a cardigan-scarf, the bangles on her arm jingling like church bells. "Hello, my dears."

"You look nice," I said.

"Went on a shopping spree today. Marlon sent me

my check." She rubbed her fingers together. "Best day of the month."

"Ah, so you'll be busy this weekend," I said.

Pia always prowled the dating sites after she got her alimony. One afternoon, Bettina and I had snooped and found her profile. She'd written that she was a "free spirit" looking for "a man who feels as comfortable on a saddle as he does in a tuxedo." We had laughed at that for days. The only problem was that I'd had to create an account to view it, and I was still getting emails about my perfect matches, no matter that I deleted the account or how many times I clicked Unsubscribe.

"What did you get Sloane?" I asked.

"What every girl needs. A fast-drying hair towel and some face masks." She winked, then said, not subtly to me, "We have to talk by the way. I heard from Jimmy-O."

"Jimmy-O? About what?" Alice asked.

Pia gave me an *are-you-kidding-me* look, but I ignored it, relieved that Bettina, who had gotten the tablecloth under control, was heading straight for us and distracted Alice. We gave her the obligatory comments about how nice the party was going.

"Oh this is just part one. I'm taking her downtown to the Mandarin next weekend for a girls' spa day and afternoon tea. Joe has no idea how much it's costing or his brains would splat out of his ears." She smoothed her hair, then said to me, "Paul's not here?"

I shook my head. "He wasn't feeling well."

"He's been sick a lot lately, hasn't he?" Alice asked, chewing on a celery stick. "I saw his car the other day in the drive."

"When?" I asked, puzzled. Truth was, Paul hated

neighborhood gatherings. Always had. It was a chore to drag him along, so I'd given up on it entirely. But before I could pry further, Theresa rounded the corner into the yard, tapping a pink birthday card in her palm. I waved her over.

"Hey, guys." She handed Bettina the card. "Sorry Adam and Lily couldn't make it. They're on their way back from Philly now."

"Oh my god, y'all did such a great job with the decorations at your house, by the way," Alice gushed. "I love them so much."

"Thanks," Theresa said. "I'd like to pick up some of those extras from your shed, if that's still okay?"

"Sure," Alice said. "You've got Kendra's key for the shed?"

Theresa nodded, pulling her hair back behind her, then swirling it all to one side in front of her shoulder, revealing the leaf pin.

I cringed. Did she really have to wear it so soon?

Bettina noticed it, too. Her face twitched, and she stiffened.

But Alice, our sweet Alice, was predictably chipper. She pointed at the pin. "I love it! We all have them, you know."

"We all *did*." I glared at Pia.

"I lost mine," Pia said flatly. She shrugged.

Yeah, right. More like hid it away somewhere because it wasn't *her thing*. That said, Pia had been the one who had gotten Jackie's pin back for me. I still remembered her bringing it to my house, clutched in her palm, a satisfied look on her face. Victory.

"Let's talk costumes," I said, not wishing to dwell

on the pins any longer. "You all saw the link I sent? Any questions?"

I didn't expect any. It wasn't like anyone else had come up with a better idea. As usual, I'd done all the work. But I'd much rather it be that way. The party was my baby, after all.

"I'll take the squirrel," Bettina said quickly. I knew she'd want to get her pick in before the others. Bettina did not like leftovers—she wanted dibs.

"And I'm the fox," I said. "The orange and brown will go best with my hair."

"What else was there?" Pia asked blankly.

"Wait, the fox? Don't you hate foxes?" Bettina asked, half-distracted watching some relatives arguing over the punch bowl.

"No," I said. "I just hate some of the things they do. Like stalk the poor mourning doves."

"She thinks their mating call sounds like a woman screaming," Pia explained to Theresa.

"Can we please focus here?" I asked, my annoyance sharpening like a lead point on a pencil.

Alice plucked a piece of cheese from a platter and nibbled it. "This will be sooooo cute. I want to be Bambi."

"That would be perfect for you," I said. *Skittish, fragile, easily frightened.* "And, Pia, the raccoon would be good with your hair."

"Raccoon, good. Black mask, striped tights." She tapped her behind. "As long as the dress is big enough to cover this, I'm in."

Bettina motioned to Theresa. "That leaves the skunk."

Pia tried to turn her laugh into a cough, but we all caught it.

"What?" I demanded. "That's a good one, actually. A sleek black suit with the black-and-white tail?"

"I think I'd like to be an owl," Theresa said.

"There wasn't an owl in the costumes I sent around." If my voice sounded bossy, I didn't care.

"I could probably find something. I'm sure there are owl costumes out there. I just thought that would be— cute. Wise old owl?"

"Sounds like a hoot," Bettina said, and she and Pia did snicker this time.

"I'll look into it," I said. "The company might have something. I want us all to match." She seemed wounded, but I could only help her so much. If she was going to hang out with us, she needed to grow thicker skin.

"Oh, y'all. This will be fun." Alice touched her nose with her finger. "I get a little brown nose. And a fluffy little tail."

"I've got to go," Bettina said, taking a step back from the group. "Joe's mother is in town for this. She's driving me bat-shit— Oh! Henrietta! How are you? Be right over!"

We mingled. Alice stepped away to keep Jonah from injuring himself climbing a tree. Theresa took a phone call from Adam. My headache was still raging, so I left Pia talking animatedly with one of Bettina's sisters about the latest episode of a trashy reality show so I could get a breather.

I went inside, found Advil in Bettina's medicine cabinet, and then slipped into the small guest room off the kitchen to rest for a minute.

I lay on the bed and put my hand over my eyes, trying to ignore the murmurs of the party outside. I hadn't been sleeping well. I was doing too much again. *You need to learn to delegate tasks*, my boss used to tell me at each annual review. *You can't do anything well if you try to do everything.* But what the fuck did he know? He was single, no kids, and he *inserted mistakes* into my press releases whenever he reviewed them.

But the no sleeping was a problem.

Pia was right. I couldn't stand the sound of the foxes. That high-pitched scream. A young woman's cry, echoing through the forest. It was always in my nightmare. The same nightmare I'd been having for years. That scream, coming out of the blackness, terrified. Hollow. It clawed beneath my skin, waking me each time in a cold sweat.

"Here she is." Light and noise burst into the room.

I sat up, blinking as my pupils adjusted. Alice and Bettina and Pia came storming in, shutting the door behind them. There was barely enough space for all of them to stand at the foot of the bed.

"What the—"

Bettina crossed her arms. "You got a photo, and you didn't tell us?"

Pia, standing by the door, had the grace at least to look guilty when her eyes met mine. "I felt like they needed to know."

"What did the message say?" Alice demanded, her voice cracking.

"I was going to tell you guys." It sounded weak, even to me.

"When? When I found someone tip-toeing outside my kitchen window?" Alice asked.

"Oh please," I said angrily, shifting to the edge of the bed. The theatrics were getting on my nerves. Also the fact that she was right—that they were all right for being angry with me. I hated being wrong. "This is exactly why I didn't want to say anything about it."

"I think it's our business to know if some creep is taking pictures of us," Bettina said. She tightened her scarf and glanced out the window.

"I'm with Bettina. Somethin' is brewing here, y'all, and I don't like it." Alice picked up a picture frame, put it down again. She looked like she might start crying. "What did it say, Kendra?"

I took my phone out and showed them the message.

Oh, dearest Queen Bee. Just 28 days until Halloween! Enjoy the spotlight while you still can—soon you will be nothing. Are you going to tell everyone what you did? Or should I do it for you?

I'm watching you! Don't screw this up.

"Twenty-eight days? You didn't show me this," Pia said. "What's with the tick-tock countdown?"

"And '*What you did?*'" Alice quoted, snatching the phone from my hand. She sat down on the bed next to me, deflated. "Sweet Jesus."

But it was Bettina who got the reference. I knew she would. Bettina, who I knew would get the reference. "'*Dearest Queen Bee...*'" she murmured. "Shit."

"What?" Alice asked.

"That's what Jackie used to call me. Remember?" I said.

Alice's hand flew to her mouth. "So it *is* her." She looked at Bettina. "We were right."

"I just can't decide why now," I said. "With everything we have to hold over her?"

"It's got to be her," Alice snapped. "No one else knows what happened. Did you tell anyone?" she asked Pia. "Did you?" she asked Bettina. "Did you?" She settled on me. "Because I sure didn't. And if none of us did, then *she* is the one—"

Pia held up a finger. "Alice—"

"No. Do not interrupt me." Alice handed me back the phone and stood. "I know we never speak of her. I know it's all hush-hush quiet, pretend she doesn't exist. But she's still out there."

Pia tried again. "Well—"

"And all this business has already brought fire and brimstone to my door. I cannot handle any more of it."

"The drama is just too much, Alice."

"Hello?" Pia called, waving her hands. "I have news about Jackie. If you'll all just shut up for one second."

That stopped us.

"Jesus." She adjusted her bangles. "So, Jimmy-O did a check on her—"

"You guys checked up on her?" Alice blinked tears away.

"And?" This was the first time I was hearing the outcome of Jimmy-O's investigation.

"—and she's been living in New York. She was working as a receptionist for this talent agency."

"Was?" Bettina raised an eyebrow. To Alice, she added, "They kept it from me, too."

"For fuck's sake," I said. "We didn't want to needlessly upset anyone."

"What does *was* mean?" Bettina repeated at Pia.

"Jimmy-O said that she quit the job this summer," Pia said. "And he can't find a current place of address."

"So, then *where* is she?" Alice asked impatiently.

Pia rubbed her temples. "It's a pattern with her, apparently," she finally said. "She's had on-and-off jobs, some acting ones, too, but then she sort of goes off radar for a while."

"So she could be here then, right? Is that what y'all are saying? Jackie could be right here in Ivy Woods?" Alice asked.

None of us had to answer that.

EIGHTEEN

Theresa

My mother had one good dress. She'd gotten it as a hand-me-down from one of the women whose houses she cleaned, a sleek black Azzedine Alaïa frock that made her look like she ruled the world. I'd only seen her wear it a few times, whenever she needed to transform from a working-class single mom to a queen. Under a blazer, when she had to go to court to file charges against our landlord. And the time her friend from church had set her up with a lawyer and he'd taken her downtown for steak and potatoes. And last, the day of my high school graduation.

If you project the confidence that you belong, Theresa Ann, then you will belong, she'd always told me.

When she died, I kept the dress. It didn't fit me, but I hung it in my closet as a reminder.

I thought about the dress as I took the metro into DC

for my job interview in my best suit. Reporters often went more business casual at the office, and I probably could've gotten away with a nice sweater and black skirt, but it was always better to aim high and impress.

When I stepped onto the street, I was swept away by the rush of being back in a city. Crowds of people, pastry shops, clothing stores, delis, office buildings. I missed my friends at the *Inquirer*—our lunch walks, coffee runs, complaining about our bosses. I'd been so terrible at staying in touch, stuck in my new sleepy cul-de-sac life. How self-absorbed I'd been, so caught up in Ivy Woods.

I was early. There was a Starbucks on the corner, and I bought a scone and coffee and sat in the window, trying to envision myself here, every day.

This would be a good move for me. I wasn't just Adam's arm candy. I could be a loving, supportive mom and also have a career. Be a role model for Lily. Be like Kendra with her high-profile communications job and Bettina, who was a drug rep for a pharmaceutical company. Working moms. Powerful women.

I bought one more small coffee and walked to the *Post*'s office. Here in the city, the world seemed bigger. Dramas were diminished. I needed to focus, to push my nerves aside and turn "on."

After signing in and getting a badge, I waited in the lobby for Bettina's friend Sharita. When the elevator doors opened, a stylish woman, lanyard around her neck, emerged. She gave a jaunty wave, swiping her security badge as she pushed through the turnstile toward me.

"Theresa. I'm Sharita. I'm sorry it took so long. Had a call that went on longer than I expected. Did you find us okay?" She helped me sign in and whisked me into the elevator, talking as though on a timer that was about to run out.

"Yes. Thanks so much for putting in a good word for me."

This was how it worked. Hadn't Greg said as much? It was all about who you knew. That didn't guarantee you anything, but it got you in the door.

"Of course." She smiled. "Any friend of Bettina's is a friend of mine. Even if she's living a million miles away from me, the big jerk. I always knew when she got married she would rush out into the suburbs." She laughed and paused to catch her breath.

"How long have you known her?" I asked as we left the elevator. We passed one of the newsrooms, where reporters sat at long tables, typing furiously on their laptops, headphones on to shut out distractions. Above them, a line of muted televisions were tuned to various news stations. There was a steady hum of energy, the sense that important things were happening.

Sharita led me inside a conference room. "An eternity? Ha. No, since college. We were in the same sorority. Sisters for life, right? That girl knows all my embarrassing moments. It's a good thing I know hers, too." She chuckled and opened the blinds, letting light into the room. "But anyway, you like living there, right? She's always telling me how wonderful it is. Good group of friends."

If she lived in Ivy Woods, she'd realize it was more than just good.

I knew I hadn't entirely earned my place yet. I'd seen them disappear inside Bettina's house during the birthday party without me. But, as Mom always said,

You may deserve the best, Theresa, but you still have to work for it.

And I was willing to work.

First step? Acing this interview. Proving that I could capitalize on a favor just as well as I could ask for one.

A rap on the door, and an older man poked his head in and introduced himself as Ben, followed by four others, two men and two women, all dressed much more casually than me. Panel interview. Great.

They took seats across the table, Ben at the head. He pulled out my résumé, then glanced up. "You ready, Theresa?"

I swallowed. Thought of my mother's dress. Of Kendra's hoop earrings. Of my reflection in the glass at the coffee shop. Of everything I'd done to get to this moment. It had been worth it. All of it.

"Absolutely," I said. "Born ready."

NINETEEN

Kendra

Halloween was near. You couldn't flip through three channels on the television without seeing a man with a weapon walking slowly or hear a woman's high-pitched scream. Word had gotten out that our decorations were done, too. Each time I glanced out the front window, there was at least one car driving slowly around the cul-de-sac, windows down, cell phones out, recording video.

Bettina met me for a walk after dinner. It was midweek, a few days since Sloane's birthday party, and yet Bettina was still sulking that I'd kept the photo from her. I tried to ignore it—sometimes the best course of action with her—but it was there, her anger, simmering under the surface.

As we were coming back onto the cul-de-sac from our jaunt around the block, I decided to be direct. "Are you still pissed at me?"

She opened her mouth to respond, but a mini-van rolled onto the street, blasting Michael Jackson's "Thriller," its headlights blinding us. We lifted our hands to shield our eyes.

"Someone nearly hit Mrs. Orloff as she was backing out of her driveway yesterday," Bettina said, rolling her eyes. "I don't know if I can take three more weeks of the 'tourists.' They're so rude sometimes."

Tick-tock. Twenty-one days.

I tried to ignore the dull worry that swept over me whenever I thought about the messages, about Jimmy-O failing to track down Jackie for us. "You should be proud we're so popular."

"Not this year. I'd do just fine without people sticking their heads out their windows to take pictures of me and my house."

"So you are still pissed," I said.

"I'm not pissed at you, Kendra. I'm just worried. That's understandable, isn't it?" She glanced over at me. "Jesus, it's not always about you, you know."

I took offense to that, but let it pass. Bettina did have a right to be pissy with me, after all.

"So, is Mrs. Little Perfect joining us for Full Moon, too?" Bettina asked as we passed Theresa's house. This was how we often bickered. Like an old married couple. Picking at other scabs instead of addressing the open wound.

"What's your problem with her?"

Barney found something to sniff in Mrs. Tressle's lawn, and we stopped.

"I was just surprised you gave her a pin," Bettina said. "Seems...sudden."

Was Bettina...jealous?

"It's a piece of jewelry." I tugged at Barney, who had started to wedge his way into Mrs. Tressle's bushes. "One that you don't apparently like to wear much anymore, I've noticed."

"Oh I'm sorry. Do you have a spreadsheet for that, too?"

I sighed, trying not to take the bait. "She's not a vampire, for fuck's sake. Besides, is it a terrible thing to have the wife of Woodard's principal on our side?"

Bettina shrugged. "I just don't like secrets, I guess." She rubbed her upper arms. "Not now."

I knew she wasn't talking about Theresa anymore. "I'm sorry, okay? I should've told you about the message. Will you ever ever ever forgive me?"

The minivan stopped in front of Alice's house, and a family hopped out, snapping pictures. Alice's porch looked amazing. Bettina and I crossed the street to avoid the gawkers.

"I just want to make sure we're all okay," Bettina said.

The leaves crunched under our feet, and Barney sniffed the ground ahead, a dog with a purpose, never straying from his path. I didn't blame him. I didn't want to look to the side either. Into the night. I was afraid of what I might see.

"I do, too," I finally said. I'd been contemplating our next move, since Jimmy-O was no help. He was either terrible at his job, or not taking us seriously. It wasn't like Jackie was some master secret agent or survivalist. She couldn't be that hard to track down.

"So what do we do?" Bettina asked.

I waited until Bettina met my eye, then said quietly, "We need to find her ourselves."

Or, rather, *I* would have to find her. Because once again, *Kendra* was going to have to step in and get the job done. *Kendra* was going to have to confront our former friend and figure out what the hell she was up to. Why she wanted to ruin everything—again.

"And how do you think we'll do that?" Bettina asked, stepping to the curb as the sidewalks narrowed. She had her guard up, I could tell, but unlike Alice, Bettina got stronger in a crisis. I remembered her steadiness that long-ago night. She could be hard to win over, but once she was your friend, she was loyal for life.

"I don't know," I admitted. I'd been stewing about it the past few days, poking at the problem with a big, sharp stick, and getting nowhere. "I can't think of anyone she'd stay in touch with."

When Jackie left, she cut all ties. Plus, if we asked too many questions of too many people, wouldn't that look suspicious?

Bettina bent over and picked up a small twig, snapped it in half. "It's not like we know her ex-husband well enough anymore to walk up to him and be like, 'Hey, have you heard from Jackie lately?'"

That made me smile. But it also gave me an idea. *Of course.*

"No, but I think I know someone who does."

TWENTY

Theresa

The Barn felt different when no one else was there. It took me a few minutes to figure out how to open the door. I had to use Kendra's key to remove the padlock and then slide a plank from a metal latch, which looked way more complicated than it was.

Alice wasn't home, but when I'd texted her about stopping by for the leftover decorations, she'd told me to come anyway. I hoped to surprise Lily with extra gravestones and a glow-in-the-dark zombie that I didn't think anyone else had claimed. And I needed to keep myself busy while I waited to hear about the job at the *Post*. I felt pretty good about it, but waiting was the hardest part. All of the Ivies had texted me to check how it went, which was sweet, but also added pressure. Were they genuinely concerned as friends? Or was it a test to determine if I was worthy of my pin? I couldn't tell, but whichever it was, I couldn't afford to disappoint.

I pulled open the heavy door, which scraped on the concrete pad, and stepped inside. It was cold and dark. I found a small rock to shove under the door to keep it from swinging shut behind me and cutting off the outside light. How had Alice turned on the lights in here, again? I activated my phone's flashlight, found the chain, and tugged.

The Barn wasn't a place I wanted to spend a ton of time. For one thing, hanging on a hook right next to the door was Alice's beekeeper's suit, and the big hat and netting looked rather intimidating. Sharp garden tools and the random Halloween stuff that remained made it feel like the perfect horror movie setting.

Many of the decorations we'd sorted through together were gone now, and a bunch of empty boxes were stacked against the wall. I spotted more gravestones for Lily's cemetery and dragged those out into the yard. But there was still plenty of other junk left. I sifted through boxes—lots of fake spider web material, black tablecloths, an unopened bag of paper lanterns. Half-burned candles, pumpkin-carving tools. A hideous rubber mask of a man with a scar across his cheek. *Take whatever you want—honestly. Get it out of there, there's too much*, Alice had said. But there was nothing that would fit Lily's theme.

Then I spied the zombie I'd come for, shoved in the very back near a tall bookcase. As I leaned over to pick him up, I stubbed my pinkie toe on a box that had been half-hidden in the shadows.

"Dammit." I knelt to rub my toe through my sneaker, letting the ripples of pain subside. From there, I could read the black magic marker label on the side of the box.

SCRAPBOOKS

I opened it, lifted out the book on top. It was dated five years before, an album from the Ivy Woods Halloween party. Alice with a baby, probably Greta, and her oldest, Jonah, in a ninja costume. Kendra pouring a glass of punch, her face painted like the Queen of Hearts. Poorly lit shots of the decked-out cul-de-sac.

I set it on the floor and flipped through a few other scrapbooks—more from past block parties, others from vacations Alice and her family had taken to the beach.

An alert tone from my phone reminded me I had an appointment to review wallpaper samples for our powder room. I stacked the books I'd removed and tried to pack them back in, but my grip slipped, their weight knocking the box on its side. The rest of its contents skittered onto the floor. Cursing again, I righted the box, stuffing them all back inside.

The one that ended up on top was smaller than the others and seemed older. *Ivy Five Halloween Bash*, Alice had written on the front in her loopy cursive. Curious, I opened it and noted the year: 2005. Wow, they *had* done these parties for a long time.

It was fun to see them younger. Alice's hair was much longer—she looked barely older than Lily in some of the photos. Kendra still had the same haircut, but Bettina's was just past her shoulders with short bangs and the ends flipped out for body. I didn't even recognize Pia at first because she had reddish-brown hair and none of the gray streaks.

Then I came across a group shot—all of them dressed as witches in black dresses and capes and big hats that shadowed their faces. Alice, Kendra, Pia, Bettina, and a fifth woman, standing on the edge, slightly apart from the others as if she didn't really want to be there. I squinted to see her better, but the photo was grainy and had been taken from far away.

In the corner, Alice had written in black Sharpie:

The Ivy Five!
Halloween 2005

The fifth mother.

My heartbeat increased. I rubbed my finger over her face, as if that would clear it. Something about her posture seemed familiar, rounded shoulders. That thin, pointed chin.

I carefully plucked the photo from the transparent corners that held it to the page. On the back, Alice's handwriting again, this time fainter, faded, though I could still make out all the names.

Bettina Price
Kendra McCaul
Me!
Pia Burman
Jackie Hendricks

Jackie Hendricks.
Greg's wife.
I felt like I'd been hit by a two-by-four in the gut.
Bam!
The sound echoed through my body. Then I realized I'd actually heard a noise.

I looked up. The Barn had gotten a lot darker suddenly. I dropped the photo and moved to the door, which had closed. My rock had given way.

I pushed at it, but the door didn't budge. Had it really been that heavy? Heart now pounding, I pressed my whole body against it. But nothing. Not even an inch.

I grabbed hold of one of the hooks on the back of the door and shook it. No luck.

The door hadn't just closed. Someone had re-latched the plank on the other side.

I was locked in.

HALLOWEEN

She's trapped.

She's stuck in Ivy Woods. Look at that face, staring off into the distance. Do you feel sorry for her? She doesn't want to be here. She hates this place, even though she does a good job of acting the part.

She wore the stupid witch costume, didn't she? She made the Rice Krispies treats. Bought her daughter the superhero costume she wanted, even though she'll only wear it once and probably tear it before the night is over.

She's playing her best role tonight—loving wife, doting mother, best friend. She's pretending that her life isn't falling apart around her, that she hasn't lost everything. She doesn't want to believe that her choice to move here—the perfect neighborhood—wasn't the worst mistake of all.

But even though she's a good actress—always has been—she can't bear it anymore.

Not now that she knows about the betrayal.

But please, don't feel sorry for her. Not tonight, on Halloween, the night of the spirits, when everything dead comes alive. She is no more innocent than anyone else here at this party, dancing and drinking and flirting with danger. Look at them all. How far they'll go to feel this way.

She needs them.

She is just like them.

Maybe that's why she hates herself the most.

Her friends (are they her friends?)—Alice, Bettina, Pia, and Kendra—are wrapped up in their own power and glory, drunk not only on the sweet punch, but on their own pride.

"Oh my god," Alice exclaims suddenly, bouncing up from her chair. "Oh my god. We almost forgot a picture." She waves her arms, her long black cloak billowing about her. "Ladies, come. Come here. Quick."

And they obey, of course they do, scooting together, arms entwined, their sweet perfumes co-mingling. Someone hands her flip phone to her husband. "Honey, take it, won't you?" And they toss their hair and fix their bangs and throw their shoulders back and stick out their chins and smile—the most beaming, beautiful, wicked fucking smiles you'd ever see, so dazzling you can't sense the poison behind them.

"Say boo," the husband says, that charmer.

"Here's to 2005," shouts another husband, holding up his plastic cup and sloshing it on himself.

And they all say boo. The Ivy Five.

Five witches, lined up in a row. Five witches, with little kids, with babies, with almost-babies. With high mortgage payments, with fears, with the kind of confidence that guarantees a fall.

Kendra McCaul. Alice Swanson. Bettina Price. Pia Burman.

And on the end, nearly dwarfed by them all, is the last one. Her witch cape billows open, exposing the cleavage underneath. She isn't smiling quite as hard. She is still panicked she knocked the phone into the fire. She is still distracted by so many things.

Her eyes shift at the last second, as the camera flashes.

The fifth mother.

Jacqueline Hendricks.

EIGHTEEN
DAYS UNTIL
HALLOWEEN

TWENTY-ONE

Kendra

Whenever we were in Pia's walk-out basement, I made sure to sit as far away as possible from the doors. It was my aunt Patty's fucking fault. My father's sister had enjoyed scaring the shit out of my sister and me when we were kids. Don't get me wrong, I loved spooky things and horror movies, but I despised practical jokes. They were Aunt Patty's specialty—the mean kind. Running out of the kitchen with ketchup dripping from her hand, pretending she'd cut herself with a knife. Leaving fake spiders in our beds. And once, when we'd been in her basement playing *Monopoly*, she'd snuck outside and gone around to the back wearing a rubber dog mask, pounding on the glass doors and howling.

No wonder she had died alone.

We were here to stuff the bags for the trick-or-treaters, since my online order had finally arrived. Pia was making drinks upstairs, and Bettina and Alice sat around the coffee table, which was covered with a Ouija board tablecloth. I huddled next to the fireplace. It was a gray afternoon, making it seem later, and the glint of the thick black candles on the mantel reflected in the cold glass of the doors like the bright eyes of an animal.

Watching.

If Pia had had drapes, I'd have pulled them tight.

Alice turned on her Halloween playlist and skipped around, adorning us each with glow-in-the-dark skeleton necklaces.

"Is Theresa coming?" Bettina asked, checking her phone. She still had the radiance from yesterday's spa day with Sloane. I'd checked the prices for a massage and facial at that place and nearly fainted. One good thing about my boys—they weren't fussy. Their idea of a birthday was pizza and cheese fries and whatever latest video game was hot.

"I hope so," I said, throwing her a meaningful look. "We have things to discuss."

Namely, a favor I was going to gently *ask* of Theresa. Since she was so *chummy* with Greg Hendricks, maybe I could use her to get to Jackie. I'd thought about stopping by her house but decided to wait until this gathering and bring it up naturally, so she wouldn't get suspicious and ruin the only idea I had.

"Well, in the meantime, let's get stuffing," Pia said as she came downstairs with mugs of hot apple cider, flavored with Indian spices her grandmother had shipped from Delhi. Even the warm drink couldn't evaporate the deep chill of the basement air.

I'd begun to sort out the candy when the front door opened and Theresa glided down the stairs, that red hair of hers just-out-of-the-shower wet. She resembled a drowned rat.

"Sorry I'm late."

Bettina leaned back on her elbows like a lazy cat. "We were starting to worry you'd locked yourself in another shed."

Theresa unwound the scarf from her neck and shrugged off her coat. As soon as she did, Alice attacked her with a skeleton necklace.

"I'm going to have Justin take that dead bolt off the door," Alice said. "That was just—not good. If any of the kids ever got locked in there…"

Alice truly believed the door had fallen shut and the plank had slid down of its own accord. I was doubtful—that thing was rusty and definitely wouldn't just close without someone encouraging it—but I didn't want to go accusing her little darlings of imprisoning the neighbor. And Theresa hadn't seemed too fazed by it. She'd only been stuck for twenty minutes before Alice discovered her.

"I was on the phone with the contractor. The sink faucet is delayed *again*, which means we still don't have a working bathroom on the main level." Theresa sat cross-legged on the floor, fluffing out her hair.

"Any home project is always insufferable," Pia said. "Just accept it and ride that wave out. It'll look good when it's done."

"I guess." Theresa frowned. "It doesn't help that Adam has zero interest in any of it. He can make things out of wood like a master but zones out the second I start asking about countertops."

"Same here," I said. "Our house could be crumbling

around our ears and Paul would be like, 'Eh, the TV still works.'"

Alice laughed. "I swear Justin thinks the magical fairies come by for months while he's gone to keep the house clean and feed the kids. He thinks *he's* got the hard job."

"They have no clue, do they?" Bettina asked. "It's all just taken for granted. Part of the routine. Not even a thanks for all the sacrifices we make."

"Well, the ones they know about anyway." I glanced at Theresa, who was picking at the carpet. Was she thinking about her own little sacrifice? The favor that had gotten her here? Good. I needed her to keep it front of mind.

Bettina got the reference—I'd told her how Adam got his job. Which meant eventually they'd all know. We passed gossip around our group like a bottle of wine— plenty for everyone.

"Let's get this show on the road, darlings." Pia took her seat next to me. "I've got a Skype date later tonight."

"Isn't that kind of late for the high school boys to be up?" Bettina asked.

We worked in an assembly line—I added a bite-size candy bar, Bettina a glow-in-the-dark necklace, Alice a gummy ghost candy, Pia an orange-and-black bouncing rubber ball. Theresa put a temporary tattoo on top and drew the bag closed.

"Seriously, how's what's-his-name? Michael?" Alice asked Pia. "Y'all seeing much of each other?"

"Michael's old news. He was way too immature."

Bettina cleared her throat, smirking.

Pia ignored her. "This one's my age, in fact. He's a lawyer, too."

"Ooh so he can bankroll all your expensive tastes." Alice grinned as she tossed a candy in a bag and shifted it down the line.

"Only trouble is, he is really into the outdoors. Like, camping." Pia pointed at her chest. "Can you imagine me sleeping on the ground?"

Alice giggled. "Never."

"And I suspect he might be married still." Pia sighed. "All the good ones are."

"Doesn't have to stop you," Bettina said. "Why let a small sacred vow of matrimony get in your way?"

Theresa had become quiet. I watched her tug a draw-string too hard and break a bag. When she let a bouncing ball loose, I snatched it before it flew under the couch and handed it back to her. She barely looked at me as she took it.

I snapped my fingers in front of her face. "Earth to Theresa?"

Everyone stopped chattering.

She set down the bags and stack of tattoos and got up. "I need to use the bathroom?"

Pia pointed up the stairs. "Top of the stairs, first right." Once Theresa had gone, Pia made a face and said what we'd all been thinking. "What's with her?"

I wasn't sure. But now was the chance to get her one-on-one and see if she was as good at granting favors as she was asking for them.

I stood. "I'll go find out."

———

In the kitchen, I set out the cheese and crackers I'd brought. Theresa emerged from the bathroom as I was slicing the Monterey Jack. She was pale, with dark circles under her eyes that I hadn't noticed in the dimmer basement light. Maybe I wasn't the only one not sleeping well.

"Hey, can you help me for a sec?" I asked as she passed.

She picked up a knife and started cutting next to me at the counter.

"Everything okay?" I asked. "You seem quiet today."

Theresa dropped the knife and crossed her arms. "How come you didn't tell me you guys were friends with Greg's wife?"

"What?" I hadn't been expecting that. I squeezed a stack of crackers, and they crumpled between my fingers.

She picked up the knife again and began cutting very aggressively. "The Ivy Five. I saw a picture in the shed." Each time the knife smacked into the cutting board I gave a little jump.

"That was ages ago," I said, caught off-guard. I'd been looking for a way to bring up Jackie, and Theresa had gone and done it for me. But it was irritating that it wasn't on my terms—I'd have to guide the conversation back under my control. "And now we have you in our group." I smiled, but she continued the hack-slicing. Why would it bother her so much that we were once friends with her professor's ex-wife?

"I'm just surprised you guys never told me the connection."

Well, we were too busy trying to find out if she was stalking us.

"Actually, the weird thing is—I was about to ask *you* about her," I said truthfully. "We must be on the same wavelength."

"Me? Why?" Theresa put the knife down again, and I subtly stuck it in the sink.

"Well." I put on a tragic expression. "It's kind of complicated, but I need to talk to her. And I can't seem to get in touch with her. But since you know Greg so well, I thought…"

"Oh I don't know her at all," she said. Defensive tone. "I mean, we were at their house a few times as a class, but I only spoke a couple of words to her."

I frowned. Rearranged the cheese. "Okay. That's too bad. I really hoped you'd be able to help." I waited, wondering if I should give the message more time to get through. *How's the* Post *thing going, Theresa?*

"I wish I could. I do," Theresa said. She ran her fingers through her still-damp curls, looking disconcerted.

I started scrubbing Theresa's knife with Pia's dish soap. "Never mind," I said. "I can try to find someone else. I just feel like I owe it to Ellen…"

"Ellen?" Theresa's voice rose. "Did something happen?"

I dried my hands, faced Theresa. "Okay, fine. I'll tell you." Like she'd been twisting my arm. "Keep this to yourself. I don't like to speak ill of people." I held off until she nodded. I had to choose my words wisely since Theresa and Greg were obviously still friendly. "Let's just say it wasn't exactly shocking to us when Jackie left. She wasn't happy. I'm sure Greg did everything he could, but it just didn't work. Which, fine, right? Marriages don't always have staying power. But to abandon your child? That's just something I don't understand."

"Wait," Theresa said. "Abandoned? You mean because she moved out of state?"

"No. I mean abandoned. No contact."

"She doesn't even talk to Ellen?"

"Not that I know of."

"Damn." Theresa was dejected. "What caused her to leave?" she asked, chewing a fingernail.

A burst of laughter from downstairs. I'm sure they were all curious how it was going up here. They'd better have the sense to leave us alone.

"Anyway, with graduation this year and everything… Parent Team often does a special mother-daughter tea right before it. And we were just thinking that maybe we could at least reach out to her. Mother to mother…" I sighed heavily. "I don't know. Maybe that's meddling. But I wouldn't feel good about myself if I didn't try, you know?" I pressed my hand to my heart. Thank you, high school acting class.

Theresa ran her finger across the kitchen counter. "No, I can see that. That's generous of you. It's just…"

"What?"

"Well, if she really did leave like that, then maybe it's good she's not in Ellen's life. Maybe it's good she's not"—she whirled her finger in the air—"here anymore."

"See? That's why I thought I'd ask *you* for advice." I poked her in the arm. "I figured you'd have perspective on the situation. And I thought maybe you might even know something more about their…family situation. If anything's changed. I'm not close enough with Greg to ask him about all of it." I picked up a cracker and nibbled the edge of it.

But you are.

It took a minute for her to get it. "I see, yeah. I don't know that I am either, but—"

"I wouldn't want to put you on the spot," I said

quickly. "This would just be if it came up, you know. Organically."

She was thinking about it. Her shoulders were still squared defensively, but I'd worked my magic. "I could try," she said finally.

"Really? Thanks so much." I hugged her. "I'm sorry I didn't tell you about Jackie earlier. I hope you're not mad."

We pulled back. I smoothed my hair, lifted the tray of cheese and crackers.

"It's okay," Theresa said. "It seems like it was… complicated."

Oh, girlfriend, if only you knew.

TWENTY-TWO

Theresa

I was showered and waiting for Lily when she came downstairs Wednesday morning, residual anger from the day before still rolling off me like fumes. After years and years of good behavior, it had only taken Lily a month and a half at her new school to get in trouble.

"What are you doing?" she asked, eyeing me suspiciously. She had her hair twisted up in a bun like Ellen wore hers. But who was I to judge about "borrowing" style? I'd taken to wearing hoop earrings and an ivy leaf pin everywhere. Maybe we were both chameleons, just desiring to fit in with our environment.

"I'm driving you the rest of this week," I said. "Just to make sure you get there alright."

I'd gotten the call yesterday afternoon from Adam that Lily was on the absentee list. It hadn't been a great week to begin with, after I'd gotten locked in Alice's horror shed and had to wait for what felt like an eternity to get her to answer her phone and let me out. And then Lily misbehaving. Skipping school when your stepfather was principal—that took pluck. With a generous helping of stupidity.

"You're joking, right?" She was running late, as usual, pulling on her Converse sneakers while finishing the rest of a breakfast bar. She'd spent all of her time on the hairdo, no doubt. And the eye makeup.

"Nope. It's either that or you can get up extra early and ride with Adam."

She looked like she wanted to stab me with a nail file. Adam was naturally tuned to handle teenage emotions and whims, but I was not. He had slowly and systematically won Lily over when we'd started dating—giving her attention, but not trying to be her best friend. He'd ignored her rudeness when she pushed back, but didn't let her steamroll him. I'd been furious with her on many occasions, but he'd approached it with a calm and grace and compassion that I lacked.

"It's the lying that gets to me," I said once we were in the car.

There was a time, not long ago, when Lily would've been mortified about lying to me. I still remembered her crafting me a three-page apology letter when she'd stuffed her Barbie in the trash because she'd burned the doll's hair with my curling iron and hadn't wanted to confess it.

"Ellen said that kids skip all the time and it isn't a big deal."

Sure, because Ellen doesn't have a mother who cares about her. I wanted to snatch the thought back as soon as it came. It was unfair. I didn't quite know what the situation was there, but it's not like it was Ellen's fault.

Lily flipped down the sun visor and used the mirror to add a few bobby pins to her hair. "Besides, it was for a good cause."

"So you skipped school to volunteer at the nursing home?"

She gave a big, deep, you-don't-understand-anything sigh. "We were looking for my costume. A wedding dress. Ellen knows this really great vintage store, but it's only open during school hours."

I bit my lip, not wanting to get into how wrong her rationale was. I knew from experience, after all, that when you really wanted to do something, you were going to find any way to justify it. Like my relationship with Greg. Hadn't I been really good at convincing myself it was okay?

I thought about the photo in Alice's scrapbook of the Ivy Five from 2005. That was the year Greg and I had been together. While Jackie had been sitting with the Ivies in their matching costumes, I'd been across town with my fiancé, thinking about her husband. Ironically, we'd *all* been witches that year. Them in their capes and hats and me in the Good Witch/Bad Witch costume.

I still couldn't believe Kendra hadn't mentioned they were best friends with Greg's ex-wife. Though, why would they? Kendra knew I was friends with Greg. Maybe she'd even figured I'd already made the connection.

Besides, I couldn't expect them to spill *all* their histories right away.

I certainly hadn't.

At the front of the school, the flow of traffic confused me, and I didn't want to admit I had no idea where to go. I'd never driven Lily in the mornings.

"I'm grounding you this weekend," I said as I tried to read the school signs. "You can't just skip school without consequences."

Lily's eyes widened. "But there's a football game on Friday!"

"Exactly. And you can listen to it through your bedroom window."

A glare, nice and nasty.

I took a road that wound around the flat gray building. "Well, I hope you have a good"—Lily unbuckled her seat belt and slid out the door before I could even fully stop the car—"day," but my words were drowned out by the slam of the door.

That went well.

I hated punishing her—I'd skipped school myself as a kid—but it seemed like every conversation we'd had over the past few weeks, from leaving laundry wet in the washer to coming home late on a school night, had ended in an explosion. And now the lying?

But it's okay for you to lie to her, Theresa?

I focused on getting out of there and followed the road along the side of the school building. But around the corner, I got stuck behind two school buses. Kids swarmed my car, talking loudly, on their phones, headphones in place. I wasn't used to this side of our new community, the noise and clamor.

Knock. Knock.

Two short raps on my car window startled me. Greg Hendricks was leaning in, waving. I rolled down my window. "Hey," I said, glad to see a familiar face. "What are you doing here?"

"Debate team has a tournament next week. We're prepping." He was freshly shaved, a blue-checked collar peeking out from his gray jacket. He pointed at the unmoving buses. "I don't think you're going anywhere for a while. And I'm on my way to get coffee across the street. Why don't you pull over and walk with me?"

Why not? I needed a reprieve from my fight with Lily before I went back to my glamorous day of home improvement projects. And I'd meant to reach out to Greg anyway after talking to Kendra on Sunday, but had been too distracted by Lily's misbehavior. I swung my car to the curb and shut off the engine.

"It's weird to run into you here," I said as we started walking. "I always think of GU campus as your domain."

"Ah, yes. Well, it still is," he said. "You know, you should stop by sometime. I'll give you a tour. A lot has changed since you were there."

"I'll bet," I said.

"Your turn," he said. "How'd you get stuck at the school?"

"I was torturing Lily." I hesitated, realizing the reason I was here actually had everything to do with his daughter. "I don't know if you heard, but she and Ellen skipped yesterday."

Greg gave a quick bark of laughter. "I suppose I should apologize for my bad influence daughter."

"Lily can make her own decisions," I said. "And apparently she makes terrible ones."

"Well, Ellen needs to take responsibility, too. This doesn't shock me, tragically. She's been suffering from ennui. She says school doesn't challenge her. I really

think she'll excel in college." He smiled. "Or die trying."

He opened the door of the coffee shop, and I caught
a whiff of his woodsy cologne as I passed. I remembered all the times we'd gone to a coffee shop on campus, sitting close, pretending to discuss a research paper.
The table had been carved over the years with student
names, cryptic messages, stick figures. If it was still
there, somewhere along the side, in a small corner, was
the GH + TP Greg had etched one day with his pocket-
knife, cheesy as it was.

But that was a long time ago. I'd been a different
person. We both had been.

The shop was packed. It was a local chain, with lots
of small tables of solo customers with laptops and ear-
buds, quirky artwork on the walls, and free Wi-Fi.

Still, the buzz of a few group conversations and artsy
jazz created a circle of privacy as we ordered our coffees—French roast for me and black as midnight for
Greg—and snagged a table in the back. It was cozy—
maybe too cozy. I prayed no teachers from Woodard
would wander in and spy us. The last thing we needed
was gossip about the principal's wife.

"I don't approve of them skipping school, but I am
glad Lily and Ellen are getting along so well," I said as
we scooted our chairs up to the small table.

He grinned. "It's weird, isn't it? After everything.
That you end up back here, and our kids are good
friends?"

"I just wish she and *I* were getting along better," I
said. "I feel like I can't do anything right by her lately."

"Story of my life," Greg said, taking the top off his
coffee, adding six packets of sugar, and stirring with

a small straw. "Perhaps I've given Eleanora too much leeway. She's always been so independent."

Abandoned was the word Kendra had used to describe Ellen. Surely she must have been exaggerating or mistaken. What Brad did to Lily and me—*that* was abandonment. But Jackie must've maintained some kind of relationship with her daughter over the years, even if it was minimal. People get divorced all the time, but that didn't mean they stopped spending time with their kids.

"How often does she see her mom?" I asked.

He snorted. "Never."

"Oh, Greg." I frowned. So Kendra hadn't been exaggerating. "Not even during summers or whatever?"

Greg shook his head. "Believe me, we've tried. Sometimes Jacqueline makes a half-hearted attempt, but she always ends up ghosting." He sounded bitter.

"Poor Ellen," I said. No matter how strained our relations were lately, at least I was still there for Lily. Trying. And always would be.

"Yeah, well, it is what it is." He shrugged. "And honestly, I can't blame her. I made my bed…you know. I was the asshole."

We were the assholes. Memories played out in my mind: of him stopping by my place when Brad had a three-hour night class. Me airing out the apartment after he left—cold blast of night air through the window, a lavender candle burning—to get rid of that strong smell of cologne. I'd been a cheater, and I'd been the other woman.

There had been shame in it. I knew what we were doing was wrong. But I didn't really understand *how* wrong then. It seemed exotic—like living the part of a movie where love conquered all. Like playing with fire.

A pretty little secret I could twirl around and hold in the palm of my hand. A thrill of the forbidden.

If I hadn't inserted myself into their lives, would Ellen have grown up with a mother? Would Jackie have stayed in Ivy Woods?

"Where is your ex-wife now?" I sipped my coffee.

"New York, last I heard," he said. "Last time I talked to her, she made one of those half-hearted attempts and said she wanted Ellen to stay with her for a while. Or come here to visit. I have no idea if she'll actually follow through, so I haven't said anything to Ellen, but who knows?"

I imagined reporting that news to Kendra. It didn't sound like Jackie was reliable, but what if this time was different? What if she really was trying to make amends? What if Kendra reached out, convinced her to come back? Two moms, both with graduating seniors. Planning events, growing closer again…

I felt my chest tighten, but tried not to show my anxiety. "Maybe she's having regrets?" I asked. "About leaving?"

Greg shrugged. "It's possible." He took a sip of his drink and, satisfied with the sweetness, pushed the plastic top back on. "I'm not holding my breath, though. Jacqueline always seemed to love Ivy Woods, to love being a mother, but then she ran away from it. Like she runs away from everything. She enjoys the mirage of the high life. In New York, she sponges off people, stays with friends, borrows money. She hasn't had a home address in years." He sighed. "I shouldn't dump all this on you."

The coffees steamed curlicues in the air between us. I reached across and squeezed his wrist. "Ellen seems to be doing well without—I mean, you've done a really good job with her, Greg."

"Thanks." He sat back in his chair. "As you know, it's not easy. God, that was a tough time," he murmured. "First you, then Jackie. Like two bullet wounds. Bam bam."

"But you broke up with *me*," I said, then wished I hadn't. It made me sound like I wasn't over him, when I was.

"Ah, I did," he agreed. "It was the only way I could think to try to save my marriage, Theresa. For Ellen's sake. Clearly, it didn't work."

Wow. I'd known they'd broken up soon after we'd ended our affair, but I hadn't realized Jackie had left town then, too.

"You don't have to justify anything," I said. I hadn't wanted our conversation to turn into a rehash of the past. "It was wrong, what we did. I'm sorry for my part in it."

Greg, the few times he'd mentioned his marriage, always called it a mismatch. But I had been someone who fit with him, he'd said. The puzzle piece with just the right angles and curves.

He'd been flattering me, of course. But it was easy to remember how I'd fallen for it. Greg was charming, easy to talk to. I didn't feel like I needed to perform for him or worry about how I was coming off.

"Stop apologizing," Greg said. "The problems between my wife and me started long before you."

I thought again about Alice's Halloween block party photo—probably the last photo Jackie had taken with the Ivy Five. What if she did regret it all now? What if she did want to come back?

It's too late, Jackie. You're not going to ruin every-thing now. You had your chance.

Greg finished his coffee and got up to use the bath-room. While he was gone, I typed out a text to Kendra.

Just talked to Greg… He says Jackie's in Europe!

My thumb hovered over the message, hesitating. A small lie, yes. But Jackie had been the one to leave. She had chosen to run away from her problems—from her child. She'd cut off those ties. Hurt Greg and Ellen. Why should she get to come back now and upset everything? She was gone, and I was here.

I sent it. Then added:

Doesn't know when she'll be back

Some acting thing? Doesn't sound like she's in touch unless she needs money.

Will fill you in later. Sorry not better news. ☹

I hadn't known Jackie Hendricks very well. I'd only seen her a few times, during our monthly class get-to-gethers at Greg's house, where she'd often make a quick appearance and then disappear. But the more I learned about her, the more I was of the opinion she should stay far, far away. It was best for everyone.

HALLOWEEN

The moms relax once the trick-or-treaters get their fill, once it's just the Ivy Woods neighbors remaining at the party. Their kiddos are with the babysitter. They take seats around the fire. Pour drinks. Slowly, their chairs move closer together. The Ivy Five segregate themselves. They have things to discuss, wounds to lick. They are so close, and it's so dark, that it's hard to tell them apart.

"I've never trusted him," Alice whispers.

"I just can't believe he'd do this to me," says Jackie.

"He can't," says Bettina in a thick voice, so thick you could cut it with a saber. "We won't let him."

"What do you mean?" Jackie, the wounded one, is crying now. She's always been unstable.

"He won't get away with this behavior."

"And neither will she," says Kendra, hissing the words like a snake, her dark eyes glittering in the reflection of the blaze. "She parades around like she's

better than us. Like our kids love her more than us. I cannot stand it."

Pia, who up until now has been quiet, chuckles. She has no real stake in this game, but she's willing to throw a few punches if needed. That's what friends are for.

"Are you sure, though?" Alice asks. "Are you sure it's true?"

Jackie tears up again as a response. "My baby told me so. She saw them together. 'Daddy and the babysitter,' she said. I could strangle her."

The moms focus on the babysitter. They sharpen their darts, make her the target. They all agree they hate her. She has no place in this neighborhood. She is marring the Ivy Woods name. She revels in all the attention, dotes on it. They call her names to make themselves feel better. They call her names because they worry that they are getting older and uglier, because they worry they are losing control, because she represents what they've lost. They work themselves up, drowning in vodka and bourbon and sugar. Their voices crackle as loud as the flames beside them.

"But what can I do?" Jackie wrings her hands. The makeup on her face has smeared. It looks like she has a black eye.

"You've already had your chance," Kendra snaps. She has never had the patience. She's tired of having to clean up everyone's messes, though she's the only one capable of doing so. "Now it's up to us."

TWENTY-THREE

Kendra

I headed toward the cafeteria, a box of donuts in my arms. Class at Woodard had already let out for the day, but after-school activities echoed in the halls—a blubbering tuba, cheerleader shouts, laughter.

Someone could blindfold me, drive me around in circles for hours, then lead me inside that high school, and I'd be still able to tell where I was in an instant. Because of the smell. Industrial, bleach-mop, squeaky floor, plastic bitterness. Gym shorts sweat. Cheap teenage perfume and cologne that took me back to my hairsprayed, high-top sneaker days.

God, I missed those days.

Halfway down a locker-lined hall, my purse strap slid off my shoulder, landing awkwardly in the crook of my elbow. As I set the donuts on the floor to adjust it, I noticed my phone, tucked in a side pocket, light up with a Facebook notification.

Ivy Woods commented on your post.

An eerie feeling traveled all the way up and back down my spine. But before I could click the notification, a call came. Sam. It would be around lunch time in California.

I took a deep breath and answered, balancing the phone between my ear and shoulder. "He lives."

"Mom, I don't have long." He never did. I imagined Sam striding across campus, the sun streaming through his blond mop. Always on a mission, just like his mama. "I tried to call Dad at work, but no answer. You guys haven't paid my room and board yet this semester? I tried to get a burger at the grill just now and they told me my account was suspended."

"What?" My voice echoed loudly in the hall. *Tone it down.*

"She let me eat, no worries. I won't starve. But we need to take care of that."

Goddamn Paul. I'd entrusted him to handle the college bills—the only bills he had to deal with, mind you. So much for delegating.

"I'll take care of it tonight."

"Thanks, Mom. You're the best."

Normally I'd try to squeeze something out of him about his life, but I opted to let him go and angrily texted Paul. The exchange *almost* made me forget that Facebook notification. Almost. Still squatting, I opened it with the kind of dreaded precision of a bomb squad.

It was my post about Full Moon. I'd invited everyone to donate to the merit scholarship and to wear white for the fundraiser, as was tradition. Several friends had commented they would donate (some who would, some who were just posing). At the end of the list, just two minutes before, Ivy Woods had commented:

What REALLY happened to Daphne Brown? 14 days 'til Halloween...

What. The. Fuck. Yesterday Theresa told me about Jackie gallivanting around Europe, and I'd had to take half a goddamn sleeping pill to fall asleep last night. If Jackie was abroad, it was much less likely that she was this taunting creep "Ivy Woods." And she certainly wasn't the one stalking us in Alice's backyard.

If it wasn't Jackie sending us the messages, then who—

"Just the person I wanted to see." Maggie Lewis's syrupy voice came out of nowhere.

I looked up to find her posed in an ill-fitting suit and her TV makeup. I slipped my phone back into the side pocket of my purse. I needed to get somewhere private, stat, and delete that comment before Alice or any of the others saw it.

"Am I?" I asked as I took my time standing.

"Yes," Maggie said. "I need you for background. For my story on the Halloween party."

The bright blue of her suit showed off the cat hair nicely, and she was tugging down the skirt, probably too vain to order her real size.

"I don't know about that," I said.

"Come on, Kendra." Maggie fake-frowned, cocked

her head. "You know *all* the history. Surely you won't pass up a chance for publicity. No camera. For now."

All the history. Like Daphne?

Had I underestimated Maggie Lewis? Could it be more than coincidence that she'd showed up minutes after that Facebook comment appeared?

"What exactly is your story about, Maggie?" I asked, suspicious, shifting the donuts to my other hand.

She adjusted her bag, a heavy-looking computer tote. White papers threatened to spill over the top. "I'll fill you in on all of it, don't worry. How about tomorrow evening after the boys' swim meet? I'll buy you whatever you want at Starbucks."

The bitch. Strong-arming me. I knew the tactic. I'd done it myself.

"Maybe…" I trilled. *Never.* "Though me and the fam might be going out to dinner."

Maggie nodded, as if she knew I was lying. "I'll text you tomorrow." Just as I was getting ready to pull my phone out again, she turned. "Oh one more thing, Kendra. Do you stay in touch with Jacqueline Hendricks?"

The endless rows of lockers, gray and solemn, had never seemed so claustrophobic. "Excuse me?"

Maggie grinned. "Just a little something I'm following up on. But we can talk tomorrow." She gave a finger-wave, pivoted on her heel, and sauntered off.

The cafeteria was empty except for the scholarship committee meeting. As I strolled in, one fluorescent light flickered like a twitching eye above a sign that said EAT HEALTHY, PLAY HARD.

My committee volunteers—Debbie Pincheon, Zoe Taylor, Kelly Conville, and Beth Posniak—were sitting at a long table, flipping through essays written by the juniors and seniors who'd applied, their giant paper coffee cups stained with various shades of lipstick. The committee was always a prestigious role—Alice would be on it when Jonah was old enough to attend Woodard. I picked the team with an eye toward future PT officers.

"I brought you all some sugar for the midafternoon crash." I placed the box of donuts before them. Food was always a good way to keep people on your side.

"Thanks," Zoe said, though I knew she was on the latest fad diet and wouldn't touch the sweets.

"There are so so so so so so many good applications this year," Kelly said. "I just don't know how we're going to choose a winner."

"Well, choose we must." I picked up a stack of applications. "Are these the rejects?"

"That's the *yes* pile," Kelly said, taking a sip of her coffee. Kelly was new blood. I'd recruited her for Parent Team this year, and so far she seemed to be working out.

"So, I hear Full Moon is coming up?" Beth asked. "I saw your Facebook post."

Had she also seen the Ivy Woods comment? I didn't think so. Her phone wasn't out, and I'd deleted it as soon as Maggie had walked away.

"I hope you'll be there," I said. "We'll be collecting for the scholarship, and it would be nice to have the committee represented."

"Wouldn't miss it," Kelly said. I knew she was hoping she'd have an inside track when her daughter was a junior. So be it. Knowledge was power.

"Maggie's covering it for the news, you know," Beth said, plucking a chocolate donut with sprinkles out of the box.

"Yes. I heard that," I said. "So kind of her."

I let them eat while I scoured through the *yes* pile casually, looking for number 122. When I'd entered the applications into the system, I'd made a mental note of Maggie's son Bo's number. I pulled it to the top now, trying not to roll my eyes at Bo's bragging in the essay.

"Well, you all have your work cut out for you. These *are* good," I said, putting down the *yes* pile.

If Maggie Lewis was playing some kind of game with me, she was going to be sorry. I was still in charge in this town.

I waited until all the moms were looking down and slid Bo's application into the middle of the rejects.

Too bad, so sad, Maggie. Can't be winners all the time.

TWENTY-FOUR

Theresa

Whenever I felt guilty, I got productive.

So I was checking everything off my to-do list the day after I saw Greg. I ordered new curtains for the living room. Sent Trixie a card for her birthday with a gift certificate to her and my brother's favorite restaurant in Philly. Finished a freelance story about charter schools and sent it off to my editor—one day early—then turned to the block party.

Kendra had tasked me with finding entertainment options for little kids, and I spent thirty minutes on Google. I had no idea what she wanted, but I'd heard Kendra bitch before about how she always had to do things herself, so I didn't want her to think she had to step in and do this for me. I wanted to be extra helpful to make up for my lie, even if she didn't know about it.

Finally, I came across something that looked simple and inexpensive. I texted her.

I think I found the kid entertainment for the party! There's a place that does movies. Like, brings the screen, projector, all that jazz, sets it up. They have a whole bunch of kid-friendly movies to choose from. Coraline! ☺

Hmm... Maybe.

Low maintenance!

Wouldn't that interfere with the band?

A new text from Kendra popped up before I could reply.

Think inflatables. A giant slide? Ball pit or something?

On it. ☺

I stood, stretching my back, rolling my neck, which was stiff from leaning into the computer screen all morning. Through the window, I noticed the mailman pulling away.

I jogged down to the end of our driveway. Our cul-de-sac was impressive even midday in the bright sun. Nearly every house was decorated for Halloween now. Even my crabby neighbor, Mrs. Tressle, had a small skeleton standing in the front with a sign that seemed directed at me. YOU ARE DOOMED.

My mailbox, too, seemed to be judging me. Erect on its post, a slight dent halfway up its door like a haughty nose turned up at me.

Liar.

"Shut up," I said to it, then looked around to make sure no one heard. All I needed were rumors about the new neighbor talking to her mailbox. But as I opened the latch, I couldn't help but hiss, "I deserve to be here."

And I did. My mother had wanted a different life for me and my brother. She pushed me to be the best I could, to not settle for less than perfect. *You don't need friends, Theresa Ann. You need influencers. People who will open doors.* It had taken me a long time to get here, but, now, finally, I had it. No one was taking that away.

The mailman had shoved in a parcel instead of walking up the driveway to drop it at our door. I wrangled the bag out. When I saw the return label, I knew immediately what it was. The owl Halloween costume Kendra had ordered. The Ivies had all been busy getting ready for Full Moon, the scholarship event, this past week, and I was bummed I hadn't seen them, despite our proximity. I was getting lonely. But the costume was a good reminder of the upcoming party, and I felt a twinge of anticipation. I was part of it. A big part of it.

I hustled up the driveway, tossed the rest of the mail on the side table, and took the package up to our bedroom.

The costume was a dress made of tiny felt triangles to evoke feathers. Holding it up, it seemed no bigger than a hand towel, stretchy and thin. Did Kendra really want me to wear *this*? It came with a matching cape—maybe to keep me warm?—and a creepy, feathered Mardi Gras–style mask. My first Halloween block party here in our new neighborhood, with the Ivies, and this was what I would be wearing?

Suck it up, Theresa Ann.

I wiggled my way into the dress—it didn't have a

zipper—and stared at myself in our full-length mirror. The bottom of the costume came barely halfway
down my thighs. At least the triangle "feathers" hid
any flaws, but the top had flimsy spaghetti straps and
a neckline that plunged deeper than a scuba diver looking for treasure.

But they'd asked *me* to be part of their group costume. No way I was going to back out now. Even if it
meant dressing like I was about to go onstage at Club
Risqué.

"Mom?"

I turned, startled to see Lily in the doorway with
Ellen Hendricks, backpacks slung over one shoulder.
Ellen clamped her hand over her mouth. A giggle es-
caped.

"What the hell *is* that?" Lily asked.

"Watch your language," I said, but it was drowned
out by Lily's bark of laughter.

She picked up the packaging from the floor with two
fingers. "Hooty? Seriously?"

"More like Hooters," Ellen said.

I grabbed the cape and wrapped it around me. Why
hadn't I closed the bedroom door? "I didn't know it was
going to look like this," I said.

"Why an animal at all, though?" Lily asked. "I
mean… I could think of much cooler things, Mom."

"It's for the block party," I said.

"All the moms are doing it," Ellen said in a strange
voice. Was she mocking me? She plopped down on the
edge of my bed and leaned back on her elbows, studying
me. "You guys are like a cult or something, you know?"

I saw it again, that flick of something behind
her eyes. A judging, a bitterness. I pictured us from

her perspective, our pins and our party. Old and out of touch. I wondered if Ellen had said anything to Lily about seeing me in the woods that night with Greg. Probably not—teenagers were too self-absorbed.

"It's just for fun." I caught my reflection in the mirror. "Oh god, it's really horrible, isn't it?"

Lily circled me. "I don't know. I think it's fixable. I mean…" She looked thoughtful. "If you wore a turtleneck under it and really dark tights and your cute ankle boots, it wouldn't be that bad." She held up the mask. "And the mask is kind of cool."

"I guess. I just can't sit down all night unless I want to flash the neighbors." We both looked at each other. Then burst into laughter.

It felt good to joke with Lily. She'd been a bear to deal with lately, but underneath the hormones, she was still my girl. And she was right. I'd make it work.

"I should probably go," Ellen said, getting up from my bed.

I suddenly saw us through Ellen's eyes. Here we were, goofing off and making her feel left out. She was just a kid, after all, a kid who'd grown up without a mother and had only Greg as a role model. It was a wonder she was as successful as she was.

Lily's smile faded. "But I thought we were going to watch *Amityville*?"

"I can't," Ellen said. "I've got to study for my chemistry test."

"Oh don't leave," I said. "It's early. I'm sure you can watch the movie and still have time to study later, right? The kinetic formula bonds and formula test tube whatever-they-are equations can wait."

Ellen stared at me like I'd grown a third head. "Thanks, but another time."

As soon as she left, Lily turned to me, her sweetness gone. "Why do you have to be so weird?"

"Me?"

"Yes, you. You freaked her out."

"I freaked *her* out? This is the girl you are planning on dressing up as ghost brides with, but *I'm* the weird one?" I worried again about Lily's status at Woodard. With the principal as her dad and her charming personality, Lily should've had no problems mingling in any social circles, and I didn't want her to get pigeonholed. "Lily, I really think you might want to hang out with other kids. What about Sloane Price? Or, I don't know, some of those girls in your English class that you like?"

Her eyes narrowed. "Why don't you say what you really mean, Mom? *Normal* kids. *Popular* kids." She threw the costume's bag at me. "Not everyone needs to be in the cool crowd."

And before I could respond, she turned on her heel and slammed the bedroom door.

ELEVEN
DAYS UNTIL
HALLOWEEN

TWENTY-FIVE

Kendra

Bettina ran because she liked it; I ran because I needed to not look pudgy in my fox costume. I had a week and a half left to burn off as much as I could, which was the reason, and the only reason, I'd been rolling out of bed at an ungodly hour to meet her. Belly fat. It was a real motivator.

We converged at the bottom of the path behind my house, down by the lake. The very spot where we would be holding Full Moon in a few days. Bettina was setting her Fitbit, already lightly jogging in place, a black knit cap on her head that made her seem, from a distance, like a very small man.

She looked up, waved. Bettina I could always count on. If you were fighting an enemy, she would be the person you wanted backing you up. She'd always go for blood, no questions asked.

"Twice around?" she asked when I was closer.

We took the first lap in silence, which was good because I was breathing too hard to talk.

It was quiet, slightly foggy. Everything wet with dew. No one was out save for a few ducks in the water and squirrels in the branches. My muscles resisted at first, then relaxed into a rhythm.

On the far side of the lake, when we ran past the trail that led up to the railroad bridge, I picked up my pace.

The bridge wasn't a pleasant place. The police occasionally patrolled it, especially this time of year when the high schoolers tended to get high and regale each other with ghost stories up there. A bride with no eyes. Unexplained sounds of weeping or screaming. Such bullshit.

Reality was much more horrifying than a ghost story.

"Hey, Speedy, wait up," Bettina called. I pretended not to hear. She was usually the one who bested me, but today my adrenaline had kicked in. The faster I went, the harder it would be to think. The cold air filled my lungs like the fumes of a strong peppermint candy.

Crack. Pop.

A branch breaking. A rustling in the trees to my right. I looked over, slowed, peered into the trees. It was then I caught a flash of someone traipsing through the brush. A woman, her hair loose around her shoulders. She'd stopped and was peeking around a tree. Watching me.

A jogger, just catching her breath, I told myself. But a jogger wouldn't be wandering through the trees.

Not in all white.

I moved off the path, up toward the group of trees

where I'd seen her. I thought about the photo. The countdowns. The messages. *I'm watching you!*

"Kendra!" Bettina called again.

I rushed up to the tree the girl had been behind. Stepped around it.

But no one was there. Nothing was there.

"Hey! What's wrong?" Bettina said from the path. She was breathing heavy, hands on her lower back.

I shook my head, meeting her back there. "Nothing," I said. "I just thought I saw a deer."

As we walked the rest of the loop, I tried to focus on other things. "Did you see what they did to Mrs. Tressle's house?" I asked.

Bettina nodded. "I sent Sloane over there to help clean it up."

I bit my lip. "I can't say she doesn't entirely deserve it, because she's a troll half the time, but all that egg… on her siding. That is going to be a bitch to clean up."

"Well…'tis the season," Bettina said.

"Yeah." I paused. "Been kind of a shitty one so far."

"Tell me about it." Bettina stopped, retied her sneaker, then stood and stretched. "So you're worried, too? I just keep thinking—if Jackie's abroad, then who the hell took our picture?"

"And who keeps writing to us?" I added, referring to the latest comment I'd gotten from "Ivy Woods."

The million-dollar questions.

Someone else was lurking in our woods, someone unknown. We didn't know what they wanted. It meant we were back at square one, with less than two weeks to go until Halloween.

"Did you ever think maybe we should just cancel

Full Moon or the party?" Bettina asked. "Maybe this year is too much?"

"Are you kidding?" I gaped at her. "You're going to let some jerk taunt us into canceling everything?"

"We could come up with a good reason," she said. "Something—"

"No." I stomped my foot. "Absolutely not. No one is ruining this for us, Bettina. Did you ever think that's exactly what they want?" As I said those words, I realized it made perfect sense. "In fact—yes. Think about it. People throw around the term 'Queen Bee' all the time. Especially jealous bitches who hate that we throw an amazing party every year."

A golden retriever came around the bend, huffing, followed by a woman wrangling the leash. We shifted to the side, said our hellos as they passed.

When the woman had gone, I continued, "Like Maggie Lewis. She's been trying to shove her way into the spotlight with this party. Trying to make it some trashy weekend TV news feature." *You should tell her that Maggie mentioned Jackie.* "She pouts every year that she's not part of the planning. I wouldn't be surprised if it was her spying on us around the bonfire, hoping to outdo us."

Bettina looked dubious. She was walking fast. I had to push to keep up with her.

"I mean, what's the worst that can happen here?" I asked. *Eleven days left.* "Come on, B. This is *our* neighborhood."

"Yeah. You're right." We were back at the start of our lap. Bettina took a deep breath, then punched me lightly on the arm. "Come on. Let's do another before I get stiff."

We ran again, both of us faster.

This time I kept my gaze ahead, eyes forward. No more ghost woman in the trees. No more memories of the past.

Just my breath, my muscles, my will. Building stamina.

TWENTY-SIX

Theresa

A TV van pulled up to the curb outside our house just as I was finishing raking leaves. Maggie from the bake sale hopped out, waving enthusiastically.

"Nice work, sister," she said. "Looks like you've been busy."

I wasn't sure if she was referring to the bags of leaves, knotted and fat like blob creatures waiting for the bus, or our extensive Halloween decorations, but either way, she was right. I had been busy, and I was tired.

"Getting ready for the big block party?" she asked.

"You know it," I said with a small smile.

"That's why I'm here, actually. Halloween. I'm doing a segment."

Maggie's driver, who I suspected was also the cameraman, got out of the van and began fiddling with something in the back.

"Oh right." I smoothed my ponytail. "I don't think Kendra's home now, though. You probably want to talk to her. Or maybe Bettina?"

"Actually, I really wanted to talk to you," Maggie said. "You know, as the new neighbor coming in. Stuff like *so glad to be part of this community*, *keeping tradition alive*...all that jazz."

She glanced up at our house, and I imagined our place as a story backdrop. It did have that imposing look to it, especially with the attic window.

"I'm not really camera-worthy right now," I said, wiping my dusty jeans. I smelled like decaying leaves.

Maggie waved her hand in dismissal. "You look great. Seriously. In fact, I'd hire you. If you ever wanted to come to the Dark Side." She did a good Darth Vader voice. "Broadcast is where it's at."

I laughed. "I appreciate the offer. I've got a lead, so we'll see."

In fact, I'd been mentally prepping. The *Post* had called me to come in for a second interview, and I'd been mulling over potential answers to the hard question, *What's your biggest weakness?*

"I'll give you some time to freshen up if you'd like. Doug wants to grab some B-roll outside anyway."

I hesitated. I wasn't a fan of the way I presented on camera.

"Come on," Maggie said. "It'll be fun. You'll be famous."

I considered that. Kendra *had* said she wanted attention for the party. Local celebrities. Media coverage. Maybe Maggie would even do a live feed the night of the party.

"Okay," I relented. "As long as it's brief?"

Maggie held up her palm. "You won't even remember I was here."

I led Maggie inside the house and made us tea—Maggie wanted hers with no sugar or honey. I left her in the kitchen, on a call, while I ran upstairs to fix my makeup and hair, then fastened the ivy leaf pin to my shirt for good luck. When I returned, she was typing on her phone, tea untouched on the counter.

"So, where did you want to do this? Outside?" I asked. Lily would be so excited to have her front graveyard on the news.

"Can we go upstairs?" Maggie asked. "You've got a great window up there."

"The attic?"

"Atmosphere, Theresa." Maggie grinned. She unwrapped a stick of chewing gum and popped it in her mouth.

Smelly socks and five hundred bottles of nail polish? "It's a teenager's bedroom. I'm afraid that's not the kind of atmosphere you're looking for."

But Maggie insisted, and I found myself agreeing. She was in reporter mode, very persuasive. It was like I was watching myself, another braver Theresa, leading them up the stairs. Would Lily be thrilled or mortified I'd brought reporters into her room? And what would Adam think about me letting a camera in our house for party publicity?

"Whoa. This is cool," Maggie said, spinning around, mouth open, as I frantically made Lily's bed and picked up the clothes strewn on the floor. But Maggie didn't seem to care about any of that. She brushed her hand across the beams like she was in a museum, and directed the cameraman, Doug, to take a wide shot from the corner.

Maggie walked over to a stuffed mummy doll Lily had on her bed and noted the horror poster on the wall. "Your daughter's really into the dark stuff, huh?"

"She never was the unicorn and rainbows kind of girl," I said, smiling.

"Bo's the same way—that horror shit. I think all the teenagers are." Maggie set the mummy down. "I'm guessing she's really into Ghost Girl, then?"

"That urban legend?" I rolled my eyes. "It's all she can talk about."

Maggie nodded. She stepped to the other side of the room and gazed down from the large round window. "I figured that's why she picked this place as her bedroom."

"What do you mean?" I joined Maggie at the window. Could you see the railroad bridge from here? No. At least, I couldn't. All I could see beyond our street were the trees that shielded the lake.

"So you don't know." Maggie was close enough that I could smell her chewing gum—peppermint. Her eyelashes had clumped from the large amount of black mascara, making them look like little daggers. "Ghost Girl was a real person. Her name was Daphne." She pushed off the window ledge and stopped in the center of the room, the light from outside casting odd shadows on her face. "And she lived right here. In this bedroom."

"What?" As far as I knew, the Browns had owned this house for decades.

"Weird, right?" Maggie said. "She was staying with her aunt and uncle."

I tried to remember everything Lily and Ellen had

mentioned, but I only half listened whenever they'd brought it up. A young girl. A wedding dress. Jumping off the railroad bridge. And Ellen's words, coming out of the darkness. *I've seen her. Many times.* "Seriously? It's real? I thought it was just a story?"

Doug snorted. I'd forgotten he was there.

"A lot of people do," Maggie said. "Maybe because Ghost Girl is such a stupid name. She wasn't even a *girl*. She was twenty years old."

Daphne. Daphne Brown. Of course. That name had sounded familiar, and now I knew why. "The scholarship," I murmured.

"That's right. The Daphne Brown Merit Scholarship that the Hive put their little Full Moon show on for." Maggie seemed exhilarated. She sat down on Lily's bed, rubbing her hands along the comforter. "It happened on Halloween, you know. During one of their block parties, about a dozen years ago. Daphne was babysitting all their kids that night. She left the kids"—she made a sweeping gesture with her arm—"right here in this very room. They were the last ones to see her alive."

A chill crept over me, thinking of the kids. They'd all been so young. Who had been there? Kendra's sons, Cole and Sam? Bettina's daughter, Sloane? Pia's son and daughter, Rachna and Jason?

And Ellen—well, Nora?

How had I never heard this story before?

But Maggie wasn't done. She pointed at my pin, her face hard now. "They gave you an ivy leaf, but didn't tell you all their little secrets, I guess." She tapped her fingertips together. "I wonder why."

EIGHT DAYS UNTIL HALLOWEEN

TWENTY-SEVEN

Kendra

I took the day off work without telling Cole or Paul. I liked the idea of no one knowing where I was. I had to drop in on the vendor who always supplied free snacks for the kids at the Full Moon fundraiser and stop at the zoning office to grab the permit to close the street off for the party on Halloween.

I had another errand, too. One that I didn't want anyone else to know about.

I drove out west on the highway. Tall commercial buildings and malls gave way to rural farmland and small towns. It reminded me of my hometown, which reminded me I hadn't talked to my sister in ages.

I called Chrissie, envisioning her in her farmhouse-style home just outside Milwaukee, acres of land surrounding her.

"You must be a mind reader," she said when she answered. "Ma was just here, and we were talking about you."

"Ah. So that was the ringing in my ears." I put on my blinker, switching lanes to pass a large tractor trailer carrying logs.

Chrissie ignored that. "Ma was wondering if you were coming here for Christmas this year."

We hadn't been back to Wisconsin in a few years. We owed them a visit. But I was not excited about it. Traveling to see my family was like slipping back in time. It wasn't me anymore. I'd long ago grown away from it. "I'll have to talk to Paul about it. First I have to get through Halloween."

"Oh right." Her screen door slammed shut. I could hear barking in the background, her dogs tearing off into the field behind her house. Her two oldest kids were in college, like my Sam, and only her daughter was still home. My niece was a year younger than Cole, and rumor had it she was probably going to be engaged before she graduated from high school. "I don't know how you do it, Kendra," Chrissie said. "But you know, Halloween's never been my cup of tea."

Chrissie had never liked dressing up, and she couldn't stomach a horror movie. She was too scared even to walk at night in the dark.

"I blame Aunt Patty for that," I said.

"Aunt Patty? Why?"

"Don't you remember when she scared us with the dog mask?" I asked incredulously.

A pause. Dishes clanked. "Gosh, I'd forgotten about that," Chrissie finally said.

"Forgotten about it? How could you? You slept with me for weeks after, refusing to be alone." Like it was happening right now, I could feel my sister's weight up against me in the darkness of my bedroom. She'd made me hang her fleece Care Bear blanket over my window so that no one could look in.

"Did I?" My sister sighed. "Well, gosh, Kendra. I was just a kid when Aunt Patty died. I barely remember her."

After getting updates on my niece and nephews, and promising Chrissie I'd let her know about holiday plans soon, I hung up and took the exit off the highway. Headed right, down a two-lane road a few miles to the cemetery.

I couldn't believe my sister didn't remember the dog mask. That she wasn't scarred by it. After all those nights I'd whispered to her that it was going to be okay? That I, her big sister, would take care of it?

But there were two sides to every story. Two people could experience the same thing and interpret it in very different ways.

The cemetery was small, with gentle rolling hills. It'd almost be quaint if it wasn't concealing rows of decay. I pulled into the front lot, parked, and picked up the wildflower bouquet from the passenger side.

I only visited once a year, but I knew where I was going.

Daphne Brown's parents hadn't paid much for her grave. She didn't even have a stone, just a small plate in the ground with her name and dates. Every year, we used some of the money raised at Full Moon for the merit scholarship to buy flowers for her grave.

The other moms thought I had them shipped to the cemetery. They didn't know I delivered them personally.

It was a cold, gray day, threatening to rain. I could

hear thunder rumbling in the distance as I arranged the flowers.

Daphne Brown had gotten carried away, in over her head. She'd been too confident. Too trusting.

She'd made bad choices.

Still, everyone's gravesite deserved flowers.

———

By the time I got home, the skies had opened up, and it felt more like midnight than noon. My wipers couldn't work fast enough to clear the rain off the windshield. I was about to turn into our driveway when I noticed our house was as lit up as the Biltmore mansion at Christmas. I saw Paul's Honda in his spot in the driveway.

I circled the cul-de-sac. What the hell was he doing home? I distinctly remembered him telling me this morning he had two back-to-back meetings and that it was going to be a busy day. That if I called him, he might not be able to answer.

He'd been distracted lately, forgetting to pay Sam's college bills. Unreachable at times.

I tried to slow the boil of suspicion building inside me. Maybe he'd come down with a cold, gone home, and passed out from NyQuil on the couch. Or had a doctor's appointment he hadn't told me about and took the rest of the day off.

Or maybe he was cheating on me.

I parked on the street. I was panicked at the thought of Paul—that balding head of his, those age spots on his arms—with another woman. In our house.

No. There was no fucking way I was going to end up like Jacqueline. I wasn't going to sit around and let that happen right under my nose.

But if that bastard was…

I didn't even bother with an umbrella. I was a stumbling wet mess as I walked to the front. We never came in the front door, only visitors, but I fished out my key and flung open that door.

TWENTY-EIGHT

Kendra

I heard female laughter from the back of the house. In the living room, Paul's suit jacket was tossed on the couch. *The People's Court* was on the television, and the bagged lunch I'd made him last night was spread out on the coffee table like a crime scene. Thin bits of crumpled white bread. The tops of strawberries staining a napkin red.

I heard the deep tenor of his voice rise into a question. The woman answered. I barreled forward, slinging open the French doors.

And there were Theresa and Paul standing in my kitchen. She was wearing a dark green raincoat, her umbrella dripping on the back door mat. Paul was still in his dress shirt, tie loosened around his neck. But the look on his face was as if I'd caught him bare-assed, bending her over the counter.

"What the hell is this?" I asked.

"Kendra. You startled me." Theresa's smile dwindled. Her red hair was pulled back, but small tendrils curled around her ears from the humidity.

"You're home early," Paul said brightly. He wouldn't meet my eyes.

"So are you," I said pointedly. "Having lots of fun, I see."

Theresa blinked. "Oh no. I just stopped by to drop off the money I owed you for the trick-or-treat candy." She backed up, checked the clock on the wall. "I interrupted poor Paul's lunch. And then it started pouring." She glanced out the window. "But I think there's a break in the rain now, so I should go."

She grabbed her soggy umbrella and skittered out the back door like a cockroach.

"What are you doing home?" I asked him as soon as she disappeared.

"What was that all about?" He gestured. "You swooped in here like you were about to stab us all."

"I'm sorry. I guess I was just surprised that you *lied* to me about all those work meetings you had today."

He shook his head. "Never mind." He left the kitchen, and I followed him into the living room.

"Why are you home, Paul?" I asked from behind him.

But I figured it out as soon as I asked the question. Maybe a part of me had been suspecting for weeks now, and I'd let it go because I hadn't wanted to look too closely. It was how I'd been dealing with everything these days.

I thought maybe if I didn't see it, it wouldn't fall apart.

He turned, shoulders sagged in defeat.

Paul wasn't having an affair. He'd lost his job.

"How long?" I asked him.

Paul sat on the couch, picked up the remote, and shut off the court show. He sighed. Why was he always so calm? I wanted to shake him, to make him scream or cry or grip me. Anything to show some sort of passion.

"One month. They eliminated my whole department."

An entire month? I flashed back to all the signs— him coming home on time, drinking more. Having a greater interest in exactly which days I'd be working from home. No wonder I'd had that feeling someone had been in the house—*he'd* been there and split before I came home.

"Where've you been going every morning?"

He shrugged. "Some days the library. Some days into the city, walk around."

Paul, sauntering around the city, lying to me, while I worked my ass off on everything...

"Or come home and hit on the neighbor," I added.

I didn't really think there was anything going on with them, but I made a note to keep my guard up.

Paul sat back, took off his tie, and rolled it up over his hand. "Come on, Kendra. I can't right now. You're doing that thing where you want to pick a fight for the sake of picking a fight. I'm not playing."

"Picking a fight? I don't have to pick very far. Considering you've been lying straight to my face for a month."

"I didn't want you to worry," he said. "I was working on a lead. I thought I could secure something before I had to tell you. But it fell through, just yesterday in fact. I'm sorry."

Paul was right. I was crabby, picking a fight for no reason other than to control something. Because everything else felt *very* out of control.

I sat down next to him, weary. I wanted to laugh. I wanted to sob. But somehow, I managed to shut out my thoughts. I was always good at compartmentalizing.

"We'll figure it out," I said.

I'd figure it out, at least. I always did. But not until after Halloween.

"I have to admit, it's a relief I don't have to hide it anymore," Paul said. "Do you know how horrible it is to have such a terrible secret?"

TWENTY-NINE

Theresa

All the kids were there, sitting in a circle on the floor. They were in their Halloween costumes—a vampire, a Disney princess, a police officer, a robot. Half of them were falling asleep. It was late.

So late.

They were looking up, eyes wide. *What now?* their faces asked.

Their babysitter glided around the room like an ice skater, in a long wedding dress costume, her hair pulled up in a soft bun.

Shh, she said, pressing her finger to her lips. *We're going to play a game. I'm going to leave for just a little while, and you all are going to have to help each other. Okay?* She kissed the tops of their heads, telling them *good night, good night, good night.*

Then she slipped away, down the stairs, her train

bouncing behind her. The last thing they saw was her hand, so pale, so white, waving, before it, too, disappeared.

I shook my head, and the scene evaporated as quickly as it had come, leaving only the messy remains of Lily's bedroom. But the chilling air lingered. I lifted Lily's cashmere sweater to my face, inhaling the strawberry scent of her shampoo.

Ever since Maggie told me about Daphne a couple of days ago, I'd felt strange being in the house alone. As if every corner I turned, I might catch her hovering in the next room. As if every creak and groan of the house was a sign. Maggie had gotten to me. She'd transformed Lily's vague, silly legend into reality and dropped it into my lap. My house. My life.

No one else in my family seemed bothered by it. "Duh, yeah. Urban legends are almost always based on some sort of truth, Mom," Lily had said.

"Don't you remember our real estate agent telling us about that? That the previous owners had a teenager who died?" Adam had asked me.

I hadn't.

I'd wanted us to come here so Lily had opportunities. So she could grow and be happy and become her own person. I'd brought her back to our past so she could have a future. Not so she could go chasing ghosts with Ellen.

I couldn't wait for Halloween to be over.

I walked over to the big round window and looked out. A few people were milling about the cul-de-sac. A young couple, holding hands, wandered the path behind Kendra's house toward the Full Moon festival. Lily was already there with Ellen and a few other girls from school and had texted me to bring the sweater.

The idea of Full Moon suddenly seemed very creepy. I had assumed it was just a nice fundraiser for a school scholarship. In fact, at one point I'd felt left out for not being a part of it. But now I wasn't so sure. How could everyone revisit the memory of that terrible night each year? Wouldn't they want to forget it?

Maybe that's why the Ivies had never told me the full story—it was painful for them. Someone *died* during one of their parties, after all, and their own children had been left to fend for themselves in that dark, shadowy room. Plus, they'd probably assumed I'd already heard it. Everyone in town seemed to know it.

About a dozen years ago, Maggie had said to me when she was here.

I went to my bedroom and did a search on my laptop. *Daphne Brown, Ivy Woods, suicide Halloween.*

A bunch of articles from paranormal blogs appeared with mentions of Ghost Girl. But about five or six hits down was a local newspaper story about the tragic death. Young Girl Jumps to Death Off Railroad Bridge.

Halloween 2005.

Just before Greg had ended our relationship, before I'd broken up his marriage, Daphne killed herself in the same woods that bordered Greg's house, just a few miles from campus, and somehow I'd heard nothing about it. I'd thought this was such a pretty place to live—so peaceful and safe. Big houses with large, tall windows to bring in lots of light. Cats sleeping in sun patches in the doorways. Kids kicking balls in their backyards.

"Theresa? You ready to go?" Adam, from downstairs.

You were too wrapped up in your own dramas, Theresa Ann.

All along I'd been missing the tragedy unfolding right nearby.

HALLOWEEN

*The iffiest member of the Ivy Five, Jacqueline, aka
Jackie Glitter, who once played Audrey in an off-off-off-
off-Broadway production of* Little Shop of Horrors, *isn't
happy with the way the evening is going. She hates these
kinds of gatherings, hates this fake suburban nonsense
and all these people who care about nothing but their
kids. All the talk, every conversation, is about the kids,
about their poop and their dance skills and what they
said five minutes ago that was so adorable it should've
been filmed, as though once you become a mother you
lose every ounce of yourself. You cease to be.*

*Jacqueline can't handle that. It was hard enough,
carrying around all that weight for nine months. It was
hard enough having to hear everyone tell her how she
glowed, when she felt like there was a parasite inside
her feeding and feeding and feeding, more more more,
and destroying her body.*

Do you see her even now, shifting her attention away

from her friends, from the other mothers, as they talk about their kids' teachers? She's scanning the crowd, trying to make out the figures in the night. Looking for her husband. She longs to be alone with him and her daughter, somewhere far away. A vacation, maybe. Or more. Away from all this. Away from inane conversations and meaningless days. She wants them to live glamourous lives—sail around the world or caravan across the desert. Anywhere but here.

But it's too late for that. Things are already beyond her repair.

She wishes she could sneak away and take another hit of nose candy, as the line she'd snorted before coming out here is starting to wear off and she's feeling twitchy.

Where the hell is Greg? The man she gave it all up for?

She is swallowed for a moment by the thought he's gone forever.

Then he is there, swaggering through the crowd, dressed like some literary figure—she can't remember who—and the cape and weird discolored collar embarrass her. Jacqueline stands and crosses the cul-de-sac to meet him.

"My dear," he says in a bad accent, bowing to her, and she wants to smack him. She wants to scream as he leans in to kiss her cheek. She smells perfume on him, a dusty, heady scent that reminds her of a club she used to go to in Brooklyn, of some other time, some other life, but one thing she knows for sure: it's not her perfume.

"Where have you been?" she asks, daring him to lie.

If you turn and look, you'll see the rest of the Ivy Five are suddenly interested in this exchange. They are watching by the fire. They know what Greg Hendricks has been doing, and they are tired of it. They don't stand for that kind of behavior here on Ivy Woods.

Jacqueline feels that they are judging her. She's never good enough and she knows it. Part of her wants to please them and another part wants to burn it all down.

"Getting my costume ready," he says, chuckling. He's not a big drinker, Greg, but she can tell he's had something. "Want to dance?"

Jacqueline does not want to dance. She walks away from him, toward the drink table. She thinks about going home, but the trail down and around the lake to her house feels very far away. Instead, she refills her cup with the rosé she brought. She likes her wine the kind of sweet that hurts your teeth.

Someone's opened a small bag of M&M's and left them scattered across the tablecloth, and Jacqueline presses a fingernail into a green one, crushing it to dust. She licks the chocolate from her finger and surveys the place, her neighborhood, her home. This was not how it was supposed to end up.

A small body tackles her, hugging her around her knees, and she nearly falls.

"Mommy. Mommy." Nora throws her head up and gazes at her, that white-blond hair spilling over her shoulders.

She is Wonder Woman, though the mask and the sword are long-lost by now.

"Where's your babysitter?" Jacqueline asks, then feels bad that that's the first thing she's thought of. "She may be worried about you."

"She's over there with Daddy."

Those words send a cool chill down Jacqueline's spine. She looks up, and indeed, there is Shakespeare—that's who Greg is dressed as, she remembers in a flash—with the bride. Are they dancing? Just like that, in front of everyone? She turns and sees Kendra whispering to Bettina. They've lost their pointed hats but still—as always—look just like witches.

"I see."

"Mommy, can I stay with you? Please? I want to be with you. For always."

"Oh, hon. You're always with me. Go play with your friends." Jacqueline swigs down her wine and untangles herself from her daughter. She sends her back to Greg and the sitter.

She is slowly burning—a ball of hot ash. Things can't go on like this, she thinks. Guzzles more wine.

Thinking.

Plotting.

Smoldering.

And Daphne Brown has only one and a half hours left to live.

THIRTY

Kendra

Full Moon, too, had been my idea.

The event started out as a vigil for Daphne Brown, but after the first few years it had morphed into a festival to raise money for the student merit scholarship in her honor. For most people, Full Moon was popcorn and hot chocolate, donated by a local cafe in town.

For the four of us, Full Moon was about tradition and remembrance.

The weather was cold and clear, and when night fell, the moon would be a perfect circle high above the nearly leafless trees. We always held Full Moon down by the lake. Select members of the Woodard marching band played haunting music, and now, from my screened-in back porch, I could hear them starting up with the theme from *The Addams Family*. It was almost our turn.

"Sloane's so excited to show you guys their routine."

Bettina had recruited the dance team to perform this year. "They are amazing. Wait 'til you see."

Paul stuck his head out the back door and grinned, his cheeks pink from the temperature. "Ladies!"

Since he'd come clean about his job yesterday, he'd been a different person. Happy, jolly. Too happy. A little stress wouldn't hurt. It might motivate him to fix it faster.

"What's the crowd like?" I asked.

Paul gave us two thumbs up. "They're ready whenever you all are." He paused. "You guys look great as usual."

"Thank you, darling. You are so sweet." Pia, who I suspected had been sipping from a flask, actually stood on tiptoe and kissed Paul on the cheek. If it wasn't so ridiculous, I might've been offended. Paul smiled and patted her on the arm awkwardly, then left.

I took a deep breath, squared my shoulders. In the kitchen window that overlooked the porch, our reflections caught my eye. Four women in white, the flickering candles in our hands illuminating our faces.

Angels.

Ghosts.

"Ready?" I asked, turning to face the others.

All at once, all four of our candles went out.

"Wind," I said impatiently. "Bettina, you have the lighter?"

"I do." Her voice was quiet. She relit her candle. "There wasn't a breeze," she said.

"No, it was demon breath," Pia said. "The evil spirits don't want us collecting money for the children."

"Do you have to be the biggest bitch about everything?" Bettina snapped at Pia.

"No, I leave some things for you, my dear."

"Guys!" I said.

"Can we please not pick at each other?" Alice asked. "Please? And remember, I have to be done by nine or my mother-in-law will kill me. She gets tired so early."

With our candles lit again, I led them out into the night.

We walked solemnly down the path to the lake, holding our hands in front of our candles so the flames wouldn't extinguish again. Paul had been right—good turnout, I noticed as we descended. Volunteer students and parents from Ivy Woods had distributed small candles, complete with a white cardboard circle around them to catch wax drippings. Everyone would help light each other's candles once the program began.

The crowd turned and watched as we approached. *Stand straight, shoulders back. Suck in the tummy.* I scanned the faces. There was Maggie Lewis moving through the crowd like a toxic sludge, in an ill-fitting button-down black shirt and puffy vest.

Was she really here to cover this event for an innocent feature? Or was it more sinister?

I swallowed the wave of doubt that lapped inside and stuck my chin out. No one was going to control us.

We were the Ivy Five, glowing in white as dusk fell. My tunic was long-sleeved, but the thin material allowed the brisk wind to push right through. I knew the others were chilly, too—but it was always better to look good than to feel good. Pia's dress was long and flowy. Bettina had chosen skinny white jeans, a white T-shirt, and a white jean jacket. And Alice was wearing a white sweater and skirt that hit mid-calf, with white furry boots she'd found on clearance at Ross last year.

We were always the star attraction at Full Moon.

The marching band finished its song as we glided to the podium. I took the microphone first, addressing the crowd.

"Thank you all so much for coming once again," I said, my voice echoing across the water. "Happy Full Moon to everyone. As you know, this is a time for us to reflect on our community, to come together as a group to celebrate and remember and to raise money to help one lucky, deserving Woodard student attend college."

Applause. We took turns giving our speeches, explaining the scholarship, pointing out the buckets at the food stand where people could donate.

"As you all know, thirteen years ago, a young girl lost her life right here in these woods," Alice finished up. "It was a tragedy, a promising life cut short, but our community rallied together, and tonight we remember how fragile life is."

We never went into details about the bridge or the suicide—we didn't want to be downers.

Alice stepped to the side and passed me the mic again to finish up. I always ended with a quote about the moon. "Thank you all for your generous contributions to the scholarship. As an old saying goes—"

Maggie's cameraman stepped forward, kneeling down to take footage.

"—'Always remember we are under the same sky, looking at—'"

Beside him, Maggie whipped out a notepad and started scribbling, a smirk on her face.

Oh, dearest Queen Bee. Enjoy the spotlight while you still can.

"You okay?" Bettina whispered next to me, nudging me with her elbow.

I shook my head to clear it. "As I was saying, 'Always remember we are under the same sky, looking at the same moon.' Be kind to one another, tonight and always."

Stronger applause this time as we moved into the crowd and lit everyone's candles. The lights blinked off the still, black lake, and I felt, for a moment, that we were doing something good. Releasing positive vibes into the universe, to help counter the bad ones.

Someone announced the dance team, and the four of us shifted to the side of the stage as the girls filed out in their usual blue-and-black dance leotards with skirts, their hair back in tight buns. They seemed somber as they lined up, Sloane in the middle, all serious and dignified, like tragedy had struck her.

The dancers fell to the ground in poses reminiscent of the dead. I flinched. Poor taste. But Bettina looked on in awe, clasping her hands in front of her. Someone started up their Bluetooth speaker, and a bad recording of a song started. I recognized it as "I Will Remember You" by Sarah McLachlan. Her mournful wail began, as the dancers, one by one, stood up and started waving their hands in an odd, drunken sway.

When the song was finally ending, Sloane skittered to the edge of the performance area to grab a rolled-up parchment. She held the end, and the other dancers unrolled it. It spelled out, WE WILL NEVER FORGET.

I was mortified by the overwrought display, but Bettina applauded rapturously. Pia looked like she'd eaten a lemon.

"Ladies. Another dramatic event." Maggie approached

through the once-again-mingling crowd. She still had her stupid notebook, pen poised. "Raising a lot of money?"

"We always do," I said coolly.

"Nice dance," she said to Bettina, then turned to me again. "And I'm hoping you'll agree to a quick interview on camera." She smiled. "Surely you aren't afraid this time."

"I never was."

"Good." Maggie tapped her cheek with her finger. "I've got a very interesting source for my story, you know."

Something caught my eye coming out of the woods behind Maggie. A girl, all white, walking slowly. "Ghost Girl," someone gasped, and someone else giggled. Then the light caught Ellen Hendricks's face. She was dressed in a ridiculous lace wedding gown, veil on her head.

"Hang on a minute," I said to Maggie, and I saw her motion to her cameraman to start filming.

Ellen had something cradled in her hands. She asked a random person for their candle and lit the object, a paper boat. I followed her over to the lake's shore as she kneeled, set the boat down and pushed it out into the water. The rest of the crowd went back to their conversations.

"I'm sending her spirit out into the universe," she told me as she straightened.

I could hear Maggie breathing behind me, but I ignored her.

Ellen lowered the veil over her face. "Let's just hope she takes the offering and doesn't come back to haunt the ones who wronged her," she said. The hem of her dress floated on the lake's surface.

"Kendra?"

"What?" I whirled, ready to yell at Maggie to back off, but it was just Theresa. She jumped. "Sorry. I thought you were someone else."

"That was great," Theresa said as Bettina strolled up beside me. "I can't believe you guys never told me any of this. I had no idea. What a sad story."

Someone lit a sparkler nearby, handed it to a young boy. He squealed as it sizzled, twirling it in the air in wild, wide circles. Hopefully he wouldn't set himself on fire.

"It is sad," Bettina said, crossing her arms over her chest. "But you wouldn't think that the way Maggie Lewis is walking around, shoving her microphone in people's faces."

"If she tries to talk to you, don't do it. We are *not* encouraging her," I said to Theresa.

She zipped and unzipped her jacket. "Oh?" she asked, looking from me to Bettina.

"Have you met her?" I asked. "Maggie Lewis? From Channel 7?"

"But I thought you guys wanted media coverage?" She tugged on her ponytail. "I thought you'd...like that?"

"Not from *her*," Bettina said.

I drew myself up taller. "We are not going to be part of some...trashy news segment she's doing for ratings, got it? So if she tries to bug you about it, you tell her no."

"Oh yeah. Definitely." Theresa nodded.

I smelled patchouli, thick and oily, as Ellen stepped between us, her hands pressed together in prayer. She hummed as she marched past, then through the crowd and toward the woods. Everyone murmured as she strode by.

Behind Theresa, Maggie and her cameraman were talking quietly to each other, headed our way again.

"Here she comes," Bettina announced.

Theresa turned, then stammered that she had to go find Adam.

As she scampered off, Alice rushed up from behind, grabbing both our shoulders. "Y'all," she whispered. "Come here. Now."

Her face was as pale as her skirt as she ushered us over to a nearby tree.

"What is wrong?" I asked impatiently.

"I just had a conversation with Mrs. Vancavage, you know, that dear old woman who lives over in the town houses?" Alice was tripping over her words, like she couldn't get them out fast enough. "She's a peach, I love her to pieces, but lord she goes on about theater and opera and whatnot and I don't know a blasted thing about any of it but"—she stopped, took a breath—"she was all excited because she recently heard from her old neighbor, Jackie Hendricks."

"What?" Bettina burst out.

"Apparently they email now and again? And she was so excited to hear Jackie got some new part. Some revival of an Edward Albany play or something—"

"Albee," I corrected her.

"Whatever. Point is, I said, 'Oh is that in London?' And she got all puzzled and said, 'No. New York City.'"

I stared at Alice. "She must've gotten it wrong."

Alice shook her head so fast her hair flew around her like a skirt. "She was sure as sugar. Even said Jackie was thrilled because the theater was easy to get to from the apartment she was staying at."

I looked over to the crowd, where Theresa was standing with her husband, cheery face, shaking someone's hand.

Jackie wasn't unreachable. She was here, on the East Coast. A train ride away.

Had Theresa lied to me?

"What the flying fuck?" I whispered.

FOUR DAYS
UNTIL
HALLOWEEN

THIRTY-ONE

Theresa

"Maggie? This is Theresa Pressley?"

I cringed. My voice was nowhere near as authoritative as I'd hoped. I sounded like a child trying to convince the usher that I was allowed in the R-rated movie theater.

"Theresa, yes of course. About to head out for a story. What's up?" Maggie seemed to have me on speakerphone. I could hear the hum of other people in the background, static, a radio. It had taken several calls to the newsroom to even get through to her.

"About your story," I said quickly. "Listen, I really would prefer you not use any images of our house. It's just—with Adam being the principal and all, well, we've decided we don't want to be part of it."

A pause. "Well, Theresa. Unfortunately, we've already edited the segment. I can't change it at this point. You *did* give your consent for us to film."

I got up from behind my desk, walked the length of my office and back, thinking furiously. Out my window, an orange fox was slinking across the street in broad daylight, tail raised proudly.

Be a bitch, Theresa. Pretend you have power.

"I'm sure you can understand our dilemma," I said firmly. "You do something you regret. Like, you know, when Bo got into that little fight with Cole McCaul at school recently?" *Taunting*, Adam had technically said. And he wasn't supposed to talk about discipline issues, but I could've heard it from Kendra. I needed the leverage. "I'm sure he wouldn't want that on his record and endanger his status on the swim team, right?"

If I didn't get myself out of that story, I was done for with the Ivies. They'd think I betrayed them.

"Anyway," I continued. "I'm sure you have other B-roll you can use. It would really be in everyone's best interests if you could swap that out."

The second pause was even worse than the first. I thought I'd gotten cut off. Then Maggie spoke, her voice even brisker than before. "I'm sorry, Theresa. The story's done. And you don't have to worry about Bo. He'll be just fine."

She hung up.

I collapsed at my desk. I'd gone too far. Screwed up royally. It was dumb enough to lie about Jackie—but now, how was I going to explain the story? When it aired, what would the Ivies think? I'd only seen them at Full Moon, though I suspected that party prep would switch into high gear over the next few days and I wouldn't be able to avoid them for much longer. I'd just have to be honest—that I'd talked to Maggie before I knew they didn't want a story. That I'd gotten confused when they asked if I knew her—maybe less honest. But they'd understand. I'd *make* them understand.

The front door opened. Adam was hanging his coat in the closet as I came down.

When he leaned in and kissed me, he smelled like pine. "Guess what?" he said. "That fox is still burrowing under our porch."

"I just saw it run across the yard," I said. "Maybe it's looking for a home for winter."

A week ago, Adam had found the hole in the side of the porch, a pile of dirt behind it. He'd tried to cover it back up, but each morning it was dug out again.

He closed the closet door. "I think we have to figure out how to deal with them."

I wrapped my arms around him, pressing my cheek to his chest. Trying to absorb some of his positive energy, his strength. "I really like the foxes."

"You won't like them when they destroy our house," he said. "Mess with the foundation. Once they settle in there, it'll be very hard to get rid of them." He pulled away, opened his briefcase, and drew out some folders. "Oh here. I found this in the mailbox."

"I already got the mail," I said, taking the yellow envelope from him.

He shrugged. "It was the only thing in there. You must've missed it." Whistling, Adam went into the kitchen.

The envelope was addressed to me, no return address or stamp. Inside was a baby shower invitation. On the front, a smiling baby in a diaper grabbing at her feet. Someone had written LILY? and drawn an arrow to the baby's head.

I opened the card and read the message.

"Theresa?" Adam had returned, a bottle of beer in hand. He tilted it at the card. "What is it?"

"Nothing," I said quickly. I felt a dull roar between my ears.

No no no no no.

"Nothing? You look like someone just died."

"It's just a baby shower invitation for someone down the street." I heard the lie leave my mouth. "I don't even know if I know them. I probably won't go."

I stuck the card in the back pocket of my jeans.

Adam took a swig of beer, wiped his mouth with the back of his hand. "Maybe you should. Good opportunity to meet more people, right?"

I nodded. "Sure. I'll think about it. That beer looks tasty. I think I'll get myself one. Meet you in the living room."

In the kitchen, I rested my palms against the counter, inhaling deeply. Closed my eyes. When I could, I drew out the card again, read the message that had already burned its way into my brain.

Who knows the truth about Lily, Theresa?
Are you going to tell her? Or should I?

HALLOWEEN

Some women cannot handle jealousy. It ensnares, wraps its tentacles around them, and squeezes.

Until they pop!

Queen Kendra. Our leader. Her party is a success, but it's not enough. It's never quite enough.

Daphne Brown, the babysitter for so many of the kiddos on the street, is playing tag with the children. She laughs, gathers the skirt of her wedding dress, and runs, chasing them as best she can.

Someone says, "Look at her. She's so good with them." It's a neighbor, an older woman, someone Kendra dismisses as not understanding the struggle.

Kendra says, "Well, that is her only job. You do know why she's here, right? Where she came from?" Our Queen raises her eyebrows expectantly. She can't help herself. She's tired of everyone treating the sitter like some kind of saint. Not now. Not now that she knows how she really is.

The neighbor backs off, shrugging. "She seems like a nice girl to me."

"Of course she's nice," Kendra snaps. "I wouldn't trust her with my boys if she weren't. It's just—you have to watch her closely, if you know what I mean."

Kendra walks off to check the ice. Grabs a bag from the freezer in her garage and hauls it down to the cooler to refill, tossing it onto the beer bottles inside, burying them. She balls up the empty plastic bag and carries it to the trash can under the tree.

Two of the neighborhood men are standing a few feet away, sipping from their plastic cups. They are watching Daphne, and Kendra is watching them.

"I'd hit that," one says.

The other laughs, tips his cup up, finishing it. He turns and softball pitches it into the trash can.

He doesn't even see Kendra.

She might as well be invisible.

THIRTY-TWO

Theresa

Greg was right. Gunston University's campus had completely changed since I'd last been there. The university had put up new buildings and torn down old ones, added roads and walking paths, and I had a hard time even finding a parking space. The campus had always been an oasis in the middle of a busy city, its green lawns and center quad an oasis of calm against the concrete strip malls and department stores on its outskirts. But in the decade I'd been gone, the structures had shot up like looming monsters and everything felt busier and more impersonal.

I had no idea where Greg's class was held, so I first had to go to the English department, talk to the nice but impatient and vaguely suspicious receptionist who smelled like chicken soup, and then trek across campus to a new building. I was worried I would miss him, but when I found the room and peered through the pane of glass in the door, he was still there wrapping up.

The classroom looked like a conference room, with wall-to-wall industrial gray carpeting and a number of round tables instead of rows of desks. Students sat around them in various states, checking phones, leaning forward, chins propped in hands, scribbling notes. When I took my Literature and Society course with Greg, it had been in an old building, wood floors that creaked, smudged windows. He had never stood in front of us but gathered our desks in a circle. It always felt intimate.

As I spied through the door, I noticed the women tended to be paying more attention. I suppose some things *hadn't* changed after all.

My cell phone rang. Adam. I moved away and answered with a quiet hello.

"Theresa?"

"Hey, babe. Everything okay?"

Adam hardly ever called during the school day. I could picture him at his desk, papers piled high. Emails from parents and teachers pinging in.

"Where are you? Are you home?"

"Uh, no. Why?" I kept my voice low, though the hall was empty.

"The contractor just called. He says he's at the front door, but no one's answering."

Shit. I'd completely forgotten they were supposed to come by to put in the faucet finally.

"Dammit," I said. "They said they'd call first."

"He said they did call you. No answer. Where are you?"

I checked my notifications. Sure enough, missed call. They must've called while I was driving.

"I, uh—I stopped at the library, actually, to pick up a couple of books." The lies were becoming easier and easier these days. Once you started, you had to keep going.

Greg's students started filtering out of the classroom. "I'll call him right now and reschedule," I said into the phone. "Sorry they bothered you."

"No problem. Love you."

Greg was at the front podium packing up when I slipped in. A blonde student in a long floral dress took her sweet time gathering her belongings.

Greg looked up as I approached, and when he saw me, he threw a million-dollar grin my way.

"To what do I owe this honor?" He gave me a big hug.

"I was hoping you had time to talk?" I asked. "Can I buy you coffee?"

He lifted his wrist—Greg was still a faithful watch-wearer—and checked the time. "I've got a faculty meeting in twenty minutes, sadly. But you can walk me there?"

I waited while he finished packing up. The butterflies were fluttering in my stomach as I thought about the note I'd gotten yesterday, how I would broach it with Greg.

Greg turned off the projection screen and slung his bag over his shoulder. "Misty, did you have a question?" he asked the student.

"Oh, uh. No, not really. I just wanted to double check that our essays are due next week, start of class?" Her voice was timid, eaten up by the fabric walls designed to dull loud noises.

"That's right," he said. "I can't wait to see what you come up with. I'm sure it will be dynamite."

She flushed, tossed her hair over her shoulder, and rushed off with a triumphant look.

I turned to Greg and raised an eyebrow. "Misty?"

He laughed. "Jealous?"

"I'm certainly not," I said.

"I didn't mean you." He winked. "Come on."

We strolled across the quad, past students sitting on benches or in groups on the lawn. "Bring back memories?" he asked.

"Memories? Feels like an entirely different planet."

"Ah, yes. The new president's been very aggressive about building. Problem is, it's all for the sciences and business. Us lowly humanities people don't matter."

There was something about being on a college campus that evoked opportunity. The students around us all seemed so hopeful, so young and earnest. It made me feel ancient, a foreign body. I'd once been one of these kids, hopeful but naive. Making bad choices, even as I had the hubris to think it would all work out and not come back to bite me.

And now it had.

Someone knew everything. And they were threatening to tell Lily. I'd been stupid to think I could keep it a secret. Stupid to think I could come back here with no consequences.

"Theresa?"

"Sorry," I said as Greg led me on a shortcut through the atrium of a building.

"What's going on? You seem like you're about to burst."

I let his question hang in the air between us. How to even begin?

"'The past is never dead. It's not even past.'" I hadn't realized I'd said it out loud until Greg glanced over at me.

"William Faulkner? Now I know something's wrong. You always hated him."

"And you always loved him," I said. "I guess that quote stuck with me." I never quoted literature. Was Greg's influence starting to creep back on me after all this time? The idea made me uncomfortable.

He stopped. "Come on, now. You navigated this place, found me, for a reason."

The campus had quieted down. The time between classes had ended, everyone filing into their respective places.

"It's about Lily," I said. "Someone knows about her, Greg."

He took one look at me and nodded. "We should probably find somewhere to sit." He ushered me to an alcove with a small private table. "They won't be surprised if I'm late to my meeting."

"Greg, I'm worried that Lily and Adam are going to find out…" I couldn't say the words aloud, even to him.

"Jeez, Theresa. You make it sound like it's some dirty secret. There are a lot of people who are adopted, you know."

"I know. I just thought—I wanted her to feel loved, to feel complete. I didn't want her to think she was unwanted or anything."

"Why would she think that? You're a great mom.

You're great at everything you do." He reached across the table and touched my shoulder, then let it drop.

I hadn't thought of it as lying back then, when I'd taken Lily. I just hadn't wanted it to matter. Greg and I had broken up, and I'd gone back to Brad. We were planning to get married. And then, out of the blue, Greg had reached out a few months later about a baby. The young mother who couldn't care for her child anymore.

At first Brad had resisted. He wanted us to try to have a baby ourselves, after we were married. But something about her story compelled me. It was a sign, I thought. We were the ones who needed to help this child. I'd told Brad we should at least explore it. That it wouldn't prevent us from still having our own children, too.

So we agreed to see the baby. And then, the first time I fixed eyes on Lily—that sweet pale face, big green eyes—that was it. I was in love.

Brad was, too. He agreed to the arrangement, on one condition. That we would keep the secret that she was adopted. He didn't want that kind of stigma on his daughter, he'd said. He'd seen the way some people were treated, and he never wanted her to go through that.

And then, when Brad left, and my mother died, and it seemed like I was losing everyone I cared about, well, I decided to go on keeping the secret. That Lily would always be *mine*. *My* daughter.

"You did a really good thing," Greg continued. "You've given Lily a good life. Don't beat yourself up."

"But you never told anyone, did you? Someone sent me this…card. And I'm afraid they might tell her."

He shook his head. "Of course not. You remember the family wanted everything to be discreet."

"But do you think…her mother might…?"

He shook his head confidently, but he wouldn't meet my eye. "No. No, definitely not."

"Are you sure? I mean, I know people sometimes regret their choices."

"Theresa, she's dead. Lily's mom. She died…a few years ago."

"What?" I drew back. "You didn't tell me?"

"I didn't—no, I didn't. I'm sorry. We weren't really in touch then. I didn't think you'd want to know."

Maybe I wouldn't have. After all, we hadn't cared where she'd come from, and Greg had never offered up details about her parents.

"Well, then who would threaten me like that?" I asked. "Would her father? Grandparents?"

"Theresa," Greg said gently. "Does it really matter who? Maybe you should just tell Lily the truth."

I should. I should've told her years ago.

"I can't. She'll hate me."

"And she'll hate you worse if she finds out from someone else."

TWO DAYS
UNTIL
HALLOWEEN

THIRTY-THREE

Kendra

I filled my biggest pot with water and set the burner on high as Cole entered.

"Hello, my saintly mother," he greeted me, kicking off his shoes and leaving them in the middle of the doorway. His hair was still wet from practice, curls hanging in his face like tentacles. The boys on the team let their hair grow and grow until state championships, dying it ridiculous colors, and then they shaved it all off to reduce drag and be more competitive in the water. This was the best stage, longer but not completely shaggy.

"Oh no," I said. "What kind of trouble did you get in today? Must be serious if I'm a saint."

"No trouble." He went to the refrigerator, took out a can of Coke and salami and cheese, and piled it on the counter.

"What are you doing? Don't you see I'm making dinner?"

"I'm starving. Ravished." He unwrapped the salami and stacked a piece of cheese between two slices, then ate it like a sandwich. The dog came bounding down the stairs, looking for love from his favorite person, and Cole slipped him a bite.

At least some of us in this household were happy. At least some of us didn't have to worry about betrayal and threats to upend their entire lives.

Theresa had been so eager to be friends, right from the very beginning. All those questions about the Ivy Five—I'd thought she'd been insecure, that she just wanted to see how she fit in. She'd mastered the mother-next-door image, all grateful and awed to be here with her perfect husband and daughter. I'd have been lying if I said I wasn't impressed by how she'd wormed her way into our group.

I'd let her in. Pinned her as one of us.

She'd told me her secrets.

Did she lie about Jackie's whereabouts? Or did Greg lie to her?

If she lied, what did she have to gain from Jackie being in Europe, unreachable, versus in New York? Did Theresa somehow know Jackie from when she was Greg's student? Were they working together to threaten us?

But why, Theresa? We'd given her so much. I couldn't see the connection.

Still, now that Jackie was back in play, everything had changed again. The *Queen Bee* message loomed once again in my mind as a direct hit from Jackie to me. Jimmy-O—prodded by Pia to get his act together—had asked a friend of his in New York to track her down, based on the information Mrs. Vancavage had given

Alice at Full Moon. We needed to talk to her, set things straight. Find out what the hell she wanted.

Jimmy-O said it might take a few days to find her.

We only had two days left.

I opened a bag of salad and tossed it together while I watched the news. I wanted to catch the weather report. I could recall only two times since we'd moved to Ivy Woods that it had rained on Halloween, and they'd both been before we started the block parties. One had been when Sam was so young he didn't really comprehend trick-or-treating, and on the other, the families on the cul-de-sac had all parked our cars on the street and sat in our garages drinking and handing out candy, dumping extra chocolate bars in the kids' buckets for their courage to go out in the weather. That had been the year Pia and her husband, Marlon, had dragged their ping-pong table to Bettina's garage and we'd had an epic tournament, doing shots of pumpkin-flavored liqueur Pia's sister made until we were all so drunk it was a wonder we were able to stumble home.

I missed those days. Everything had been easier then.

"How was your calculus test?" I asked Cole.

"Okay."

Sam had excelled at math and science. They were his favorite subjects. He used to put himself to sleep thinking up complicated multiplication problems and solving them in his head. Cole, not so much.

"Did you do alright with the graphing stuff?"

He took a sip of soda. "Yep. Got them all right. And I ate all of my veggies. And I'm wearing clean underwear. Want to see?"

He turned around, started to pull down his jeans.

"No need to be vulgar," I said. "You're in a special mood."

"Just happy to see you, my dear mother." He drew close, kissed me on the cheek. I could smell the meat on his breath.

"And?"

"And nothing. Can't a son just love his mother?"

I moved past him, opened the door, and let Barney into the backyard. He ran out, barking into the darkening skies.

"No," I said. "Does this have anything to do with Lily Pressley?" I'd seen him and Lily through the window as he'd come home from school yesterday. Their heads were close—not touching, but in an intimate little conversation—and she'd thrown him a wiggly finger wave before heading inside.

He laughed. "Uh, no."

"You sure?" I cocked my head. "You two seem pretty chummy. Just be careful. She's the principal's daughter." *And her mother's a liar.* "And too young for you anyway."

"She's too young. Ellen's too weird. How am I ever going to find a girl to please you, Mother?" He batted his eyelashes.

"You can joke all you want, but you know you can't mess up this year."

"Who's messing up what?" Paul walked in, what hair he had left sticking up in all directions like he'd just woken from a nap. I had no idea how he spent his days at home now, since he still had no further leads on a job.

Just get through Halloween.

"Are you going to show yourself at the block party this year?" I asked Cole.

He shrugged. "Do I have to?" He popped another piece of salami in his mouth.

"Stop eating that." I tossed the cheese and salami packages back in the refrigerator. "And yes, it would be nice if you came. Given this might be our last one."

"Ah, give him a break, Kendra," said Paul. He picked up a bag of opened potato chips from the counter and started crunching on them. "When you were a teenager, I'm sure you didn't want to hang around with your parents on Halloween."

I snatched the bag of chips from him. "We. Are. Eating. Soon." I glared at both of them.

"Whoa. Calm down." Paul held his hands up. Behind him, I caught a glimpse of a reporter on the news, standing outside a building with police cars and fire trucks in the background. "The level of perfection is just too high sometimes. We can't live up to it."

I turned back to Paul. "I'm sorry. I didn't realize we were aiming for mediocrity here."

He let out a dramatic sigh. "Never mind. Forget I said a thing. I'll set the table." He jerked open the drawers and slammed down the silverware, his own small rebellion, and Cole used it as an opportunity to slink out.

I didn't take the bait. I switched back to the television. I'd missed the weather report, but Maggie Lewis's voice now filled the kitchen. I'd know it anywhere—nasal and lilting, like she was pinching her nose and trying to act surprised. What she said made me forget all about Cole and Paul.

"An I-Team special investigation," she said. A tacky Halloween graphic with bats flying out of a haunted house appeared on screen. Then an image of the railroad bridge, fading into a sepia tone that I guess was supposed to be frightening. Maggie's voice said, "A young woman. A tragic death. A local urban legend that comes alive each year on Halloween. But what do we really know about this story?"

Maggie appeared on screen then, doing her best to look serious. "Tonight I will take you behind the scenes to uncover the true story behind the Ghost Girl legend. We all know the rumors. But what is the truth?"

"Oh fuck," I muttered, tossing the pasta into the pot and taking a seat at the kitchen table. I was going to need vodka for this.

Maggie narrated the history for everyone. "It was an annual block party. A harmless tradition. And then it turned deadly."

I snorted as she showed more photos of the railroad bridge and interviewed teenagers on Woodard's campus (I made a note to tell Adam Wallace he should forbid reporters on school grounds) who yammered on about how scary it all was. A boy in a gray hoodie stood nervously with hands in his pockets. "If you go to the bridge at midnight and call her name, you'll see her floating," he said. "Nah, I'm too scared to go there." Three dim-witted girls giggled as they admitted they'd gone there before but seen nothing.

More tacky images, and then Maggie was on our street in a black jacket, hair whipping around her head. Theresa's house loomed in the background.

"The girl behind the Ghost Girl legend? She had a name—and she lived right here in this sleepy neighborhood we call Ivy Woods."

Maggie swooped her arm dramatically. As she explained the *tragic* history of Daphne Brown, the camera panned our cul-de-sac, then the lake, the woods. A squirrel running up a tree.

"She was a popular babysitter in the neighborhood, well-loved by the kids."

The camera cut to a somber Ellen Hendricks. "Yeah, she was a great babysitter. We loved her."

Maggie again, close-up now for drama. "But something drove Daphne Brown to her death that night. Was she really depressed and suicidal? Or was it something else that turned tragic?"

"I have my doubts." Mrs. Tressle stood on the curb, chewing her lip. "That girl always seemed happy to me. She didn't seem like the type to jump."

Maggie stared knowingly into the camera. "Some long-term residents believe that even if Daphne did get into trouble, it would be hard to find the truth in such a close-knit neighborhood."

She cut to Lynn Deeds, one of her poker buddies, in front of her house. "If something *did* happen," she said in a whiny voice, "I could totally see how no one would say anything about it. Let's just say what happens in Ivy Woods stays in Ivy Woods."

"Are you fucking kidding me?" I glared at the screen.

The television hissed. Then I smelled something burning, turned, and realized the hissing was the sound of the pasta boiling over. "Shit." I jumped up to turn off the burner. A small spit of hot water dropped onto my hand. "Shit, shit, shit."

I ran my hand under the faucet, as more graphics graced the screen. The bridge again. Lightning. "In part two, I'll investigate more of the true story behind one of our area's most famous urban legends. And we'll go behind the scenes with someone who has an interesting connection to that tragic night."

The camera focused on a black-and-white shot of a bedroom. I knew that room. Knew that circle window with the witch decoration. In fact, I could've, right then, walked across the house, peered out the window, and seen it across the street.

Theresa's house.

She'd promised she wouldn't talk to Maggie about the story. Once a liar, always a liar. She must have lied about Jackie, too.

"Did Daphne Brown really leap to her death that night? Or did something else happen? Tune in Halloween night to see this special I-Team investigation."

And then Theresa herself, the traitor, silhouetted in the frame of her front door. As the camera zoomed out, away from her, she walked inside. Reached up, tugged at the end of her ponytail and twisted it around her finger, all innocent. That gesture.

That house.

That liar.

Theresa was going to pay for her lies.

We had to confront her before the block party. I just needed a plan first.

THE NIGHT BEFORE HALLOWEEN

THIRTY-FOUR

Theresa

As I came up the stairs, Lily tried to toss the Ouija board under her bed, but she missed, and the planchette skittered toward my feet.

"Why are you sneaking up on us?" Her eyes flashed with annoyance.

They'd lit black votive candles, the only light other than Lily's small desk lamp, and were sitting cross-legged on the floor. Ellen's face was shadowed, but I could see the hint of a smug smile.

I picked up the planchette and handed it to Ellen. "I don't want that thing in my house, girls."

"Mom! What is wrong with you?"

What is wrong with me? Good question. How about everything, Lily? My life was crumbling around me. I got a call this afternoon from the *Post* saying they were canceling my second interview because they'd decided to take the job "in a different direction." Maggie's story has caused me trouble with the Ivies. And someone thinks it's funny to threaten me and I don't know who it is. How about that?

"No one should mess with these things," I said. I couldn't stop my voice from rising in pitch. "They're dangerous."

That was my mother's voice coming through. Fifth grade, my best friend Molly and me in my room with a Ouija board. Goofing around, trying it out. But my mother had heard us shrieking and came barreling in. She'd never liked Molly—thought she wasn't good enough for me. Wished I'd hung out more with Carley Aronowitz, whose parents were doctors.

Was I turning into my mother?

Lily sighed deeply, like I was the most annoying person on Earth. "It's just for fun."

"We were trying to see if we could conjure up Daphne." Ellen's tone was maddeningly calm, bored, condescending.

Daphne. Daphne. Daphne. I was so sick of hearing about *Daphne*.

"No more ghosts," I said to the girls. "Play *Monopoly* or something."

"*Monopoly*? It's Halloween." Lily stood. A large black skull ring sat like a lollipop on her middle finger.

"And you'll spend it up here alone if you don't stop talking to me in that tone."

"Unbelievable. Fine. Ruin everything. Like you always do." Lily scowled, wrapping her arms around her knees and murmuring something under her breath that made Ellen snort.

"Can I talk to you downstairs?" I asked. "Now."

She stomped down the attic stairs and followed me into my bedroom. I closed the door and turned. "How dare you talk to me like that? Anytime, but especially in front of your friend. I've been pretty lenient with you, but I'm tired of it. I'm your mother."

As soon as I said those words, I flinched. *I'm your mother.* Lily's eyes narrowed, and I half expected her to scream, *No you're not.* That whoever had sent that baby shower invitation had already gotten to her.

But she lifted her chin. "You treat me like a baby. Everyone sees it, even Adam."

"I'll treat you with respect when you act like you deserve it."

She clenched and unclenched her fists, out of breath like she'd been running.

I wanted to hug her, but I was frozen. Greg's words whispered in my ear. *Tell her, before someone else does.*

"Lily, I—"

"Lily?" Ellen's voice from the attic, echoing against the walls.

Lily reacted quickly, lunging for the doorknob. "I've got to go. Don't worry about us. We'll, like, do our nails and talk about boys all night, just like you want."

And she was gone, before I could say anything at all.

That's when my cell phone buzzed.

———

Downstairs, Adam was flipping through the TV channels. Michael Myers seemed to be murdering people on every station. I could almost relate to him.

"Ready to watch a movie?" Adam asked, a bag of candy corn in his lap. I married a man who liked *candy corn*?

"I can't, Adam. Kendra just texted me."

I stared at the message I'd gotten after Lily had left me in the bedroom.

Busy? Need you to meet us at Alice's. Bonfire meeting.

I'd texted her back: I don't know if I can. I've got Ellen sleeping over.

And then her response, almost immediately, like she'd been waiting: It's important.

"Party emergency?" He smirked, but then saw my face and dropped it.

"I don't know." I sank down on the couch next to him. I wasn't sure I could handle a crisis with Kendra right now on top of everything else.

Adam kissed my head. "Well, maybe it won't take long."

"Maybe. Lily's pissed off at me. Keep an eye on them, okay?"

"Always."

I left to get ready, my nerves at high peak. I felt like I was going to throw up. Lily's attitude. The note. My lies to the Ivies. The party tomorrow.

Just get through this goddamn holiday. Then you can work it all out.

One more day. That's all I needed. After the party and Halloween, I'd come clean to Lily and Adam.

And hope that they still loved me.

I grabbed my coat and went back into the living room to say goodbye to Adam. He'd shut the television off and was staring into space, his jaw set hard.

"You look like you saw a ghost," I joked.

He didn't laugh.

He held out my phone. "You got a message."

I took it and saw the notification that had popped up. A text from Greg.

Just checking in since you seemed so upset the other day. Let me know how you are. XO

"Where did you say you were going? To Kendra's house?" Adam's voice was low. Even.

"Adam, this isn't— I don't—"

"Save it, Theresa." He sighed, drew his fist to his forehead. "I should've known."

"Known what?" I asked.

"You and…him. I saw how he looked at you at the football game."

"Adam! Are you kidding me? He was my teacher. That's all."

Liar. Cheater.

His face was unreadable. Stone. "Then why lie?"

"Lie? About what? Kendra just texted me. I will show you." I pulled it up. "Right here."

"Not about that." He shook his head. "The library. You weren't at the library the other day when I called you. It was 10 a.m. The library doesn't open until noon on Thursdays."

I felt the trap door open.

"Adam, it's not what it seems. I swear."

"I said save it. I don't want to talk to you right now." He got up, left me alone.

The perfect house on the hill that I'd needed. The perfect house in the perfect neighborhood. I'd built a castle on top of a snake's nest.

Perfect, perfect, perfect. It's all I'd ever wanted. No—it was all my mother ever wanted for me. Pushing me to look my best, act my best, never make mistakes. All that pressure—it caused you to do things you wouldn't ordinarily do. To lie. To cover up flaws. To pretend to be someone you weren't, just to fit in. It caused you to change, until you weren't even sure who you really were anymore.

It was a windy night, the gusts howling between our house and Mrs. Tressle's. The dead brown leaves skittered around and around the cul-de-sac like noisy insects. As I shut the door behind me, something moved fast across the lawn. A dog, I thought at first, but a motion sensor kicked on, and its green eyes glittered. The fox. It stopped, staring at me. Sizing me up. A dead squirrel hung limp in its jaws.

It turned and disappeared along the side of the house, into the shadows.

Potential predators were everywhere.

I started down the porch stairs and accidentally kicked the jack-o'-lantern from Bettina's crop off its step. It rolled down into the middle of the sidewalk, laughing at me with an evil, lopsided sneer.

"Fuck you," I said, kicking it again.

Then I hoisted it up, walked over to the side of our garage, and hurled it at the brick. It smashed with a satisfying thunk, splattering into orange chunks of wreckage.

I left it there and hurried to Alice's house, licking the pulp from my thumb as I went.

HALLOWEEN

Alice Swanson adjusts her witch hat, wishing she could take it off because it itches terribly, but she's afraid of pissing off the others. She and her husband are younger than most of the families here, and Alice is self-conscious about it. This is why she reminds everyone with every breath she takes that she is with child. Once she's a mother, she thinks, she'll fit in. She'll belong.

She's made three desserts for the party. Witch hat sugar cookies, a candy corn cake, and spider cupcakes. She bought uncomfortable black booties with heels that are too high. You can tell by the way she shifts her weight, back and forth, and hasn't anyone else noticed? Won't they tell the pregnant woman to sit down? To rest? To go home, crawl in bed, and go to sleep?

Alice pats her belly underneath her black witch dress, still just the tiniest of bumps, still hardly anything at all. But she'll be such a good mother. She knows she will.

The problem is that everything feels so slippery, so precarious, and Alice worries constantly about falling. She was born to please, and she wants the other moms to love her like she loves them.

She's one of the Ivy Five. She even thought of the name and was so thrilled when Kendra liked it. Even more so when Kendra bought all of them ivy leaf pins. It reminds her of her sorority sisters. Live and love and die by the group. She knows how to be loyal. She is a very good sister. She'll be an even better mother.

And yet they've deserted her right now (of course they have, there are always tiers, rankings, even in the tightest of groups, and Alice is more disposable than others). She and Justin are alone, by the fire. She sees no other witches. Where did everyone go?

"I need another beer." Justin is not dressed up for Halloween. He doesn't think adults should wear costumes.

Alice follows him to the cooler. Her feet are really hurting now—see how she shuffles, gingerly? Poor Alice, the Good Witch.

And then she hears her name. "Alice." A whisper. A hush. She turns, and there is Kendra. Smiling. Beckoning her. There is Kendra, bringing her back.

"Come here. We need you."

She should say no, dear reader. But hindsight is everything.

She doesn't realize this decision is so important. She doesn't realize that it will seal her fate forever.

She goes. She follows Kendra to the other witches in the darkness under the tree. She's joined the coven again.

"What?" she asks eagerly, the pain in her feet forgotten now. "How can I help?"

She is useful. She is wanted. She's willing to follow them anywhere, at any cost.

"Yes," she says as they tell her their plan. "Yes."

THIRTY-FIVE

Kendra

"Are y'all sure you want to stay out here?"

Alice's voice wavered, even as she threw another log in the firepit. The wind blew the flames sideways and sent a cloud of smoke over us.

We were in the open air, surrounded by the tree shadows. Menace. Anyone could be out there, crouching. Waiting.

It was Mischief Night. Teenagers skulking around pulling pranks. Wrapping toilet paper in trees. Using the night as their cover.

Whoever was threatening us could be out there, too. I didn't want to be here, exposed. But I'd be damned if I was going to let someone send us scurrying into rabbit holes. We wouldn't give them the satisfaction.

"Yes. We're fine out here."

They all eyed me. I didn't care if they disagreed.

"It's just creepy," Alice said, rubbing her arms briskly.

"Dude, I learned how to flip someone over my back in self-defense class last week," Pia said. "So if anyone tries to sneak up on us, I'll kick their ass."

Theresa was on her way, but I knew her guard would be up. She'd lied about Jackie's whereabouts. She'd lied about not talking to Maggie and must've known we'd seen the story.

But we'd lied, too.

And now we were going to use the situation to bait the hook.

"So, like, why are we here?" Pia asked, chipping away at her nail polish. She was wearing a wool hat with a pom-pom that wobbled each time she spoke. It was hard to take her seriously.

Bettina scowled. "Really? We have to go over it again?"

Pia shrugged. "I guess I just don't get it." I couldn't tell if she was obtuse or apathetic.

Even Alice seemed impatient with Pia. She whispered, but it came out in hissy bursts. "For frick's sake, Pia. Jackie's trying to blackmail us. And Theresa told us she was *unreachable.* Then Theresa lets Maggie into her house for that absurd story after she swore on her mother's Bible she wouldn't. I don't know about you, but I reckon that's a little suspicious there."

"Don't forget the timing," Bettina added. "All these messages and things started right after Theresa moved here."

"Or that she pulled a bunch of strings to land herself here," I said.

"In *our* neighborhood," Bettina finished.

"So what?" Pia asked. "It's a nice place to live. And

we're gorgeous people. Who wouldn't want to be here?" She fluttered her eyelashes.

Bettina ignored her. "Sharita sent me her résumé after they turned her down for the job." Bettina had made sure of that. "She was in school right here, just two miles from us, the same year Daphne died, yet she claims to never have heard about it. I say bullshit. I say she and Jackie are somehow in this together."

"I can't stand it," Alice moaned. "Maybe Bettina was right and we should cancel the party."

"Oh yeah. Okay," I said. "I'll just go rip down the tent. Call the band and say thanks, but no thanks. Easy peasy."

"Alright, everybody calm down," Pia said. "I just don't get why Theresa would—"

"Shh," I said, gesturing toward the darkness.

The gate creaked. We all turned in sync. Alice's motion sensor light went on, and there was Theresa, spotlighted, trying to lift the lever.

"Okay," I said, low enough so Theresa couldn't hear. "Remember the plan."

"Hi, guys." Theresa moved into the light of the fire. Her hair was down tonight, curling over her shoulders. Coat open, scarf hanging down to her knees, like she'd rushed off without thinking.

Just how we wanted her.

"We haven't seen you in a while," I said. "Thought maybe you skipped town on us."

Theresa smiled, but it didn't quite reach her eyes.

"Well, hey, it's cold out here and we all have stuff to do for tomorrow, so I'll just get right to it," I said. "I think we should talk about Jackie."

Theresa's eyes flashed in panic, like I'd swift-kicked her in the teeth. "Jackie? Why?"

"Come." I scooted a lawn chair over for her. She sat next to me near the fire so that together we all formed a tight circle in front of it. She leaned as far back as she could without tipping over, as if we were going to bite. I kept a close watch on her face. "She's not in Europe," I said.

"She came back?" Theresa asked. Was she just trying to feel out what we already knew so she could formulate new lies?

"She was *never there*," Alice erupted. "Why did you *lie*?"

Theresa looked at all of us, wounded. "I didn't." She clearly wasn't used to being on the defensive. I almost—almost—felt bad for her. "Greg must've been mistaken. Or maybe I misheard. If I misunderstood, I'm so sorry."

I watched her face for any sign of lies. But I couldn't get a good read on her. Was it possible Greg had lied to her? Or Jackie had lied to *him* about where she was? I wasn't sure—But I wasn't about to trust Theresa Pressley again. Still, she'd denied it like I thought she would, and now I just needed to stick to the script.

"We want to trust you, Theresa," I said. "But getting this information wrong"—*or lying about it*—"and cooperating with Maggie about that story after you said you wouldn't, well, it makes us wonder."

Theresa stared into the fire. "I screwed up there. I'm sorry. I thought you'd be excited by the media attention, and then when I found out you weren't, I couldn't get Maggie to edit it out."

"You should've just told us," I said. "We didn't ask you to avoid her because we have a grudge against her or something. There's a good reason. There's a good reason for everything we do."

The large tree nearest to our fire suddenly started swaying. We all turned in that direction.

Just the wind.

Bettina jumped in, right on cue. "Kendra, I'm not sure we should—"

I held up my hand. "I think Theresa's been holding back on us because she doesn't entirely trust us. But if she's going to be one of us now, Bettina, she needs to know everything."

Theresa's curiosity was piqued. I could see the wheels whirling in her head. At first, she thought she was in trouble with us for lying. Now she sensed a secret. Irresistible.

Alice, her voice low and lilting, chimed in, "Oh, y'all. Kendra's right." She stared at Theresa. "As long as you won't repeat anything that's said here?"

"I swear," Theresa said quickly, holding up her hand.

"We have no proof of any of this," I said. "It's all just—speculation."

Theresa was rapt. Her hair could have caught on fire and she wouldn't have noticed.

"I need a cigarette for this." Pia stood off to the side and lit up, fanning the smoke away from us.

"As you know, Jacqueline Hendricks was our friend," I continued. "We all looked out for each other. But she and Greg, well, obviously, they didn't have a great marriage. And Jackie started worrying about Daphne, Ellen's babysitter. She became obsessed."

Theresa frowned. "Obsessed?" she said.

I nodded. "She thought that Daphne wanted to take her place. She thought Daphne seemed a little too...

comfortable in her home. With her daughter. And her *husband*."

I let Theresa read between the lines. "Wait, are you saying Greg was—*with Daphne*?"

We confirmed the answer with silence. Only the fire cracked.

"Oh god." Theresa's face crumpled. I was surprised how upset she seemed. Had we just killed the professor-mentor image she'd held of Greg Hendricks all these years? Big deal.

I closed my eyes as if mustering up the words. "Jackie was obviously upset. Her husband was sleeping with their babysitter—"

Theresa flinched again.

"—and she lost her senses."

Pia took a drag, knocking her ash into the fire, playing her part, too. "She was never a stable woman entirely, and this cracked it all open."

"Jackie was terrible to Daphne at the end. Mean to her. Berated her." I may have been embellishing a bit there, but what did it matter now? I had to give Theresa a secret, something that would make her feel included so she would feel loyal to us. So she would stay away from Maggie. "It took its toll on Daphne. We feel, in some ways, responsible. Perhaps if we could've stepped in earlier, or supported Daphne more, she wouldn't have… done what she did."

In the distance, a car's engine roared. Tires skidded and squealed.

Theresa tucked her hair behind her ears. "So you think Jackie drove Daphne to jump?"

"Shh." Bettina hissed sharply, gesturing out into the

dark woods. Alice actually had tears in her eyes. She was always the better actress than Jackie. We all were.

"You can see why we don't want *reporters*"—here I flashed quote marks—"poking into all this."

Would Theresa understand? I hoped I hadn't overestimated her desire to be one of us, to be a good mother and a good friend.

I pushed on. "This is why we don't want Maggie meddling. God forbid she digs up something. Think what it would do to Ellen. To our community." As I leaned in toward her, I could feel the heat of the fire on my leg. "Theresa, you have to keep this secret. It's just better for everyone if Maggie's story goes away."

HALLOWEEN,
PRESENT DAY

THIRTY-SIX

Kendra

The fox costume may have been risqué, but I rocked it.

Paul was making coffee in the kitchen. He was still wearing his flannel pajama pants, working the Keurig while reading the newspaper. On the counter sat piles of items to donate. One of his unemployment projects was to organize and clean out our basement, and he'd been going at it full-steam for the past week. My husband, somewhat useful again.

I stood in the doorway, tall. Shoulders back, chin out, hands on hips, waiting for him to turn around and notice me.

When he did, he did a double take.

I smiled coyly. "What do you think?" I gestured to my costume, a fitted orange jumpsuit with white fur for the belly and knee-high boots.

The Keurig fizzed and popped, then hissed to silence. Paul took his mug and stirred in some cream. "You look like you just came off your shift at Chuck E. Cheese," he said, smirking at the giant hood with black pointed ears and the huge tail.

I had the urge to smack the bottom of the mug and send the hot coffee spraying all over him. I was trying to suppress it, but I was still on edge after last night. Though the conversation seemed to go our way with Theresa, my anxiety was at a peak, hovering at the corners of my mind, along with a million questions. Jackie, Theresa, Maggie. Whoever sent those notes, would they expose us tonight? Or were they just taunting us simply to watch us squirm? I couldn't get excited about my own party, because when I did, the thought of the threats dragged me back down.

"I'm joking," Paul tossed over his shoulder. I smelled the pumpkin coffee I'd bought from the store as soon as the fall stuff had hit the shelves. "So, are all of you going to be foxes?"

"Woodland creatures," I said. Like I'd already told him.

I imagined the other neighborhood moms getting a look at me. The jealousy would seep through them like syrup. Sweet and sticky. It had been worth all the sit-ups and morning runs with Bettina. The annual photo would be epic this year—I'd make Paul snap us down by the water, in front of the trees, in our natural habitat.

Would our anonymous friend be watching us?

"You want any breakfast?" Paul asked.

I shook my head, lowered my knee. "You know I can't eat anything the day of the party."

Especially one where the whole world might come crashing down.

"Did you find a costume for tonight?" I asked him as I checked my day-of to-do list affixed to the front of the refrigerator.

"Not yet. Maybe I'll run out to Party City or something."

Paul was last-minute about everything. Shopped the weekend before Christmas. Preferred to stand in an hour-long line for whatever stupid shit was left in the Halloween aisle rather than plan ahead. It irritated me to no end, but there was no use trying to change him after twenty years of marriage.

"Fine, but while you're out, I need you to run an errand for me," I said. "Someone smashed the pumpkins last night."

He looked up. "Bettina's Autumn Golds?"

I nodded. "All of them. They went around from porch to porch."

He whistled. "She must be pissed."

"She is." *Pissed* wasn't the right word. *Enraged* was more like it. I could still see her face when we'd left Alice's the night before and found the pieces scattered in the middle of the street. Fucking teenagers.

I pushed the hood off my head. "Can you drive down to the church and see if they've got any left for sale? We need five. And if you and Cole have time to carve ours for tonight, that would be grand."

He saluted. "Yes, ma'am." Then picked up his newspaper again.

I frowned. Was it that hard to have a conversation with me? Weren't we supposed to be happily married? We needed to make a good impression at the party, show everyone that despite his job loss, the McCauls were just fine.

"What is this?" I picked up a small backpack that was on the counter next to Paul.

Paul peered over the newspaper. "Our old bee sting kit. I found it in the basement when I was cleaning up. Thought I'd give it to Theresa."

"Theresa?" My husband was getting awfully chummy with our new neighbor. But I had enough to worry about today.

"She's got a bad allergy."

"Oh right." I recalled her reaction to the bees in Alice's shed.

"Swells up, just like Franny used to when she was a kid," Paul said about his sister. "Remember when she forgot her EpiPen at the family reunion and we had to take her to the hospital? Franny's got that little scar, too, on her finger from that. Can't fit her wedding band there anymore."

Something clicked then. A white flash connection. "What did you just say?" I asked him.

"She had to get her wedding band resized."

"No, not that. The hospital."

Paul's brow furrowed. "Don't you remember? Franny got stung in the field, with all that clover. And she'd forgotten her EpiPen." He went to grab his mug, but overshot the handle and knocked it over. "Shit." Coffee spilled everywhere, dotting his pajama pants. I jumped back, and luckily it missed my costume.

I helped him mop it up, but something was still nagging at me.

His sister. The family reunion. *Don't you remember?* But I couldn't. Whatever had been there, was gone.

THIRTY-SEVEN

Theresa

The cul-de-sac was already buzzing with activity late morning. A small tent had been erected in the grassy field between two houses, where the band Kendra had hired would play. Construction horses blocked off the street, and someone had looped black and orange streamers around them and tied balloons on.

But my shoulders hung heavy as I made chicken wings—my mother's special recipe. They were one of Adam's favorites, too, though he didn't even acknowledge the delicious smell that filled the house. He was keeping busy, hauling out the card tables and the lawn chairs I'd bought on clearance at Lowe's at the end of summer back when he hadn't hated me. The cloud of anger hovering over him tainted any hope I'd had of making happy memories tonight. Lily wasn't much better. She had holed up in her room with Ellen the rest of the night after our fight, and now they seemed to be sleeping in late.

And the bonfire last night. What the Ivies had told me about Jackie. I didn't want to think about that. No wonder the Ivies hadn't brought her up originally. No wonder they never mentioned that night. It must be horrible to suspect your friend might've driven someone to do something so awful.

They were just trying to protect Ellen, after all. To keep Ivy Woods from being marred by scandal, from people like Maggie Lewis who wanted to dig up things that should stay buried for everyone's sake. I'd almost ruined all that. I should've never lied to them. I should've never lied to anyone. It was all coming back to burn me.

If I could just get through this day, this party, I felt sure I could fix things. Show the Ivies I could keep their secret. Come clean to Lily. Explain everything to Adam. Beg forgiveness.

I left the chicken wings cooking and stepped outside to see if anyone needed help. You couldn't miss Kendra the fox in her bright orange costume. She was busy, weaving in and out of groups of neighbors, giving orders.

"Can I help?" I asked when I was able to snag her alone.

"Yes," she said, and motioned toward a group of pumpkins on a nearby picnic table. "Take one to carve for tonight since none of the others survived Mischief Night."

"None of them?" I gaped, remembering the satisfaction I'd felt smashing mine. But only mine. Who had destroyed the others?

"Where's your costume?" Kendra snapped. I couldn't tell if her tone was abrupt because she didn't actually trust me, or if she was just stressed. Either way, I'd been hoping for a more promising start.

"I've got it. I just thought it was easier to set up without—"

"Well, just make sure you're dressed by three o'clock. I want us to all get pictures together down by the lake."

I wandered over to the other side of the cul-de-sac to help some of the neighborhood moms set up a small scavenger hunt for the kids. Georgeann Wilkins was there, dressed like a scarecrow, orange braided wig, freckles, and some sort of mouth thing that made it seem like she had gapped teeth. It wasn't a great look, and I wished she had the decency to know it. But I was still glad to see her. Finally, someone who wasn't pissed off at me.

"Don't you look cute," I said.

"This?" She laughed. "It's an old costume. I'm surprised it still fits." She took a small toy out of a plastic bag and hid it in a crook of a tree. "Maggie was looking for you, by the way," she said. "She was just here... I don't know where she went." Georgeann's wig shifted; she tried to straighten it.

I felt sick to my stomach. "What did she want me for?"

"I think the story she's doing? She was going on about something—I didn't catch it all, don't tell her. I think it's about the party? And that haunted bridge. Though she was also going on about Jackie, a woman who hasn't lived here in years, so I don't—"

"You knew Jackie?" I asked.

Georgeann stopped. "Well, yeah. Did you? You

wouldn't have. She moved away a long time ago. She was great. You would've loved her, Theresa."

Great? That was the first time I'd heard anyone say anything nice about Jackie Hendricks.

"Wow," I said. "When Kendra talked about her, she made her sound like the devil."

"Really?" Georgeann tugged on a braid. "I didn't feel that way at all. I was sad when she left."

If only you knew the half of it.

"She was so pretty. And fun. I mean, it makes sense, doesn't it?" She gestured to me. "That's why they recruited *you*, I'm sure."

————

When I got back to the house a half hour later, I hustled upstairs to put on my owl costume.

It was still a nightmare, but with Lily's suggestions—a turtleneck, dark tights, and boots—plus the spooky black-and-gold owl mask and an owl ears headband I'd found online, it was salvageable. And once it got dark outside, no one would be able to tell the difference anyway.

Skipping down the stairs, I tried to psyche myself up. *Everything's going to be fine. The party will be great. You—*

I nearly fell over when I spotted Maggie Lewis sitting calmly in my living room, dressed as a fairy godmother, as though she'd just blown in from the fireplace.

"What are you doing here?" I asked her.

"Your hubby let me in. He said to wait for you here."

"I can't really chat now, Maggie." *Or ever.* "I've got to get ready for the party."

She eyed me up and down. "The wise owl, huh? And Kendra McCaul. The sly fox." Maggie laughed, her cheeks streaked with glitter makeup. "You know, you really should wear better shoes. Your feet are going to be killing you by the end of the night."

I looked down at my ankle boots. She was probably right, but while flats were safe and comfortable, they were never going to get you any second looks.

When I didn't say anything, Maggie got back to business. "Listen, I'm sorry about the story. I tried to get them to re-edit, but they wouldn't do it. I hope Adam wasn't upset?"

"It's fine."

"Do you want to hear what the second part of my story's going to be about?"

I shook my head. "Nope." The whole thing had already caused me enough trouble. "It's okay. I can find out when the world does. But I need you to leave now."

She didn't stand. She let out a deep disappointed sigh. "So, they got to you, eh?" She rubbed her palms on her poufy pink dress. "I figured they would. I'd just hoped you were smarter than that."

You know nothing about me, I wanted to say. But I kept silent. I wanted to go upstairs and crawl under our weighted blanket and sleep for a very long time. I didn't want to play these games anymore.

"Okay, I'll go. But isn't there a part of you that thinks it's odd? Why would Daphne leave all those kids up in the attic alone and go off to kill herself? It just doesn't make sense." Now Maggie did stand, tapping her index finger against her lips. She paced my living room like we were playing a murder-mystery game and she was in the role of the detective. "Why not wait until the moms came to get their kids? The party was wrapping up by that point anyway."

"I have no idea," I said.

"I'm talking to someone who knows what really happened. It's all going to come out, Theresa," Maggie said. "Don't you want to be on the right side of history?"

Kendra's words from last night echoed in my head. *It's just better for everyone if Maggie's story goes away.*

"Let it be, Maggie. It's a sad thing. The girl was depressed. End of story."

"But see, she was actually pretty happy."

"And you have proof of this?"

A slow smile curled up Maggie's face, but she didn't answer my question. She slung her bag over her shoulder. I was relieved she was finally going.

"I think you sense it." Maggie's gaze was direct, and I couldn't look away. "You know something's off. Why don't you ask them? They are your best friends now, aren't they? Ask them more about that night on the bridge. If they are innocent, then they should have nothing to hide, right?"

My heart thudded. What was Maggie hinting at? Did she know about Jackie's obsession with Daphne? Did she also believe that Daphne was driven to jump because of Jackie? Georgeann had said Jackie was great, but I bet she was just being nice. Or was Maggie fishing for a story that didn't exist? Poking her nose around where she shouldn't? "Why do you hate them so much?" I asked.

Maggie's jaw set hard. "Because they always win."

She was right. They did always win. They made sure of that, didn't they? That was how it all worked. And people like Maggie, when they tried to change that, just ended up looking foolish.

Maggie slid a business card from her pocket and

handed it to me. "My cell phone number's on there. Text me when you realize I'm right." She held it out until I took it. "Daphne wasn't depressed, Theresa. She liked it here. And she loved her baby. Why would she leave her?"

Her baby? Daphne had a child?

"And have you talked to her child?" I asked with a straight face. "For your story?"

"Well, no. I couldn't find her." Maggie looked right at me. "Her family won't even acknowledge it happened. Her parents kicked her out when she got preggers. The Browns, who took her in, who you bought this very house from, won't talk about it either."

That dull roar of panic rose inside me again.

"So they didn't raise the baby?" I asked.

But I already knew the answer.

HALLOWEEN

"Daphne."

The voice calls from downstairs. Daphne is up in the attic. In her bedroom. She loves it, can hardly believe her luck, so big and bright and plenty of room for her and the baby. She has the crib close to her bed so she can reach over in the middle of the night and make sure her daughter is still breathing.

Tonight, the big room offers plenty of space for all the neighborhood kids to spread out blankets and lie down after their long day. They had a good time at the party, as always.

She had a good time, too. Except that the mothers in the neighborhood have been cold to her tonight. She's worried she did something wrong. She likes the work— it's easy, hanging out with the kids—and she would never want to do anything to upset them.

She turned on the television so they could watch It's the Great Pumpkin, Charlie Brown. *They love this story, no matter how many times they see it, and Daphne loves it, too. She is sitting on the floor with them, holding Nora Hendricks's hand. They are just at the part where the gang goes trick-or-treating in their sad ghost costumes when the voice calls her.*

A mom is coming up the stairs. Daphne checks the time. It's early. She thought they'd be at the party for longer. She's disappointed because this is the easiest time to babysit, this here, when they are quiet and settled. When they are all on the verge of sleep.

But here is the mom, still dressed as a witch. Which witch is she? Daphne can't tell at first. It's hard to distinguish them with those pointed hats and big brims that shadow their faces.

"Daphne," the witch says. "Mrs. Hendricks needs you to take Nora home now. She asked if you could walk her back to her house."

"Now?"

The witch nods. She comes closer, tipping up her hat, and Daphne sees her. It's Alice, the younger woman, the pregnant one. The one who keeps asking her about helping out once her child comes into the world.

"I—I can't leave them," Daphne says, gesturing to the kids sprawled out on their sleeping bags and blankets, watching as Snoopy appears in the pumpkin patch and makes poor Linus faint.

"It's okay. I'll stay with them. Go now. Quick. I'll watch them."

Something's not right, but she doesn't know what. She doesn't want to upset the moms, so she gathers her long bridal skirt.

"Come on, Care Bear," she says to Nora. "Time to go home."

"No!" cries Cole. He and Nora are inseparable lately. He grabs her hand. He doesn't want to let go.

Daphne walks over to the crib and kisses her own sleeping baby girl on the head. "I'll be right back," she whispers.

She gently tugs Cole from Nora and helps her down the stairs. She doesn't turn back. She doesn't see the witch fall into her chair, remove her pointy shoes with a sigh.

She doesn't sense Cole slip away, follow her quietly down and out of the house.

She doesn't hear her baby cry.

THIRTY-EIGHT

Theresa

I raced upstairs after Maggie left. Found my phone. Texted Greg.

I need to talk to you. Can we meet in our spot by the lake?

I deleted the text as soon as I sent it so no one would see it. I felt terrible. If Adam found out… But also, I needed to know. And I couldn't very well talk to him at the party, in front of everyone.

Not about this.

Greg had been evasive about Lily's parents, and I hadn't pressed much. I'd assumed it had been a bad situation—abuse or drugs. It hadn't mattered to me then— I'd just wanted her. But what if Lily's mom hadn't died "a few years ago" like Greg had said on campus? What if she'd already been dead when I'd adopted Lily?

My heart was pounding. I felt like I'd shrunk to doll size and someone above was pulling the strings, manipulating me just for the fun of seeing what could happen.

Let's fit her here, in this house.

Let's give her this—and this. And then take it away. Take it all away.

"Lily?" I hadn't seen her since last night. I jogged up to her bedroom. She wasn't there. Her bed was unmade, sheets hanging half off and slumping to the floor. Ellen's sleeping bag had been rolled up and pushed to the corner, but the girls' costumes that had been hanging on the closet door were gone.

I sent her a text. Where are you? Don't forget about babysitting tonight!

The Ouija box was shoved partly under the bed. I picked it up to put it in Ellen's bag so she wouldn't forget it, and the board fell out. It was the generic Hasbro version, but those thick black block letters and numbers still gave me the shivers.

If my mother was here, she'd snatch it out of my hand. Furious. *Make a bargain with the devil, Theresa Ann, and you'll lose your soul. Is that what you want?*

And yet, I found myself sitting on the floor before the board, resting my index and middle fingers on the planchette. I closed my eyes.

Waited.

Imagining Lily and Ellen doing this very thing.

Imagining it moving, swirling, spelling out a message.

Who's there? Lily, whispering. *Talk to us.*

D-A-P-H-N-E

What do you want to tell us?

I opened my eyes. The planchette was still in the same spot.

As I tossed it back in the box, the board skidded against the instruction booklet, and a scrap of paper underneath peeked out.

Lily's handwriting, tall and slim letters in a teal sparkly marker:

DIED

BRIDGE.

And then, in the corner of the page, diagonal, was written largest of all:

WOW

I'd told her not to play the stupid game. She hadn't listened, same as usual these days.

My phone buzzed. I stood, pocketed the paper. It was Greg.

See you there in 10?

———

Slate-gray sky. Barely any leaves left on the trees.

Ivy Woods was different now than it had been in the summer when we'd first moved here, when it had been bright and sunny. Even in August, with the high humidity swelling the door frames and breeding insects, it had felt full of promise.

Now everything seemed cold. Dark. Dead.

Greg was already at the bench, wearing dark jeans and an army-green jacket, a striped scarf knotted around his neck. He shot me a wary look as I approached.

"You know there are easier ways to meet," he said. "I feel like I'm in a Hardy Boys novel. Did you leave me a secret code in the hollow of a tree?"

I'd thrown a coat on over my owl costume and stuffed

the mask inside my pocket so I wouldn't feel ridiculous. Hardly anyone had seemed to be paying attention as I'd slipped off the cul-de-sac, but I still felt conspicuous.

Guilty.

I hadn't said a word to Adam when I'd left. And really, what could I tell him that wouldn't be more lies? If I was lucky, no one would miss me while I was gone.

If.

"Sit," Greg told me, patting the bench.

I shook my head. There he was, my professor, my lover. The man who knew all my secrets.

He stood, hands in pockets. "You're so serious. Is it my kid? Did she burn down your house last night and you can't bring yourself to tell me?"

"No, she's fine. It's something else."

You did a really good thing, Greg had told me on campus.

I decided to be direct. "Daphne Brown was Lily's mother, wasn't she?"

I studied his face. He didn't blink. Didn't even act surprised. I wondered if he knew this was coming. "Yes."

Even though I'd already made the connection, Greg's casual admission still hit me like a boulder.

"The Browns were good friends with my parents," Greg continued. "They didn't know what to do after she died. Daphne's parents were awful—they wanted nothing to do with her. And the Browns couldn't take on a baby. They didn't want to, and I didn't blame them. They'd already done so much for Daphne."

"So you thought of me and Brad," I said, the sarcasm dripping. "How sweet."

"Daphne loved Lily," Greg said. "We wanted to find

her a good home, where she'd be loved. I knew that was you." He made it sound so simple. So innocent.

"Really, Greg?" I asked. "Or was I just the convenient solution to your dilemma?"

Greg flinched at the venom in my voice. "My dilemma?"

It all added up. Why Greg had broken up with me. Why Jackie had left him anyway. Why he'd asked me to take Lily months later.

"You were sleeping with her, too."

"With Daphne?" He put on his best offended face. "What? No. Of course not."

"Don't lie to me, Greg."

"I'm not lying. Theresa. I'm not."

"That's why Jackie dumped you, isn't it? The real reason? Because Lily is your daughter, too? She didn't want to raise someone else's child?"

Greg grabbed my shoulders. Hard. Fear sliced through me. We were here, alone. How long would it take for someone to come if I screamed?

"No, Theresa. Stop. You're not making sense."

Greg released me and drew back. "Jesus Christ. I'm sorry, Theresa. It's just—this is all getting twisted around. There was nothing going on with me and Daphne. I swear. She was…a complicated soul. I liked her. I thought she was a good kid. But I was not sleeping with her, for god's sakes. And I'm certainly not Lily's biological father. He was some kid, lived out in western Virginia, where Daphne grew up. I have the goddamn papers, Theresa."

I stared at him, unsure. "I just thought…"

"You thought I was fooling around with everyone?"

He laughed bitterly. "That's what everyone thinks, apparently."

My phone vibrated. I pulled it from my pocket, and the paper from the Ouija board fluttered out. Greg chased it.

Lily had sent me a text.

Since you didn't tell me the truth, I found someone who did.

Do not try to find me.

Greg handed me back the paper. I felt the color draining from my face.

"What's wrong?" he asked.

I looked down at the paper. He'd handed it back to me upside down. I saw it now, what I hadn't seen before.

Lily hadn't written *WOW*. She'd written *MOM*.

There'd been no return address on the envelope with the baby invitation. No stamp. Whoever had delivered it had walked up to my mailbox, casually tucked it in.

And now they'd told Lily about the adoption.

Maybe someone who wanted revenge because she'd realized *I* was the one who'd stolen her husband from her. Who had been biding her time to use this perfect piece of evidence against me.

"Are you sure Jackie is in New York, Greg?"

"Why?"

"Could she be here? In Ivy Woods?" The shed. Someone locking me in.

"Not that I'm aware of. She hasn't been back in a decade."

"Did she know about Lily's adoption? Could she have sent me the card?"

"Jesus, Theresa. Why would Jackie send that to you?"

A woman scorned. How easy it would be to get to Lily. To tell her a story. Destroy the life I'd worked so hard for.

"I've got to go, Greg."

Moving here had been a dream.

But I'd ended up in the middle of a nightmare.

HALLOWEEN

It's so dark on the path. And here she comes, Daphne, our single mother, so young, so full of hope, holding Nora's hand by the lake. Nora is scared. She doesn't like being out this late, not now, not on Halloween night when all the images of spiders and bats and monsters swirl up inside her head and threaten to overwhelm her. She squeezes Daphne's hand oh so tight. She doesn't want to lose her.

The witches materialize. They come out of the woods, black cloaks blending into the shadows, and Daphne screams. Nora buries her head in the folds of Daphne's skirt. She imagines the witches taking her away into the shadows, baking her into a pastry. Eating her.

Or worse, making her one of them.

But the witches aren't interested in the little girl. They want her to go home. They have other business to attend to.

Nora's mother takes her, tugs her away from Daphne.

She murmurs and mimics the things mothers say—"Time for bed, it's late, too much sugar"—but it's clear, dear reader, that she is distracted.

Jacqueline's hand is cold as she leads Nora away. "Hurry, hurry," she says now, rushing her along the path to their house. Inside, Nora expects her mother to bring her upstairs, help her to bed, but instead she is brought into the living room, where her father has changed out of his costume and is reading a book.

"I'm going back out," Nora's mom says. She is angry, but her voice breaks as she tries not to cry. This makes her angrier. "Take care of our daughter for once."

Jacqueline whirls before her husband can answer. She adjusts her cape. Secures her pointy hat. She does not look back, does not say goodbye. Then the mother, the witch, is gone. Just like that.

Poof.

A magic trick.

THIRTY-NINE

Kendra

It was definitely a party everyone would remember.

The decorations were spectacular. Parents were tipsy. Kids ran around wide-eyed. An abundance of food and drinks. Even Mrs. Tressle was out and about, chatting and looking less like she'd just sat on a tack.

And the band—Oh the band! How had I never thought to hire a band before now? They weren't great—just some kids who played decent enough '80s rock covers—but the live music added so much to the atmosphere. What other neighborhood around here had a Halloween party with live music?

None of them, I tell you. None of them.

I was well on my way to being good and buzzed, dipping my black Solo cup over and over again in Bettina's spiked apple cider. The alcohol had taken the edge off my nerves, and I was beginning to feel like it had all been one giant misunderstanding. Alice had made us all paranoid—and for what? We were fine. Everything was fine. There was no one here who could hurt us.

I took another swig of punch. Around me people were having fun, dancing, talking, eating. Paul was taking care of the trick-or-treaters so I could mingle.

I'd done it once again. The party was great. No. It was fantastic. My best yet.

The stuff of legends.

"You are amazing, Kendra. I don't know how you always pull this off." Georgeann Wilkins walked up to the drink table, her yarn braids swaying, and refilled her cup with punch.

"Thank you, Georgeann. And let's talk about that swim team party in the spring," I added, feeling generous. "I think you and I could cohost it and make it something really special."

"Really? Kendra, that would be great."

"Yes, absolutely." I turned around then, ready to grant more favors. Alice, in her fawn costume, stood behind me. Smiley. I hadn't seen the bouncy side of her in a long time.

"My god, I haven't seen you all night," I said. "Are you loving the party?"

"Does a pig love mud?" Alice asked, giggling. How much punch had she had? Not that I could judge. We deserved to let our hair down.

"Alice, I love your costume," Georgeann said. She scratched her cheek, and some of her bright red blush smeared onto her fingers. "You all look so cute."

"I know, right?" I said. "And we need a group shot before it gets too dark." I put my arm around Alice, drawing her close.

"Take our picture, Georgeann. I've hardly gotten any pictures tonight."

I angled my head to the right, my best side. Stuck out my chin, hand on hip, while Georgeann whipped out her phone. "Say cheese." Georgeann's flash blinded us. "I'll text you guys that," she said, and disappeared into the crowd with her drink.

"My littles are going to be up all blasted night." Alice took another swig of her drink, which was no small feat with her deer nose. "Bouncing off the walls. I should go find them."

She kissed my cheek, then wandered off. I pivoted to find food and almost bumped right into our dear owl. Theresa.

Talk about buzzkill.

"Have you seen Lily?" Her dress was way shorter than it had looked online, but I gave her credit for leaving the house in it. She was on her toes, searching the crowd, distracted.

"No," I said flatly. I wanted to forget about all the threats, the worries, the lies. Just for one night. Was that too goddamn much?

"I need to find her."

That would be difficult in the dark, with all these people milling about. Especially if Lily didn't want to be found.

"Chill," I said. "I'm sure she's running around here somewhere. Do you need a drink?" I guzzled from my punch.

"I don't know..." Theresa trailed off. In her owl mask, I couldn't see her face, and I didn't like that. "Kendra, there's something I need to..." She paused.

A group of kids rushed between us, and we had to back apart.

"What did you say?" I asked her once they'd passed.

I leaned over and pushed up her owl mask, revealing her eyes. She was tearing up.

"I think Jackie got to Lily." Her voice was just above a whisper. I had to lean in even farther to hear her, so that to anyone else it might've looked like we were kissing. "Lily's so mad at me."

Jackie? Lily? She wasn't making any sense at all. Maybe she *had* been dipping into the punch. Or perhaps we'd pushed her too much last night at the bonfire, made her paranoid. I tried to find another Ivy, but no one was in sight.

"Everything's wrong." Theresa clasped her hands together, looking around at the party. "I just need to talk to Lily. If you see her, text me, okay? She was supposed to be the babysitter."

Supposed to be the babysitter.

As Theresa walked into the crowd, it all clicked.

The way she always tugged at the end of her ponytail.

Paul's bee sting kit. Theresa's allergy.

"Theresa!" I called, but the band started up with another song, and she didn't hear me.

The lake. The clover. A young woman babysitting Ellen all those years ago. Breathing shallow. Her face white as a sheet.

You have to help. It's a bad allergy.

Someone I would've completely forgotten otherwise. If she'd never come back.

But she had returned. She knew the neighborhood. She'd been here before. The bees.

The fucking *bees*.

Theresa Pressley was the one who'd been sleeping with Greg Hendricks. *She* was who we'd needed to deal with. Not Daphne. *Theresa* was the one who'd nearly destroyed our lives. And now she was back to do it again.

HALLOWEEN

If this was another fairy tale, the bride might be met by her prince and rescued. He'd swoop in at the last second, all freshly brushed velvet jacket and shiny black boots, and remove Daphne from the witches' clutches. He'd take her back to the castle and they'd both be asleep and happily-ever-aftering while the rest of the ghouls and dark knights and painfully sweet lollipop twins and ice-cream sweethearts wandered Ivy Woods with their bags and pillowcases, looking for more more more on this All Hallows' Eve.

But this is not that kind of fairy tale.

Alas, our bride is young, and her groom has long abandoned her, leaving her with their daughter to raise alone in a tower with one circular window, above all the other homes. Alas, even Shakespeare is gone, too lazy to venture too far into the night. Alas, Daphne follows the two witches as they speak in harsh whispers. They march her to the bridge. She climbs up up up even as she's reluctant to.

It is not until they are there, in the middle of the rail-road bridge, that Daphne begins to understand what they are saying, words more polite than what her own parents called her before they threw her away, but meaning the same.

"We know it's you, Daphne. We know what you've been doing with Jacqueline's husband. And it needs to stop now."

She protests, but realizes it's futile. They will never believe her. After all, she's here because she had a baby out of wedlock. She's clearly no virgin bride. Everyone can see that.

"You've been sleeping with him." Jacqueline, venom and bullets in her voice, gets close, face-to-face. "I have proof."

FORTY

Kendra

It was just like it had been thirteen years ago.

"We need to talk. Now," I told the others.

The party would go on without us.

Our tails bounced as we walked down the trail, silent, carrying our black cups. The music and voices from the party faded. I turned on my phone's flashlight, and we followed the thin bobbing beam of light around to the back of Alice's yard and into the woods.

Dark shapes swooped in the sky. Bats.

"You're freaking me out, Kendra. What happened?" Bettina, the squirrel. "Did you find something out?"

I led us to the back of Alice's fence. On the other side of us, beyond the row of trees, was her beehive. Her bees were getting ready to go dormant for the winter. Their work was nearly done.

Ours was just beginning.

"Is it Maggie?" Pia asked. "She keeps filming us. Didn't you see that? Jesus. I feel like she's watching us even now."

We'd all pulled our animal hoods down, and they bulged around the backs of our necks.

"It's Theresa," I said. "*She* was the babysitter. The one Greg was cheating with."

It took a moment to sink in.

"Holy shit," Bettina finally said. "You mean she's the one that—"

"Yes," I said.

Pia lit a cigarette. Her raccoon eye makeup smudged around her cheeks. From the folds of her costume, she withdrew a small flask and took a slow drink. Goddammit. This was eating away at all of us, bringing out the worst in us.

"What are y'all talking about?" Alice asked, watching me closely until I looked away.

We'd kept it from her. She'd had enough to worry about afterward.

I sighed. "Jackie got it wrong, Alice. Daphne never… she was never with Greg. Jackie didn't realize it until it was too late, when he was still cheating a month after Daphne died. She never told me who he was really cheating with. Just that he had her babysit a few times when Daphne wasn't available."

At that point, I hadn't cared. I didn't want to know anything else about the situation, not after the mess it had all caused. But now I knew. It had been Theresa. All the signs had been there. The way she hadn't met my eye when I'd asked if they'd been involved. And Greg Hendricks wouldn't have done a favor like that for just anyone—there had to be something between them for him to have helped with Adam's job. I was an idiot not to have seen it sooner.

"What?" Alice asked. She was too stunned to even be mad I'd never told her. "So he was carryin' on with both of them?"

I shook my head. "No. Daphne was just a kid, had been through so much. We should've seen it then. Greg's a jerk, but not that much of a jerk. That's why Jackie lost her head. Because when he told her he was never involved with Daphne, she couldn't handle that she'd fucked it all up."

"But wait," Bettina said. "I still don't get how you know it was Theresa?"

"I met her before," I said. "A very long time ago."

I told them about the day I'd been with Cole and Sam at the playground by the lake. It had been the summer before everything happened. Hot. The flowers were blooming.

Which was why it was so strange that the babysitter hadn't had her EpiPen with her when she'd been stung. *Can you help?* she'd asked, young and frazzled. Ellen—they used to call her Nora back then—had seemed both frightened and excited by the unexpected adventure as I'd driven them to the urgent clinic.

Theresa's hair had been longer and not red. But it had been her. "She's always been familiar to me in some visceral way," I said. A random babysitter, filling in for Daphne, hardly memorable at all if not for the emergency.

Pia puffed on her cigarette and blew smoke into the air. "Fuck."

"So *Theresa* sent us all those messages?" Alice asked.

"I don't know. But she's hiding something." I paused, remembering the look in Theresa's eye when she asked me where Lily was. "Just now at the party, she told me she thought Jackie was 'after' her."

"Oh please," Bettina muttered.

"Why would she say that?" I asked. Hadn't she seemed frightened, too? "Unless she's also being threatened. She said something about Lily and Jackie. What if she's getting messages, too? She did cheat with Greg. Maybe Jackie found out. Maybe she wanted to set Theresa up by making us think it was her sending those messages. Maybe that's why she used Theresa's house in the profile picture."

We stood in silence for a moment, thinking that through.

Finally Bettina spoke, confirming my own instinct. "It's got to be Jackie, then. She's the only one who knows. She's the only one who would care about all this enough to…" She trailed off.

I heard something—someone—in the woods behind us. I turned, squinted into the darkness, but saw nothing.

"What about Maggie?" Pia asked, lowering her voice.

I chewed my lip. "Jackie must be feeding her information. Maggie said she had a source."

"Oh, y'all, I can't. Think what happened to me last time. A curse. And what will happen this time?" Alice said.

"There's no curse," Bettina said curtly, staring at her in disgust.

"There is!" Alice rubbed her arms furiously with her hands. Her voice climbed. She was getting inconsolable, like she had been all those years ago when the bleeding had started. Just days after Daphne's death, Alice had miscarried.

I'd been the one who followed Alice and Justin to the hospital, held Alice's hand when she got the news. She'd been out of her mind with grief, convinced it was karma for what we'd done.

"Stop," I hissed. "No one's getting cursed." I turned, paced.

"History is repeating itself," Alice said, panicked. "It's going to happen again. Oh I can't stand it."

"Alice, there's no proof of any of this," I said. "No one saw us that night."

The wind kicked up. High above us, branches swayed like drunken hula dancers. *No one saw us except the trees.*

"This isn't my fault. All I did was watch the kids. I paid for my sins. I didn't—"

"You had no problem keeping the secret all these years." Bettina was shaking with anger. She pointed a finger at Alice. "No problem reaping the benefits of our friendship, of letting us solve your problems for you." The slick steadiness of her voice sent shots of electricity through my back. All those years ago, that same cold certainty had formed inside her when we'd made the plan. When we'd cleaned up the mess Jackie made.

But it wasn't going to help us now to alienate Alice. "Bettina," I warned.

"I always knew she was weak," Bettina said. "Her and Jacqueline. The weak links."

"Quiet," I said.

Alice was a tornado now, ready to destroy everything in her path. "This cast death upon us last time.

It will again. Do you even understand? Do you know what that means?"

"Alice, calm down. We have to keep our cool," I said. "Like we've done for the last thirteen years. And everything will be fine."

"You pushed her." Alice thrust a finger wildly into the air. "You did it. Not us. You killed her."

As I knocked her hand away, a crashing sound came from behind me. I twisted around in the direction of Alice's beehives. Someone was rushing away, through the woods.

"What the hell was that?" Bettina said loudly.

I didn't wait for the others.

HALLOWEEN

Maybe Daphne pauses here on the bridge. Maybe she looks up, or over, into the blackness on all sides of her. Maybe she thinks about the time she was baby-sitting Nora in the Hendrickses' house and, when the little girl fell asleep, came across the expensive, long, green, glamorous coat that Jacqueline Hendricks had bought in New York City. How she'd tried it on, twirling around in the full-length mirror. It had fit so perfectly.

Maybe she hears something, out there in the dark woods, and thinks it will save her.

Or maybe instead she thinks about her baby, and how she left her fast asleep in a crib with another witch.

"Have you been sleeping with all of them, Daphne?" asks Kendra, the Queen Bee, who relies on her each and every day to take care of her two boys.

And take care of them she does, better than their own mother.

"We've trusted you. With our homes. With our children."

"With our husbands," Jacqueline adds.

"And you liked it," says Kendra. "Too much."

Don't get too close, Daphne. Jacqueline Hendricks is all piss and fire, but it's just a show. Kendra is the one to fear. This witch has something poisonous running straight through her veins.

"I see the way you look at my husband, Daphne," she says. "I see the way you treat my boys. Like they are yours."

The monster inside Kendra, green, envious, has been unleashed. There is no stopping it now.

Daphne shakes her head, alarmed. She is twisting, whirling around. Looking for an escape.

Alas, there is no escape.

"Tell us!" Kendra yells. Her voice a shot through the woods, bouncing off the trees.

"There's nothing to tell," Daphne says. "Nothing. I need to get back to the children."

"Oh I bet you do. To my children? No, thank you. You think you are so good at this, don't you? You think this is all easy?"

"No, I—"

"Half the time you just sit them in front of the television. Leave all the bad bits to me."

"They love you. You're their mother."

"Oh? There's a surprise, since I heard you telling them to call you that."

"Me? No, of course not. That's a joke."

The rage boils over in the witch. Kendra raises her hands, thrusts them forward, making contact with the bride's chest.

"It's not a joke," she says, but her words are covered up by Daphne's scream.

FORTY-ONE

Theresa

"You pushed her. Not us. You killed her."

I recoiled at Alice's words, falling back against a tree trunk. Only it wasn't a tree trunk. It gave way, crashing to the ground. I'd knocked into Alice's beehive.

I'd left the party to try to find Lily at the bridge. But it was dark, and I got turned around, and that's when I saw the Ivies wandering off the lake path. When I heard them say my name, I stopped. I had no idea what I'd hear would be that sinister. Or revealing.

As Bettina shouted, I ducked and crawled as quickly as I could in my owl costume out of the beehive area and back into the woods, heading toward where I thought the lake was.

The bees were buzzing all around me. I was afraid at any moment I might feel that pain on my body, a sting. This far away from my EpiPen, it could be fatal.

Like that day at the lake.

I'd only babysat Nora—Ellen—a few times, as a favor for Greg.

The last time, right here, I'd been stung. So stupid to forget my EpiPen. We'd plopped down in the field to pick dandelions. And the pain, so sharp and sudden and unexpected. Trying not to panic, tugging Ellen back, back, back across the field. I'd called Greg, but he hadn't answered.

So I'd asked the first woman I came across for help. A young mother with two little boys. Her hair had been shorter than she wore it now, but still those carefully placed highlights. That square, commanding face. I'd forgotten the face until I heard Kendra mention that day. She'd driven me to the urgent care center, Ellen and me in the back seat, my throat swelling, tighter and tighter. Like breathing through a straw...

Kendra.

And she was a killer.

I had to get to that bridge. It was motherly instinct and sheer adrenaline guiding me, even though all the paths looked the same.

My owl dress was thin, but I appreciated the stretchy material now that I had to move fast. The low-hanging branches caught my owl ears headband and I ripped it off, annoyed, and tossed it in a pile of leaves.

My brain was floundering with all the information I'd just learned. *They'd killed Daphne.* She hadn't jumped. She hadn't left her baby. *She'd been pushed.* Kendra had killed her, and the other mothers had helped.

And it should've been me.

I pulled out my phone. Scrolled through for Maggie's number. I sent her a text.

You were right.

I didn't wait for her answer. I didn't know where
Kendra and the others were, but I had to find Lily and
get us both home before anything bad happened.

The bridge looked even more terrifying tonight, as
if it had grown in size since I'd last seen it. A black
hulking monster lurking in the distance. I couldn't see
anyone as I approached, but I heard voices.

"Lily?" I called, and the voices stopped. "Lily? Come
down from there."

Nothing.

I climbed the steep slope to the bridge. The barricade warning people away had been shifted to the side
enough for someone to slip through. The bridge spanned
the railroad tracks below and was about as wide as a
yoga mat. Two light posts on each end gave off a feeble
orange glow. I could barely make out two figures in the
middle of the bridge. Girls in white bridal dresses, long
hair flowing out around them, faces unnaturally pale.
Lily and Ellen. Gothic ghost brides.

"Leave us alone." Lily's words rang out. Cold. Angry.

"It's not safe here," I said, desperately. The other
moms could be here at any moment. "What are you
two doing here?"

"Lily and I were just talking about Daphne," Ellen
said, chillingly calm. "Want to join us? Did you ever
wonder why she'd come up here? How she even knew
about this bridge? She was new to the neighborhood,
after all."

I inched toward the barricade, loose dirt skidding
around my boots. The bridge's drop was most dangerous
halfway across. If you fell off there (or were pushed),

it would be like dropping off a tall building onto the railroad tracks below.

I stopped, resisting the urge to flatten myself on the ground.

"Lily, I've had about enough. We need to go."

"*You've* had enough? You? What about me? I know what you did, Mom. Ellen told me everything." She'd been crying.

My eyes were adjusting, and I could see the girls more clearly. Alarmingly, one of them was standing on a narrow platform extending from the bridge right above the train tracks. In the darkness, it almost looked like she was flying.

"I don't know what that means, Lily."

"You're a liar," Lily yelled. "You and Ellen's father, Mom. It's disgusting."

I maneuvered around the barricade and stepped onto the bridge. "Lily, I really need you to listen to me right now. It was a long time ago," I said. "I made a mistake. I was young."

"Bet you can't tell us apart, Theresa." I didn't like the way Ellen said my name. "We're like identical twins. Sisters, maybe."

But I could. I was only a few feet from them now. Two ghost brides, their white dresses glowing eerily in the unnatural orange light. Lily jutting out on the platform, Ellen standing in front of her.

Holding her hand.

"Ellen…"

"If Daphne were here, too, we'd all be in trouble. Who's who? It's so easy to get people mixed up in the dark, isn't it? And who knows, maybe she will show up. It is Halloween, after all. Her night."

It was a teenager's dramatic declaration, but it worked. The fear crept into my bones, and I imagined a ghost hovering somewhere nearby. I jerked my head around, half expecting to encounter a floating bride with a broken neck.

"We all make mistakes, don't we?" Ellen asked. "Some worse than others. Like Daphne's mistake, for example, in trusting everyone. In following them when they lured her out here to the bridge. It was so easy to do."

"Can we talk about this somewhere else? It's dangerous up here," I said.

"I think this is the perfect place, actually," Ellen said. "A great setting for a TV special, don't you think?"

It hit me then. Ellen was the one feeding Maggie Lewis. Her source. Ellen knew what the Ivies had done.

"Ellen?" Lily asked. "Maybe we should go down?"

"Wait." She turned back to me. "Don't you love this, Theresa? You mothers like to play with fire, don't you? It's fun, until someone gets hurt."

"I don't know—"

"No, just shut up. Just shut up for once and listen. I've already told Lily the truth, that we're sisters. We share the same father, after all."

Ellen thought Lily was Greg's daughter—with me? Is that what the card had been referring to? She wanted revenge against me for sleeping with her dad?

I could see the confusion and fear in Lily's eyes and wanted nothing but to run to her. But I couldn't, not yet.

First I needed to know what Ellen had done. The extent of the damage she'd caused.

"So you're the one who sent me that card," I said. I bet Ellen had designed the Ouija board messages, too, and it explained all the hostility from her. Why a senior would be hanging out with a freshman.

"Even if I hadn't overheard Dad talking to you, even if I hadn't seen the email you sent asking for your *favor*, I would've remembered you. The bee sting. I was scared. I thought you were *dying*."

I felt a sudden surge of anger toward this girl. What the hell did she know? The audacity, to insert herself in our lives this way.

"You have no idea what you're talking about, Ellen." My tone was even. Direct. I stepped forward. "I would've thought the valedictorian would be better about getting her facts straight."

Ellen's smirk slipped a little at that. I took another step forward, close enough now that I could grab Lily's hand, if she'd give it to me.

"Your dad is not Lily's dad."

"You liar," Ellen said. "My father saves everything. He thinks he's clever, filing things away in folders in his inbox. I saw your emails, about 'the baby.'"

I held my hand out to Lily, but she ignored it. She tried to move off the platform, but Ellen blocked her.

"Stay there, Lily," Ellen barked. "Stay right where you are."

"You got it wrong, Ellen." I offered my hand again to Lily. "Hon, you're not Greg's daughter," I said. "You're Daphne's."

That quieted them both.

"What you overheard, Ellen? It was about something that happened a long time ago. I'd— Your father and I had made a mistake, that's true. And we ended it. And he—helped me adopt a baby. Lily."

I paused, taking a deep breath, knowing that everything I was about to say was going to hurt my daughter, but knowing if I didn't explain it now, Lily could get hurt in other, worse ways.

"No," Ellen whispered. "No, that's not…"

"It is, Ellen. It is true. I didn't know it then. Your father never told me who the baby's parents were, and I didn't want to know. I only just found out myself."

"You're a liar," she said, wiping tears away. "You got pregnant. It was your fault. Only my mother blamed Daphne. They all did. And they didn't care at all about me. None of you cared about me. You like to think you're so *special* and *good*, but inside you're all monsters."

Lily lunged herself toward Ellen, attempting to get back onto the bridge. Ellen jerked, her arm swinging in an arc, hitting Lily in the stomach, pushing her back onto the platform. She fell, rolled toward the edge.

"Lily!" I screamed.

But it was too late. Lily disappeared off the platform into the abyss below.

FORTY-TWO

Kendra

I rushed through the woods. Theresa had been eaves-dropping on us. I'd caught a glimpse of her in the moon-light. And where was she now? Had she transformed into an owl, flying over me, talons outstretched? Well, if so, I was a fox. I had teeth. And claws. I could move fast. And I wasn't going down without a fight.

I heard someone ahead.

"This way," I called, turning, looking for everyone. But I was alone. My friends had scattered. Vanished. Perhaps they, too, had transformed into the forest crea-tures they were—a fawn, a squirrel, a raccoon—skit-tering into and up the trees.

The cowards.

I made my way around the lake. It was dark except for the moon skimming its yellow light on the lake's sur-face. It had been bright the night Daphne had died, too.

I needed to find Theresa. To explain what she'd over-heard, before Maggie got to her. Before she went to the police.

To explain that it was an accident. A terrible accident. I'd never meant to kill Daphne. I'd never intended to even hurt her. I'd just wanted to get her alone, away from our children, and scare her. Warn her that she wasn't going to destroy our families. Not in Ivy Woods.

We'd all assumed it was Daphne. I *wanted* it to be her. Daphne had swooped into our lives, and I began to hate her for how perfect she was, how all the dads adored her. She'd been so good with the kids, *so god-damn good.* But they were our babies, not hers. She was *not* a better mother than me, no matter how much she acted like it.

And I'd been upset that night. Drunk. I'd heard my kids call Daphne their mother. And she had let it go. *Reveled* in it. Who did she think she was?

But it wasn't her. If Jackie had only confronted Greg about his cheating before she accused Daphne, none of this would've happened. But no. She'd been so certain—*the babysitter*, she'd said. I should've known better than to trust that stupid twit. And then, after Jackie finally did accuse Greg of the affair, after Daphne's death, and discovered she was wrong—that it was someone else—she couldn't be consoled.

She'd wanted to confess everything, tell the police what we did—what *I* did. After I tried to help her, she was going to rat me out? I'd had to calm her down. Tell her to go away. Tell her if she didn't go away, we'd con-vince the authorities *she* did it. They'd believe us over her. They'd put her away.

I didn't think she'd cut off all ties with her child. She

could've chosen to have a relationship with Ellen. But she didn't. She abandoned her.

I needed to make Theresa understand.

A scream. Shouts. Coming from the direction of the bridge.

Of course. That's where Theresa had been heading, the same way I'd gone thirteen years ago. It could be the same night, almost. Like fate.

I hit the railroad tracks and turned left toward the bridge. It was even darker down here, dark shapes surrounded by darker shapes, but I knew the way. All my senses were heightened. A fox on the hunt.

A flash of white caught my attention. And then I saw her. Down below on the tracks. Running. The ghost girl. In her wedding dress.

Daphne.

Was she running? Or gliding? Her hair billowed out behind her, just like it had that night.

How many times had I woken in the middle of the night from that same dream? The one I'd never told anyone about. Where I shoved Daphne, my hands making contact with her lace dress. The burst of anger. The gasp of her breath. The fear turning to surprise in her eyes. Her small frame falling back, disappearing before my eyes like a trick, an optical illusion.

Only it wasn't a dream. It had really happened.

I could only hear my breath now, shallow and hard.

In my nightmare, I always tried to snatch Daphne back. My hand reached out, fingers stretching as she fell, snagging one thin scrap of bridal lace before it tore. Before she screamed. Before the blur of white became utter blackness.

We'd gotten the wrong babysitter.

FORTY-THREE

Theresa

Ellen's hands were pressed up to her face in shock.

"I didn't. I didn't."

She shook her head, backed up.

Then she ran. Across the bridge, to the far side, disappearing into the woods.

I had no time to worry about Ellen.

"Lily," I yelled, rushing onto the platform. I was terrified to look down. The tears were blurring my face as I caught sight of her pale dress, standing out against the blackness.

But the white was closer than I expected, swaying back and forth, undulating like a strange flag.

Lily was hanging from the platform, clutching the metal bar that lipped the edge.

"Help me," she said, just above a whisper, as if the force of speaking loudly might take her down.

"Hold on!" I knelt, grabbed her wrists. How small and delicate they seemed.

I didn't have the strength to hoist her up. She was going to fall because of me. Fall to her death.

"You're fine," I said, searching for something to help. "You're going to be fine." But there was nothing. I kept hold of her wrists, worried her grip would loosen. Praying help would come.

Then she moved, letting go.

"No, Lily, no. Stop."

But she was shimmying along the iron bar, like she was on the monkey bars on a playground, to get closer to the bridge. I had no idea how old the bar was. Or how well it would hold her weight. But if she could get closer to the bridge, she could use the side of it for leverage.

"That's it, Lily. Use your foot," I said. "Get a foothold."

She kicked out. Somehow she dug her shoe into a gap in the concrete on the side of the bridge. She used it to push up, and I lay across the platform, reaching for her arms. I felt her lift, press into me.

"Good. Use me, climb me." I gripped her upper arms.

Then her foot slipped. She fell from my grasp, screaming, but managed to hang on to the bar by one arm now.

"Get your foot in again," I said, trying not to panic. "You can do it."

"Theresa. My god. What happened?"

I turned to see her looming over us. A lone, dangerous fox.

Kendra.

Her voice sounded sincere.

But I knew better now.

"Stay away from us," I yelled. Lily had gotten both hands back on the iron bar again, but she couldn't pull up.

Kendra was too close. Just a few steps and she could easily take care of both of us. Was that why she was here? To finish the job she tried to do thirteen years ago? We'd be the next tragic accident to hit Ivy Woods. Kendra had done it before, after all. And had gotten away with it. Why not again?

"Stop being ridiculous," Kendra said. "I'm here to help." She crouched, somehow completely nimble even in knee-high boots. "We can both yank her up."

"We don't need your help," I said, focusing back on Lily. Her foot was kicking out, but every time she tried the bridge, it slipped. She wouldn't be able to hang on much longer.

Kendra was beside me now, holding out an orange-gloved hand. She was near enough that I could see her wide, black pupils. "Here, Lily." To me, she said, "You can trust me."

Like hell I could.

She took one of Lily's arms, and I had no choice but to take the other. At the same time, Lily caught her foot again. This time at a higher point, so she was able to thrust upward. Kendra hauled her up, and I clutched the back of her dress until she was on the platform.

We all moved to the center of the bridge and stood for a moment, catching our breaths. I couldn't let go of Lily's dress, worried if I did she might slip away forever.

I hugged her tight to me, feeling her body against mine. Above us, small gnats hovered in the sky, ghosts of their own kind. "I'm so glad you're okay," I whis-

pered. It occurred to me how close I'd been to losing
Lily, and my knees nearly gave out. "My girl."

Lily pushed away, tears streaming down her face.
"I'm not your girl. I'm not your anything. How could
keep that from me? Did you think I'd never find out?"

"Lily…" I was acutely aware of Kendra behind us.
But she didn't seem like a threat right now, not after
she'd just helped save Lily. And Lily was my priority
right now. She'd always been the most important. I'd
just done a terrible job of showing her that. "I wanted
to tell you," I whispered to my daughter. "I just didn't
know how. I love you so much. You have to know that.
I'd do anything for you."

Lily shook her head. "No. No. I can't." She stepped
away from me. Her white makeup gave her the look of
a porcelain doll—fragile, breakable, as if at any moment she could shatter into a million pieces. "I need to
go home. *Alone*."

She started down the bridge.

"Lily!" I called.

Kendra rested her hand on my back. "Let her go,
Theresa."

I swiped her off. "Do not touch me," I said, nar-
rowing my eyes. "You are the last person I want advice from."

Kendra lowered her arm, resigned. Humbled. I'd
never seen her that way before, and that was almost as
frightening as what she'd done.

"We never meant—to hurt Daphne."

"You mean *kill* her?"

Kendra flinched. "Yes. But it was an accident. An
awful mistake. I couldn't change—what happened to
Daphne. I couldn't fix it. But if we'd told the truth, it

would've ruined so many other lives as well. Our kids'. Can you understand that?"

No, I wanted to say. No. But the scary thing was that I could understand it. Sometimes the truth was too hard. Our instincts were to lie, to swallow our secrets, even if they ate us up inside. Maybe Ellen was right. Maybe that made us all monsters.

"I don't think Ellen sees it that way," I finally said. "She knows. She knows everything. She was here. She knew about—" I stopped, swallowed the lump that rose in my throat. "She pushed Lily."

"Ellen?" Kendra's voice rose in alarm.

Then she stopped. We heard something in the woods.

"Someone's coming," I said.

Maybe it was Lily returning. Or Ellen. Whoever it was, I didn't want to be on this bridge when they arrived.

I quickly staggered down the incline, back onto the path near the lake. There, under the light post, I could see my owl costume hadn't held up very well. The felt had torn in one place across my belly, and something had snagged my tights near the knee.

"Theresa, wait." Kendra had followed me. A sly fox, tail bent and broken now. Defeated.

I spun around. "What do you want, Kendra?"

"Please don't—" Kendra stopped. She opened her mouth, then closed it. For once, she couldn't find words. "I'm not proud of what I did, Theresa. I just want you to know—"

Kendra was interrupted by voices and the beams of flashlights.

"I see them!" someone called.

It seemed the whole block party had made its way to the bridge. And leading the charge, fairy godmother crown perched on her head, was Maggie Lewis.

FORTY-FOUR

Kendra

Classic.

Maggie Lewis leading the angry mob to catch the bad witch. Swap the cell phone flashlights for pitchforks and torches and we'd be in seventeenth-century Salem, Massachusetts.

As they came closer, my cell phone buzzed. Out of habit, I checked it. A text message from Bettina.

Maggie's coming. Be careful what you say.

But I was already fucked.

"Here they are," Maggie said, all satisfied. Behind her, a cameraman was filming, his instrument bulky on his shoulder. "Just like I told you."

And Georgeann Wilkins. Adam Wallace. Cole and Paul, looking worried. In the back, Pia, furiously typing on her cell phone, Bettina with her husband, Joe, and Horace Bennington, her lawyer friend.

"What is this all about?" I asked.

"Why don't you tell us, Kendra?" Maggie smiled triumphantly. I wanted to slap that smile right off her face. "Trespassing at the bridge?" She paused, then added dramatically, "Again?"

"What's going on, Mom?" Cole's eyes flicked from me to Theresa and back again.

"Nothing. Lily almost fell," I said, projecting authority. "But she's fine. We're all fine. We were just coming back to the party."

"Almost fell? We just saw her." Adam's concern was evident. "My god, Theresa. What happened?"

I realized we must've looked like we'd had a wrestling match up there. Theresa's dress was torn and dirty. Her hair had bits of leaves in it.

"You saw her? Was she okay?" she asked.

"She was going home," Adam said. "She seemed fine. Just in a hurry."

"I hate this place," said Cole, looking around. "I got lost here when I was a kid."

Yes, he had. He'd wandered off, following Daphne and Ellen that night. Just a little boy. My little boy. I'd found him, cold and shivering, curled in a ball by a tree, after everything. How much did he remember? I remembered it all. The night terrors, when he couldn't wake up, when he'd sit howling in my arms for what felt like hours before I could pull him back. I'd assumed over the years he'd forgotten about it, but maybe kernels of memory remained.

"This is the finale of my story." Maggie waved her wand around as if casting a spell. "And all these peo-

ple want to know the truth. About what happened to
Daphne Brown thirteen years ago." She grinned evilly.
"Do you want to tell them?"

"I have no idea what you're talking about," I said.

"Not you, Kendra." Maggie pointed with her wand.
"Theresa."

Theresa's face was shadowed. I couldn't see her expression. She was very still, rooted to the ground. A
broken owl that couldn't take flight.

Maggie held up her cell phone. "She sent me a message. She knows what you are now, too. And soon everyone else will."

Silence. I felt like dripping wax, melting into the
ground. The Wicked Witch. Theresa knew everything.
Theresa—the actual babysitter Jackie wanted to teach
a lesson to—was going to be the one to expose me for
killing the innocent babysitter.

That's karma for you.

Would Cole and Paul ever visit me in jail? Would
the nightmares stop now that it was going to all come
out? The scream I'd been reliving for thirteen years?

I was so wrapped up in my thoughts, I almost missed
Theresa's response. "Maggie, this isn't really the time
or place—"

"Oh god, of course. Doug, stop filming." Maggie
put her hand over his lens, and he sighed, lowering the
camera. "There," she said. "Go ahead. You can talk
freely now."

"What's going on, Maggie? Are you sure you…"
Georgeann Wilkins appeared to be a combination of
terrified and embarrassed, though it was hard to tell
with the bright red makeup on her cheeks.

But Maggie was rabid. So close to the takedown. I

could smell it on her. "Tell them what you heard," she demanded of Theresa. "What you wrote to me. *You were right.* That's what you said."

Theresa met my eyes. What was that look?

Then she laughed. Turned to Maggie, brow furrowed. "Oh that message?" She shook her head and kicked out one leg. "I meant my shoes. You were right that I should've worn more comfortable shoes."

It was the most beautiful sentence I'd ever heard. I felt the air go out of me. I was light. A fucking balloon.

And Maggie was lead. Sinking. "That is not it! You tell them. Or I'll get my source to do it. I have *proof.*"

"I don't know what you mean, Maggie," Theresa said. So calm. I wasn't sure I could trust it. But a desperate girl could hope.

I put my hands on my hips and drew up, ready to bring this one home. "What the hell is wrong with you?" I thundered at Maggie. "I don't know what you're implying, or what kind of circus show you're putting on, making our friends march out here like this, but I've had about enough."

Adam held his hands out, stepping forward to keep the peace. "Maybe we should all just calm down for a minute and go back to the party?"

"That seems reasonable," Horace said next to him. Our neighborhood lawyer who got us all out of speeding tickets, he looked dignified and imposing in the tuxedo that was part of his James Bond Halloween costume. "We don't want to say something we'll regret later." I was mildly irritated that the men were the ones bringing order to the night—they had contributed nothing up until now, after all—but I didn't want to be here anymore either.

"They're all in on it," Maggie said, her voice rising in hysterics. "All of them."

"If you dare try to spread any kind of lies about me or my friends"—I pointed my finger at her—"if you even air one second of something like that on TV, I will sue you and the news station and make sure you never, ever appear on camera again."

Her cameraman held his hands up. "We're cool, we're cool," he said, nudging Maggie. "Come on."

"I will do no such thing," Maggie yelled. She snapped her wand in half, throwing it into the woods.

But the group started heading back up the path. And Maggie Lewis, fairy godmother, had no magic left to transform any of us into rats.

HALLOWEEN... NOW

Ladies and gentlemen, skulls and boys...

By now you've guessed it's me: Eleanora, Nora, Ellen... Ms. Jackson if you're nasty.

I've attempted to relay the events as I understand them, as my dear mother Jacqueline told them to me when I located her this past summer. My friend Jayden's mom, Mrs. Millson, took Jayden and me to New York City to visit NYU's campus—because my own father wouldn't take the time out of his busy schedule for college visits. I told Mrs. Millson I was meeting my mother for dinner in the city, and she let me go.

Adults will let you do anything if you're confident about it.

Our neighbor had mentioned the show my mother was in, and I looked up the theater online and got there just as she was finishing a rehearsal. She had no choice but to talk to me. I wasn't going to take no for an answer.

It was my seventeenth birthday present—happy fuck-

ing birthday to me. A shitty NYC diner, a plate of french fries, and a black coffee, and the confession of my mother's deepest, darkest secret. The reason she left me. The reason Daphne Brown died the night I watched Snoopy on the television on her bedroom floor.

I decided what I was going to do on the drive home from the city that summer. I had no proof of any of it, but that didn't mean I couldn't make them all squirm. Why shouldn't I shake the foundations of their homes? Blast a bit of poison into the air. Knock a few inches off their Steve Madden stilettos. Didn't they deserve that, at least, for what they did? For who they are?

I'll admit I filled in some blanks of this story. Improvised where necessary—isn't that what a good storyteller does? Of course, the important things are all true. Those facts are set in stone. Alas, the fate of Daphne Brown cannot change, no matter how many embellishments I add to the tale.

She is dead.

My mother—and all the other mothers—are to blame.

Do you pity them for what they've lived with all these years? Weep not, for their guilt has been padded by 401(k) savings, faux leather car seats, Easter egg hunts, porch mimosa parties.

They know what they did, and they live with it. They bury it in their fancy purses, tuck it way down deep at the bottom with the lint and the flecks of chocolate, but it's there, and it gets under their fingernails. They can smell it and taste it and they dream about it.

Oh do they dream.

Do you hate me for what I've done? For my part in this game? I dangled the felt mouse above the cats, hoping for them to swipe, hoping their claws might cut skin. Hoping for some sort of redemption or vengeance. I sent the messages. I made the Daphne doll. I took the photo—it is so easy to slip into shadow, to go unnoticed in a place where everyone is only concerned about themselves. I messed with Theresa Pressley, too, my father's lover, the real slut. I read her emails to my father and I put it all together, her little secrets, all that she'd gotten away with. I locked her in the shed, hoping the bees might find her before Alice's children did. And when she was too weak to tell her daughter the truth, I did it for her. As Lily and I were slipping through the shadows, destroying the bad mothers' jack-o-lanterns, smashing them to bits, I told her all about her mother's secrets.

So yes, I confess. I did it all. And I'd do it again, and more. For nothing I did was worse than what they did. Nothing can bring back Daphne Brown. Nothing can give me back my childhood, my mother.

They'll all always have to live with that.

FORTY-FIVE

Kendra

Later, much later that night, I couldn't sleep. I went downstairs into the kitchen and poured myself a Bailey's.

I wasn't surprised when I heard the knock on the back door. It was almost as if I'd been expecting it.

I walked out onto the screened-in porch, tying my robe tighter to keep out the cold air. Ellen had changed, too, thank god. I wasn't sure I could handle the sight of her in that wedding gown.

She was in all black now, her eyes shrewd and darting around. Like a cat burglar.

A formidable opponent.

"I can't stay long," she said. "And I'm not here to say I'm sorry."

I nodded. Ellen was, if anything, blunt. I had to appreciate that. Here we were, not a parent and a neighborhood child, but two equals. In the end, I'd been half-right after all. It *had* been a teenage prank. All the "Ivy Woods" messages. The photo of us at the bonfire. It had been Ellen.

"What you guys did to Daphne—that was shitty. You deserve to rot in prison."

I could sense her hatred boiling beneath the surface. I'd always chalked it up to some sort of teenage rebellion, a feeling of superiority she seemed to sport, but now I knew the real cause.

"That's fair," I said. "She didn't deserve it."

"You *killed* her."

I flinched, turned to look into the kitchen window, to make sure Cole and Paul weren't up searching for me. Listening.

"Don't worry. I'm not going to tell Cole anything," she said. The porch floorboards groaned as Ellen paced. "Although I think on some level he knows. Something anyway."

She was right. I had to hope that if he had seen anything that night in the woods, it was long forgotten.

And would stay forgotten.

"How did you figure it out?" I asked.

"My mother told me. Wasn't that sweet of her?" Ellen's voice was tinged with bitterness as she shoved her hands in the pockets of her sweatshirt. "She wasn't innocent. But *I* was. You made my mom leave. You took her away from me."

That was for the best. But I bit my tongue. Jackie, after all, hadn't been the one sending us those notes. And it made sense. Why would Jackie risk being blamed for Daphne's death, like I'd threatened if she ever tried to come clean about what we did? She wasn't that dense.

"And what price did you pay for any of it?" Ellen continued. "You got to live your life, be successful. *Throw parties.*"

In one way, she was right. In another, very, very wrong. I paid the price every day. The nightmares. The guilt. Throwing myself full force into every project to stay busy. To keep the thoughts from creeping in.

Not that that was any excuse.

"I'm sorry. I truly am. I never meant to hurt her, certainly not to…push her. It was an accident."

Ellen considered that.

"So, are you still going to talk to Maggie Lewis?" I asked. "You were her source, weren't you?"

Ellen stopped. Faced me. Her features shifted. I recognized the expression—the same one I'm sure I displayed whenever I thought about Maggie Lewis.

"She's a moron. She thought she was talking to my mother. As if my mother would possibly be this crafty?" Ellen stepped back. The dark porch nearly swallowed her up. "No. I realized—tonight—well, let's just say I realized how easy it is to do something you'll regret forever."

"Lily's fine," I said.

"Yeah." Her voice caught for a second, but then it came back strong. She stuck her chin up. "But also, sometimes it's good to keep a secret. You never know when you might need to wield it, right?"

Ah, this girl was going places. God help anyone who stood in her way.

SEVEN MONTHS LATER

FORTY-SIX

Theresa

Adam's first graduation ceremony as principal was going to be glorious, even if it was the hottest day of the year so far and the humidity made it feel more like August than June. The football field looked beautiful with the stage and the folding chairs for the graduates, but I felt sorry for the kids under those hot synthetic fiber robes and hats. How pleasant could your high school graduation be if you spent the whole time trying not to pass out?

I helped hand out the battery-operated fans that the Parent Team had ordered, which allowed me to greet everyone as they arrived. When I was done with that, I walked around offering to take pictures for families, hugging the moms and seniors I knew. In just a few years, that would be us—Lily would be wearing the cap and gown—and each time I thought about that, I teared up myself.

But today, I was just the principal's wife.

"Don't you look amazing," Georgeann Wilkins said as she approached me. I'd found a dress on sale at Macy's that was the same shade of purple as the Woodard colors and had twirled my hair up into a loose bun to keep it off my shoulders.

"So do you," I said, noting her floral dress and sandals, which actually did look stylish for once. "Practicing your role as the new Parent Team president?"

Georgeann's face was already red from the humidity, so I couldn't tell if she was blushing. She held up a finger. "President-elect," she reminded me. "I'm not responsible for anything officially until the fall."

"Got it. I won't yell at you about anything until then."

"Yell at me? And here I thought we'd be fast friends. I'm starting up a monthly book club, you know. And now that the Ivy Five is just four again…" She trailed off, winking at me.

I knew what she was doing. Hinting around, fishing for information about the group. But I just smiled. I wasn't going to get into any of that now.

So much had changed since the fall. It was hard to believe it all.

"We'll see," I murmured.

"I'm just joking, of course. Where's Lily?"

I turned, shielded my eyes, looked out at the sea of faces in the bleachers. "Up there somewhere. With her friends." She was way up at the top, that streak of neon-pink hair standing out in the bright sun. She was giggling in the middle of a cluster of girls.

My heart both soared and sank, as if it were a boat churning on a wild sea, up and then down. My girl and I had had the roughest time of it over these last few months. My lies had been the cause of that, of course, and I was still paying the price. I hoped she'd come around, eventually, but until then I had to just give it time.

Still, I liked seeing her happy. She'd always been quick to make new friends. I wondered if her mother had been like that.

Every time I took the stairs up to Lily's bedroom. Every time I looked out through that round attic window. Every time I strolled in the woods by the lake. It was as if Daphne's ghost were hovering like a balloon above us. In some way, she always would.

I wasn't sure I'd ever get used to it. I was just learning to live *with* it.

I was also learning to go easier on myself. To not take on all the blame when things went wrong, when I made mistakes. My mother had honed the perfectionist in me to a painfully sharp point, and I was trying to dull it.

"Theresa?"

I realized Georgeann had said something to me, tried to reel myself back in. "I'm sorry. What?"

"I said I can't believe Adam let you-know-who speak," Georgeann said.

"Well, she is valedictorian," I said.

"Still. Lord knows what she'll say."

I could see Georgeann's point. Ellen wasn't the follow-the-rules type. I could fully imagine her "improvising" her speech. And after all she'd done to us—all she'd put us through—I hadn't been happy she'd been allowed to speak either. In fact, Adam and I had bickered about it. Which was mild compared to the fighting we'd done over Greg—it had taken us months for Adam to trust me again after I'd lied about meeting up with Greg—but I still hadn't wanted to push it. That girl didn't deserve the recognition, but it wasn't my decision.

"The silver lining here is she'll be gone soon," I said.

Adam had believed Ellen was truly sorry for all she'd done, but I knew she was manipulative. She'd spied on her father and read our emails. She pretended to be her mother, feeding Maggie Lewis tips through an anonymous account on NeighborWho. Sent me that card about Lily and told her about my affair with Greg. Lily had decided not to keep her adoption a secret any longer, though she—and Adam and I—weren't exactly broadcasting her genetics to the public. It was a relief not to have to worry anymore. At least not about that.

Ellen had used all this information to scare people and managed to get away with it. Even Lily's push, which she insisted was an accident in the heat of the moment. At first I'd wanted to pursue charges against her, but that would potentially have meant details about Lily's birth parents going more public than any of us wanted, and Lily voted against it. Of course, Lily and Ellen's friendship had dissolved quickly, and I'd heard Greg had found her a new therapist. Otherwise, Ellen had dropped a bomb in the middle of Ivy Woods and pretty much gone on with her life unscathed. Valedictorian, admitted to Princeton with a full ride. And, ironically, was awarded the Daphne Brown scholarship from Parent Team.

The world was decidedly messed up.

I caught Adam's eye as we walked toward the stage, and he high-fived a student passing by. I loved seeing him with students—his favorite part of the job, for sure. It killed me to think I'd done anything to put our marriage in jeopardy. I'd told him about my history with

Greg, but we were fine now. Better than fine. And I'd come to the realization that *I* hadn't been the one to drive Ellen's mother away or even to ruin Greg's marriage. He had made the choice to cheat on her, and he had to live with the consequences, just like I had lived with the fallout of my relationship with Brad. I still saw Greg in the neighborhood or at events, of course, but we kept our distance. It was for the best. Besides, I was too busy with freelance jobs and volunteering at the school. My life was full to the brim, just as I'd always hoped.

The event would be starting soon. I said goodbye to Georgeann and found a place to stand on the sidelines in the shade, where it would be cooler than baking on the hot metal bleachers. I leaned against a pillar, smoothing down my dress. Adjusted the ivy leaf pin affixed to my chest. It sparkled in the sunlight. I loved my life, and I'd fought hard to get here. My mother had always said the things that test us the most are the things that make us grow in strength.

She was right.

Mostly.

"Theresa!" a voice called.

I turned and saw the Ivy Five. Well, two anyway. Bettina, standing with Kendra and her family. Pia was on a two-week vacation with a guy she'd been dating since Christmas.

As usual, Bettina was dressed like she'd stepped out of the pages of *Vogue* in a cotton shift dress with a satin Peter Pan collar. Kendra's gold hoops looked extra shiny in the summer sun. She played the role of mother of a graduate well, cropped yellow summer cardigan and short fitted dress printed with bright sunflowers.

"Please come take our picture," Kendra said. "Bettina can't take a good shot to save her life." She winked at Bettina. "You know I still love you, though."

Then she handed me her phone and lined up with her family—Paul to her right, Cole in his robe on her left, and her oldest, Sam, next to his brother on the end. When summer was over, both of her boys would be off at college. I knew Kendra was already plotting what she'd do next. Hobbies, projects. Vacations. No way that woman could relax.

"Say cheese!"

A chorus of McCauls *cheese*'d back at me. Kendra kissed Cole on the cheek, leaving a faint trace of pink glossy lipstick that he immediately wiped off with his thumb. "Don't let that swim scholarship and ticket to UVA go to your head," she said, ruffling his hair.

"Aren't you guys just the sweetest?" I gave her back her cell phone.

"It's just so thrilling to have all my boys here," Kendra said. "And in collared shirts."

She squinted in the bright light, checking my photo skills, then locked the screen and beamed at me. "Perfect."

Kendra glanced over my shoulder, and her face changed. Behind me, a tall, thin woman I'd never seen before was approaching. Probably my age or younger. Too much makeup—were those fake eyelashes? Kendra beckoned her over.

"Kendall! I need to introduce you to someone," Kendra said. "This is Theresa Pressley, Principal Wallace's wife. They live right across the street from me in Ivy Woods."

To me, she said, "Kendall's looking into buying Alice's house." Of course. It wasn't even on the market officially yet, but word had gotten around quickly when Alice had decided to move away. Her husband had been transferred to another military base, or so she said. In the meantime, she and her kids had moved to her in-laws' house. I'd miss her optimistic take on everything.

"Can you tell her how awesome our neighborhood is?" Kendra asked.

Yes, I could. The houses. The lake. The way the trees swayed during a storm, bending but never breaking.

The family potlucks. The playgrounds and well-lit paths. Christmas caroling and neighbors who would shovel your sidewalk without asking.

The whispers in the woods, late at night. The animals, feasting and howling and learning how to survive. The history, the traditions and celebrations.

I'd seen it all once, long ago, and longed to be part of it. And now I was.

"I'm sure you'd adore it, Kendall," I said now, tossing her another million-dollar smile. *But you'll have to earn your place.* "It's very tight-knit. We help each other out."

FORTY-SEVEN

Ellen

Ladies and gentlemen, caps and gowns...by the time this ceremony is over, I will be free.

Free from the hypocrisy, free from the stains and lies and sins of this town.

Smile and look pretty, take your pictures. Keep your memories tucked close to your heart. It's all fake, every last bit of it.

But I don't care anymore.

I step up to the podium, clear my throat.

But we all know I can't say any of that.

My knees are wobbling, but a general sense of nervousness and anxiety is to be expected when one is speaking in front of such a large audience. I stare out at the sea of faces, blurring together into one giant collage. I've practiced this speech so many times I could probably recite it by heart, but it is there, typed out in front of me, double-spaced, sixteen-point Garamond, approved by the principal and vice principal ahead of time and sent to the school newspaper so those plebeians don't have to transcribe it for next week's collector's edition.

The sun is sautéing us in our dark purple robes. My hair is sweaty under the cap, and the bobby pins I used to keep it in place dig into my skull. Whose bright idea was it to have graduation in the middle of a synthetic field, in the broiling heat? Traditions are like that. They keep going, year after year, even when they become idiotic. It's easier to do things the same way, I guess, than work through how to make them better.

"Woodard High friends, family, teachers. My fellow classmates, distinguished board members, honored members of the community. Today is a celebration. It's a day to reflect on who we've become and look toward our future."

My voice is amplified through the speaker system, louder than it ever has been before. It gives me a sense of power. How much could I say before they cut off the sound? Before someone pushed me away from the microphone?

How much damage could I do?

"I stand here, proud of all we've accomplished. Knowing we have done and will go on to do great things. We have our whole lives ahead of us."

To the right, beyond the football field, a lone car turns into the parking lot. A bright red convertible, gleaming like a lollipop. It skips the rows of cars and takes a circuitous route along the edge, stopping along the curb closest to the field.

"I think we can all agree that high school wasn't

always easy." The audience murmurs. To the right of the stage, on the end of a row, I catch sight of Lexie Granger, who has tears streaming down her face and is wiping her nose with the sleeve of her gown. Many of the girls are already crying over the end of high school and all the good times they had. Except this might actually be the best it will ever get for them.

"I know it wasn't always easy for me. I wanted to be perfect. I wanted the best grades. I wanted to get into the most elite college. I wanted to do it all—"

I wanted to get revenge, too. Expose everyone for who they really are. Turn over the rocks and show the worms.

In the parking lot, a small woman gets out of the convertible. She's far off in the distance, but I can see she's wearing large, dark sunglasses, a floral scarf tied in her hair. The ends of the scarf whip like little flags in the wind. How very European. She walks to the fence, stops. Places her hands on the metal wire. Watching.

"—and in that pursuit, I lost part of myself. I forgot what was really important. Not being perfect. Not getting the best grades"—*though I did*—"not getting into the best college. No. It was about friendship. And community. It was about making memories that will last us a lifetime."

I pause, as if something caught in my throat. The football field has never in its life seen a crowd more silent. Perhaps everyone thinks I'm going to cry. Ha-ha.

Friendship. Community. More like backstabbers. Liars. Sinners.

They'd torn my family apart.

The woman by the fence is smoking a cigarette. My mother always loved her Marlboros. Convertibles, too.

She'd been the one to convince my father to buy one when they first moved to Ivy Woods. Said she never got to drive when she lived in New York City during college.

"So I say to you, graduates, my friends, as you pursue your dreams, as you go out into the world and do great things, just remember this moment here. The memories we've made."

I nearly choke on those words.

Lily's out there somewhere in the stands, with new friends. She probably hates me. I can't blame her. I know what hate feels like. I know what betrayal feels like.

I know what it's like to be blinded by rage.

And how one small move can turn into a mistake you have to live with for the rest of your life.

"We will venture out into the world. And we will make mistakes. But the important thing is that we learn from them." My voice carries out into the crowd. I can almost see the vibrations of it rippling through the thick, hot air.

I'd learned a valuable lesson that night on the bridge. I'd come close to no return. Very close. But I'd also learned that sometimes you shouldn't play your hand. Sometimes it's better to hold it to your chest.

Sometimes, when you have a conversation with someone on her back porch—and she admits she killed your babysitter—you are smart enough to record the chat with your cell phone. And even smarter to save it. To not tell anyone about it.

In case you need it someday.

The applause is loud now, bursting out. People are

standing, clusters here and there, until half the stadium is giving me a standing ovation.

In three months, I'll be in a dorm with a mini refrigerator and my own desk and bed. I'll share the room with a new friend, and we'll swap clothes and class notes and gossip.

It will be wonderful.

You see, I know how to keep a secret.

Mom turns. The sun glints off her glasses. She raises her hand. Maybe it's a wave. Maybe it's just to swat away a bug. She goes back to the car. And then she's gone, driving out of the stadium. Disappearing.

Yes, I know how to keep a secret.

For a while anyway.

* * * * *

ACKNOWLEDGMENTS

This book would not exist without both the persistence and the patience of my amazing editor, Melanie Fried. I'm eternally grateful to her for the honest feedback and for pushing me to make this book the best it could be. They say the second novel is the hardest to write, and they are very correct. Throw in a global pandemic, and you've got the perfect storm of frustration. Without Melanie, I'd be curled in a ball in a corner somewhere, weeping endlessly.

In fact, I need to thank all of the tireless team at Graydon House and HarperCollins, most especially publicist Justine Sha, marketing manager Pamela Osti, and Alexandra Niit, who designed my amazingly creepy cover.

I also need to thank my best friend, Beth Fiencke, for the initial brainstorming session over pizza that helped generate the kernels of this book. The character I named after you is nothing like you, don't worry (well, except for the sweet tooth).

Even though I haven't been able to see them in person for a very long time, I need to give virtual hugs to many people who offered words of encouragement, advice, or general inspiration. First off, my wonderful agent, Michelle Richter, who talked me down from many cliffs. Thank you to Jenn Allen and Helen Boorman for the inspiration fairies and magical unicorns. I owe so much to my writer friends, most especially Ed Aymar, John Copenhaver, Alan Orloff, and LynDee Walker. Thank you to early readers Kathleen Barber, Andrea Bartz, Alison Gaylin, Karen Hamilton, Hannah Mary McKinnon, and Lori Rader-Day for their amazing words of support for the book. Cheers to the Thursday Night Write Group in the Chessie Chapter of Sisters in Crime—I didn't get there often, but I appreciated seeing your (Zoom) faces when I did. And thank you to the bookstagrammers and book reviewers everywhere, especially Dany Drexler and Kristopher Zgorski, for being voracious readers and champions of writers.

This book is about friendship, and I'm fortunate to have a posse of women I'd totally cover up a crime for anytime—my dear friends, new and old, you know who you are. I also have the best beta readers in the universe—April Kaminski, Bernadette Murphy, Art Taylor, and Brandon Wicks. Your input made this book a hell of a lot better, and I owe you lifetime supplies of tacos and coffee.

I wrote this book during the pandemic, and so I need to give the biggest shout-out to my husband and son, who put up with me for an entire year without killing me (yet). Thank you, Art, for understanding when I said, for the 456th time, "I need to go write," and dealing with my weird obsession with *Murder, She Wrote*. Our son, Dash, has been patient and wise through this whole process. His best advice after a particularly hard day of editing was telling me to imagine a tennis ball was my book and "smash it really hard." I wouldn't have been able to get through this weird time without you two.

Finally, thank you to the moms in the world. The fixers, the helpers, the consolers. When the sky tears completely in two, they're the ones who stitch it back together.

ALICE SWANSON'S
TOTALLY SPOOKTACULAR
IVY FIVE HALLOWEEN BLOCK
PARTY PLAYLIST

"Season of the Witch" – Lana Del Rey

"Straight to Hell" – LVCRFT, Sabrina Spellman

"I Did Something Bad" – Taylor Swift

"Hell on Heels" – Pistol Annies

"Wannabe" – Spice Girls

"Psycho Killer" – Talking Heads

"Dollhouse" – Melanie Martinez

"Bad Things" – Jace Everett

"Disturbia" – Rihanna

"Superstition" – Stevie Wonder

"Bury a Friend" – Billie Eilish

"That's What Friends Are For" – Dionne Warwick, Elton John, Gladys Knight, Stevie Wonder

Find it on Spotify: http://bit.ly/MotherNextDoor

QUESTIONS FOR DISCUSSION

1. Who was your favorite member of the Ivy Five? Why? Do you have a group of friends you'd do anything for?

2. How does the theme of being a "good mother" develop over the course of the novel? What does the idea of a "good mother" mean for each character?

3. How does society put pressure on mothers to be perfect? How can communities better support mothers?

4. At one point it is said that the men are "largely invisible in this story." Do you agree? Why or why not?

5. How do Kendra's insecurities blur reality for her when it comes to what happened with Daphne? Where do you think those insecurities stem from?

6. Do the characters "get away" with their crimes and with their lies in the end? In what ways are they paying for them regardless?

7. How does the novel explore the ideas of ghosts and being haunted by the mistakes of the past?

8. Did Kendra, Theresa, or Ellen achieve what they wanted by the end of the story? Why or why not?

9. Where do you think the Ivy Five will be in five years' time? How about Ellen? Maggie?

10. Do you enjoy celebrating Halloween? What are your favorite Halloween memories, costumes, decorations, songs, etc.?

Three couples. Three days.
A family getaway to die for.
Turn the page for a preview of
Tara Laskowski's next novel,
The Weekend Retreat

W-JKA BREAKING NEWS

Tragedy strikes at Van Ness Winery

SUNDAY, October 15—Multiple people have been reported dead at the Van Ness Winery after an altercation late Saturday night, our Eyewitness Team reports. Police were dispatched around 1:00 a.m. on Sunday morning after a 9-1-1 call from the estate's main house, but they were delayed hours getting to the scene because of the torrential rainstorm that flooded Rte. 8 and many of the small roads leading up to the winery.

Our news team is on-site but has not been able to verify details with officials, who are still investigating the scene. It appears the damaged substation in Parnell affected power to the estate as well as a number of neighboring homes and businesses in the Finger Lakes area.

This tragedy is the latest to befall the Van Ness family, whose matriarch, investor and philanthropist Katrina Van Ness, died earlier this year of pancreatic cancer at the age of sixty-eight.

The Van Ness winery, known for producing high-quality, award-winning wines, has been owned by the Van Ness family for several generations. The family started the business in the 1950s, after selling their Arizona-based copper mining company founded by Benson Van Ness. The 985-acre winery and estate is now managed by the Van Ness siblings, who live full-time in New York City. Their family investment office owns interests in multiple different real estate holdings and industrial and manufacturing enterprises. The siblings are believed to have been visiting the estate for the weekend for a family celebration.

We will report more as details are confirmed.

THURSDAY

Two Days before the Party

LAUREN

Ever since Zach told me about The Weekend, it's all I've been able to focus on. Most people would naturally be at least a little nervous to meet their significant other's family for the first time.

But most people aren't dating a Van Ness.

"Earth to Lauren." Zach snaps his fingers, grinning over at me. He left work early to get on the road sooner and didn't have time to change, so he's still wearing his suit, purple tie slightly askew but knotted even after hours of driving.

"Sorry," I say, tugging the ends of my hair. "Zoning out."

"You look like I'm driving you to your death," he says, then grabs my hand and squeezes. "Don't worry. I promise it'll be fun. Even if my family's there."

All I can see out my window are trees and fields and cows, my cell phone bars ticking steadily down. We must be close. Zach is taking care on the steep, curvy roads. One bad turn could send our car into a deep ditch or crashing into a thick tree trunk.

It's so beautiful up there, my best friend Maisie said when I told her about the invitation. She had that wicked look in her eye. *All the rolling hills. A vineyard. Starry sky. Super romantic. Perfect place to propose.* My stomach flips at the thought, and I breathe in deep. This weekend is not about us. It's a birthday party for Zach's older siblings, Harper and Richard, the twins, an annual tradition to celebrate at the family's winery. I can't get ahead of myself.

We drive up a winding gravel road, through patches of dense trees. Taller ones have already gone barren for the winter, but some of the smaller trees arch over the road, their branches meeting and entangling like fingers, blotting out the remaining light.

"Ladies and gentlemen, we are now approaching the famous Van Ness estate," Zach says in a booming voice as the car's headlights flick on. "Please, no photographs, and keep all hands and feet inside the moving vehicle at all times."

Zach told me the estate is large—a thousand acres—but I didn't grasp what that meant until the tunnel of trees ends and the view opens to a sprawling expanse of green fields and rolling hills, stretching endlessly against the purple-hued sky. We cross a small stone bridge that extends over a stream, then bump along a rocky road. The vineyards creep closer to us now, eerie in their precise organization, each plant in a perfect row. We're inching toward winter, and all the grapes must have already been picked for the season, pressed and bottled, because the vines are bare and withered.

When I first moved to New York and waited tables

at an Italian restaurant, we served the Van Ness wine. I remember those dark purple labels, the name stamped big and bold on the front. A brand that said, *We are too good for you.* But Zach is nothing like that, like the Van Nesses you read about online. Sometimes I forget he's part of that family in the day-to-day rhythm of our lives. He doesn't talk about them much, offers the scantest of information, or cracks a joke, or completely changes the subject when I bring them up. All I know of them is from the press, fleeting and superficial, like the pages of a glossy magazine, but hazy enough that I can imagine slicing open my finger on the sharp edges if I'm not careful.

"Tell me about them," I say now, when there's no evading the topic.

He glances over at me. "My family? What more do you need to know?"

"I don't know. How can I win them over so they all love me forever and ever?" I say, trying to hide my nerves.

He laughs. "They're impossible to win over."

"Oh perfect," I say. "That makes it easy then."

"Nah, they aren't that bad. They're...particular is all."

We head up a slight incline. To the right, there's a gravel path marked Private—Staff Only. We pass it and stop in front of a large metal gate. Zach rolls down his window, fetches a key card from the glove compartment. "We had this installed years ago for extra security," he says. Once the machine reads his card, the gates swing open soundlessly. I turn to watch them rotate back and slam into place.

As we round a corner, I finally catch a glimpse of

the house, a stone mansion, stoic on the hill. The long
driveway curves up to an overhang in front, flanked by
a series of round potted trees.

"Here we are," says Zach as we pull up. He shuts off
the car, taps the digital clock on the dashboard. "And
on time for dinner, too. Elle will be pleased."

My stomach does another flip.

Breathe deep.

Project confidence.

They're going to love you.

I get out. The air is chilly—it's dropped at least ten
degrees since we left the city. I wrap my arms across
my body.

The massive wooden front door opens, and an older
man walks out, gray hair and beard, a deep purple polo
shirt with the Van Ness logo stitched on the pocket, two
flutes of sparkling wine in his hands.

"Bill! You are the man." Zach trades him the keys to
the car for the glasses. "Lauren, Bill and his wife Lin-
net have been taking care of the estate—and us—since
I was a snotty-nosed kid."

As Bill heads for the trunk to unload our baggage, I
survey the house. My eyes follow the three short steps
up to a wide entryway with pillars, to the archway above
the door, and then outward to the wings on either side.
Greenery climbs up the stonework between the windows, and I imagine Bill must trim it often to keep
it so nice. I touch a pillar next to me and feel its cool
smoothness.

"Where's everyone else?" Zach asks Bill. For him,
this is business as usual. I doubt he even notices the
grandness anymore.

"Oh, they're around," he says. "Miss Elle says dinner at 6:30, and you can all meet in the library."

I smooth down the gold silk top Zach picked out for me, hugging and hiding in all the right places, like expensive clothes do. What would my parents say if they saw me? They would never guess I'd be weekending with a famous family like this. They never thought I'd make it in New York, thought I'd come crawling back begging to return to my night shift writing obituaries at our small-town paper.

But I'm never going back.

I take a sip of the sparkling wine. The bubbles pop, cold and hard against the back of my throat.

HARPER

I gaze at myself powering away on the bike in the mirrored wall of the gym. I always loathed the way Mother designed this gym—who wants to watch herself sweat?—but it turns out it can also be validating to see yourself, no filters, all angles.

"You definitely do not look thirty-five," I say to myself.

"You're modest, too," calls Lucas, upside down, from across the room.

I climb off the bike and pat my face with a towel as I walk over to him. My quads are burning, but I squat down next to my husband anyway, run my finger along his stubble.

He's hanging in his gravity boots for his spine decompression therapy. I like when he's like this, tethered up and vulnerable. How easy it would be to pick up one of the weights and slam it down on his neck, crush his windpipe.

I stand. My murderous thoughts have definitely been on an uptick lately. Part of it is being back here at Mother's house. The heavy drapery and the gold statues, like we are throwback 1680s French royalty. Everywhere with the Herend ceramic cats and dogs, Versace vases gathering dust, thick Persian carpets. Even the gym can't escape gold-plated spotlights in the ceiling and a goddamn chandelier.

This house is a behemoth, needy and wanting, and Mother always enjoyed feeding the monster. But it's angry and sullen without her, listless, the shadows in the corners deeper and longer.

"You need to get out of those things. It's nearly time for dinner," I tell my husband.

Lucas pulls himself up, unlatches his boots from the pole, and flips himself down and upright. His face is beet red, his eyes puffy.

"I don't know how you can stand that," I say.

"Good for the back." He stretches upward. I hear the crack. "Besides, these boots are the closest thing I'll get to skiing this weekend."

I ignore his comment. He's still not over the fact that I canceled the ski trip he'd planned for my birthday. It didn't matter that *he's* really the skier. *You seriously would rather go there?* he'd asked me. *With your family?*

Of course, I said, but he knew I was lying. He knows how I feel about this place. My brothers love the estate, but my memories of summers here are complicated. All these walls do now is remind me of Mother's games, challenges that were always impossible for me to win, as if she'd set them up that way.

When she was alive, it was a tradition none of us could break—one long birthday weekend at the estate.

We'd sometimes bring friends from the city, one or two each for Richard and me. Mother always tried to plan a few surprises for us. When we were kids, it was horse-back riding or boat rides or, one year, a full-on circus with a tent and acrobats and a baby tiger we all got to pet until it tried to bite my friend's arm. As we got older, casino nights or live bands. And always, the nighttime games and fireworks. Once Mother got sick, though, the birthday weekend was a quieter affair, with Mother telling stories about traveling around Europe and doling out too much wine and unsolicited advice.

I'd planned on stopping it this year.

But then things changed.

I move closer to the mirror and pull the collar of my T-shirt down. In the reflection, the bruise is nearly gone now, just a faint greenish-blue outline that will barely be visible when I wear my jumpsuit tonight.

"Wear your navy suit to dinner. It'll complement my outfit," I say as I trace the bruise with my fingers.

"I still don't get why I have to wear a suit at all," Lucas says, holding a push-up. "It's just your family."

"Because it's tradition," I snap and turn away from the mirror. "We always dress up the first night for dinner."

He knows this. It's part of the package, putting up with our families' various persuasions. I put up with his family's annual beach white-out parties and cornhole tournaments. Looking nice for dinner for mine hardly seems like a big ask.

Lucas raises his hands. "Fine, fine. I just hope we get some time to just chill. You know how Elle gets about these kinds of things…"

He doesn't need to finish that sentence. My sister-in-law has always been a type A perfectionist, desperate to please—and anxious for control. This is her element, planning events, making a list and checking it twice. She prides herself on being detail-oriented, and for everyone around her, it's exhausting as hell.

I'm fine to have drinks and dinner, and I'll even smile cheerfully for the inevitable group photo. But she can't expect us all to hang out every second and sing songs by the fire. If this weekend is really supposed to be about relaxing, then we shouldn't have to deal with one another the whole time. What I need is the escape, and if Mother's house is good for anything, it's at least good for hiding away.

ELLE

I thought I forgot to pack my pill case, but here it is, under Richard's toiletry bag in our suitcase. With relief, I unroll it, pull out the CBD tincture, squeeze a few drops (and then a few extra) under my tongue. It should take effect before dinner. The edge should be good and gone by the time Harper gets her forked tongue going.

Yes, this and just a little bit of wine and I'll be good to go.

While Richard's in the shower, I run over my mental checklist again. Family time tonight and tomorrow, the big party on Saturday. We all deserve a little fun. Especially Richard. He's taken it extra hard losing Mom, burying himself in work. I want this birthday to be special, as she'd have made it. I've been in this family long enough to know there's nothing more sacred than a Van Ness tradition.

I step over to the window. Clouds are gathering, though it's not supposed to rain tonight. Bill says a big storm is coming, that the main road out of here might flood over. I'm hoping it'll hold out until after the party, and we'll be able to leave Sunday morning before it gets really bad. I would hate to have to move everything inside. I have a vision for how the terrace will look, how the food and drink stations will flow, where everyone will gather. And with our friends coming from the city, I want to show off the spectacular views, make sure the drive is worth their while.

I pick up the CBD tincture, a few more drops on the tongue, and turn from the window as Richard steps out of the bathroom, steam drifting behind him, towel wrapped around his waist. I slide the bottle quickly back into my pill case and pop a mint in my mouth. I've been using my CBD more and more lately and I don't want him to ask questions.

"Zach's here," I say brightly. I'd spotted his car in the driveway.

But Richard doesn't answer. He's using another towel to dry his hair, whistling a tune, grabbing for his phone. He probably has work on his mind. He always gets ideas in the shower, rushes out to make notes before they dissipate with the steam.

Richard's the steady one of the family—the steerer of the ship. It's what drew me to him, his stability, his predictability. We work well together. Everyone can rely on us, always. For the most part, this is how I prefer things—I know Richard will do what I expect him to—but sometimes I wish we were the spontaneous couple who showers together before dinner and shows up late holding hands, laughing, much to everyone's irritation.

Richard locks his phone and walks it over to the

charging station. "You forgot to pack my new shaving cream."

Dammit.

I encircle him from behind, lay my cheek against his back. He's still damp, but I don't mind. I like the smell of his body wash, woodsy and masculine. "I'm sorry."

"I knew I should've done it. I've been breaking out from the other one," he says. Which I know, because I'm the one who recommended the new brand—free of dyes and fragrances that irritate his skin. His comment is somewhere between a rebuke of himself and of me. He's always too hard on himself. I offered to pack for him so he'd have more time to work. He's taken on most of the responsibilities of the family business this past year. But I won't let him start out on the wrong foot this weekend.

"Did you think any more on the candle thing?" I push the error aside and lean into his weight. "I know you like to make a wish, but I just worry it's going to ruin how beautiful the cake looks."

"I'd be fine without candles, but it's whatever Harper wants."

Harper. Of course. This is how it always is when they're together. We have to endure their meaningful looks across the room and all the stories about how they can read each other's minds. I don't know how Zach's lived with it all these years.

Richard steps away, opens the closet, and tugs his pants off the hanger. I made sure to have them delivered to our town house yesterday, freshly pressed from the cleaners. "You invited Victor and his wife to the party, right?"

"If I left them off, I'd never get invited to another

one of Alicia's Sunday brunches," I joke. I would be perfectly fine if I never had to sip another mimosa with Alicia Hastings and her friends, but Victor is on the board of our investment company, so we must keep in their good graces.

"Now that would just be a *tragedy*," Richard says with a small smile as he swipes his deodorant, always three times under each arm.

"I'm so glad we're reviving the old birthday tradition," I say, fiddling my diamond earrings through their holes. "So many surprises in store for you."

"And Harper," he adds, picking up his phone again.

"And Harper," I repeat.

He tucks in his shirt, zips up his pants, and threads a leather belt through the loops. Whisks a comb through his hair and slides his wallet in his back pocket, always on the right-hand side. He'll wait to put on his suit jacket until he's heading downstairs so it doesn't wrinkle. And then he'll take it off halfway through dinner and hang it carefully on the back of a chair.

My husband is a creature of habit, a man of rules and regulations. I've been with him long enough that I know them all.

He fetches his glasses off the nightstand, slips them on, blinks as his world comes into focus. He nods his approval at my short black dress and long hair, which I've blown out into loose waves the way he loves it. "You look gorgeous, as usual."

"Thank you, my darling." I kiss his cheek, ignore the red blotches from the shaving cream.

I check my watch. "About time for drinks?"

I've also been in the Van Ness family long enough to know all their rules, traditions, quirks, desires. I know which flavor cakes to buy, which china patterns to use, which political issues they approve of, how to properly let a bottle of wine aerate. I know how to get under their skin and when to dodge the bullet. I know their sensitivities, their soft spots, their weaknesses.

I know their secrets, too.

THE PARTY GUEST

I like driving in the country. The long, quiet roads, especially at night. Gives you plenty of time to think as the miles pass with nothing but your headlights to guide you through the shadows.

And I have a lot of thinking to do.

I've waited patiently for this moment. Another person might've rushed things, acted too soon, but that would've been a mistake. I knew I had to hold out for just the right time, the right place, the right moment—there's a comfort in the plotting. A pleasure in slipping into their world, learning all about them. Gathering evidence and information.

And now here it is. This weekend. The birthday party.

Some people hate birthdays. They don't like the reminder that time, tick-tock, is clicking steadily forward, always moving, and they can't escape it. They loathe

the thought of getting old, of things failing them—their eyesight, their joints, their mind, their beauty.

Me? I've always loved birthdays. A tradition, a milestone. A reminder of how far you've come and how far you've yet to go.

Another year ahead to right the wrongs that have been committed around you—to you. Because no matter how much you try to be good, no matter how hard you try to go about things honestly, there are always people who just can't play nice.

It's so dark up here in wine country. I must go slow, watch out for wildlife that could dart into the road. Anything can be lurking in the darkness, ready to lunge out. Terrible things happen in the blink of an eye. One moment everything's fine, and the next, the world comes crashing down around you.

But I'll drive carefully. I'll arrive safe and sound.

There's a big storm coming, and I've got everything I need—rain boots, raincoat. Night-vision goggles.

Finally, the last item, right here next to me on the passenger seat, wrapped and ready to be delivered—the birthday gift.

For what's a party without gifts?

The Van Ness family knows how to throw a good party. They love to flaunt their wealth. They'll pull out all the stops. Good food, good wine, decorations, hospitality. All the details accounted for. They'll have planned for everything.

Well, nearly everything.